Prime Catch

by

Ilona Fridl

Dangerous Times

Prime Catch

Cover Art by *Rae Monet, Inc. Design*

The Wild Rose Press, Inc.
PO Box 708
Adams Basin, NY 14410-0708
Visit us at www.thewildrosepress.com

Publishing History
First Vintage Rose Edition, 2013
Print ISBN 978-1-61217-719-9
Digital ISBN 978-1-61217-905-6

Dangerous Times
Published in the United States of America

Every nerve in Amos' body was alert with a flood of adrenaline. He hated putting Sarah in danger, but she was a deputy and a good shot, so he couldn't tell her not to do her job. Halfway to the porch steps, the door banged open and Bobby stepped out with a double-barreled shotgun that he leveled at Amos. "And what would you like, Sheriff? I don't remember inviting you over."

"I have a warrant for your arrest in the killing of Mr. Thornton at the cannery. Now, we can do this easy. Just pass the shotgun to me and come along peacefully."

"The hell I will! Get off my property!"

Amos dropped and rolled as the shotgun fired, then heard answering fire and saw Bobby fold to the porch, clutching his knee. Amos ran up the steps and grabbed the abandoned shotgun while Sarah holstered her weapon and hurried to help.

Amos leaned the shotgun against the railing and slapped the handcuffs on Bobby almost simultaneously, and then he set to work cutting the knee of Bobby's trousers to check the wound.

Bobby yelled at Sarah at the top of his lungs. "You god-damned traitor! I'm shot by a turncoat woman who won't defend her own kind!"

"Who's my own kind, Bobby? A band of murderous animals who kill for what they want? No, that's not my kind." She picked up the shotgun and pointed it at Bobby. "I prefer to be on the law-abiding side."

Praise for Ilona Fridl's Desperate Times Series

***SILVER SCREEN HEROES*:**
"*Silver Screen Heroes* has it all. Suspense, romance, mystery, history....I found myself drawn into the story on several levels."

~Night Owl Romance Reviews Top Pick (4.75 Stars)
"Wow! What a story. It starts off with a bang, or should I say fire, that kept my attention and made me want to read more....Once I sat down and started reading, I couldn't stop. I got involved with the characters, related with the situations and felt I was a part of the story.... Read *Silver Screen Heroes* and join the magic of an era long past and feel the miracle of true love. Excellent read!"

~Marianne Gibson, Between the Lines (4 Stars)
***GOLDEN NORTH*:**
"Ilona Fridl's *Golden North* is truly an adventure worth joining. Take an armchair travel opportunity to go to Alaska. This wild state is a wonderful backdrop for such a great novel."

~Night Owl Reviews Top Pick (4.75 Stars)
***BRONZE SKIES*:**
"A quick and enjoyable read that drew me in from the first page to the last even without reading the first two books....There was romance, some laughter, lots of angst, and a few tears. There was family, friends, history, battles, casualties, injuries, a stalker, mystery, and suspense. I look forward to reading more books by Fridl in the future."

~Romancing the Book (4 Roses)

Dedication

To my friends and family.
And to the readers who loved Amos and Sarah
in *Golden North*.

Chapter 1

Juneau, Alaska Territory, 1923

It's amazing how broken a human body can be when plunged thirty feet onto a cement floor. A dark gel of bloody brains oozed from the split skull, and the rest of the body looked like it was held together only by its clothing. Sheriff Amos Darcy looked away from the ghastly sight when he realized sweat was forming under his mustache and his stomach was threatening to roil. Coroner Elmer Stanton hurried to the body as Amos turned and studied the wooden catwalk with its safety rail hanging at a crazy angle.

He turned to the pasty-faced cannery owner, Peter Anders, who fidgeted next to him. "Mr. Anders, this looks like an unfortunate accident. What makes you think it was anything else?"

Anders handed him a bloodstained envelope. "We found this jammed halfway into his jacket pocket."

On the front of the envelope was the number three. Amos held it to the light. "Has anyone opened it yet?" At Anders' shake of his head, Amos tore the end and extracted a folded sheet.

It read: *This is the third cannery bigwig to meet his maker. How many more before the traps are removed?*

Amos tucked it back into the envelope. "I need to hold this for evidence. Have two others died because of accidents here?"

The owner ran his fingers through his hair. "No. All the other executives of the plant are intact, as far as I know."

Elmer and his two helpers were putting the body into a shroud and strapping it onto a stretcher. Amos pointed to the corpse. "Anders, who was he?"

"Edward Thornton, Vice President of Operations."

"What are these traps mentioned in the note? And was Thornton in charge of yours?"

Anders blew a breath slowly through his lips before he continued, "Yes, he was. The traps are large wooden mazes set on the mouths of the rivers where salmon go to spawn. The fish get trapped and, at times, we can pick up an entire school."

Amos mopped his forehead with a handkerchief. "Have you had any threats before?"

"Not personally. But we have heard about Eskimos getting angry about the depletion in the number of fish making it upstream."

Amos waved Elmer over to the conversation. "Elmer, stop at the office when you're finished. I want a full report of anything you find."

"Will do, Sheriff." The coroner followed the stretcher out.

"Mr. Anders, who was in the warehouse when this happened?"

"Ted Carney was. Let me go get him." Anders returned with a large muscular man in worker's overalls.

"Mr. Carney?" The man nodded. "Tell me what you saw."

Carney fiddled with his bandanna and wiped his

mouth. "Well, Sheriff, we was loading cans into the crates, ya know, and we hears a loud crack and Mr. Thornton lands on the floor in front of us."

"Did you see anyone on the catwalk?"

"No, sir. I guess we was all starin' at Mr. Thornton."

"Did you hear anything overhead?"

"No, sir."

"Let me talk to the others who were here with you."

Carney brought his cohorts in and Amos questioned them, with the same results. Most of them were either too stunned or sickened by the fallen body to notice anything else.

Amos wrote on his pad of paper, then nodded. "Thank you, all." As the men made their way to the door, he pointed above. "Mr. Anders, take me to the catwalk."

Peter Anders led Amos into an adjoining hall and up a flight of iron stairs. The door to the catwalk was ajar. "Don't touch the door!" Amos called as he passed by Anders and stooped to study it. A smear of blood stained the wood underneath the knob. "Do you know if there was anyone in the hall when the accident happened?"

"I can check with the workers." He started down the steps while Amos went onto the walk.

The four-foot-wide catwalk was constructed of wooden planks, with a three-foot wall on either side. A safety rail was affixed on iron bars coming up through the wall boards. Amos went to inspect the break in the rail. There were splashes of blood on the plank floor. *Seems like Thornton was attacked before he went through that railing.* Amos tested the rail on the other side by leaning hard on it. *Hmm. It would take more than a falling body to break this.* He tested the broken side. The rail board was smooth on two sides and hung turned out on one of the iron posts. A small line of sawdust was trapped between the wall and the floor. Someone had hastily tried to clean it up— *This looks like it's been sawed through on both sides!* With this development, Amos decided it was premeditated murder.

Anders appeared at the door with another worker. "Sheriff, this is Jake Kennedy. He wants to tell you what he saw."

Amos readied his notes. "Yes, Mr. Kennedy?"

Kennedy glanced around before he began. "I was wheeling a pallet of cans to the warehouse and came in from the south door. Mr. Thornton was going up the stairs to the catwalk when I saw a man in a long coat and a fedora hurry up after Thornton and follow him through the door."

"When was this?"

"About an hour ago. Mr. Thornton always inspects the warehouse around the same time."

"By himself?"

"Yes."

"Did either of them see you?"

"I don't think so. Their backs were to me."

"Then you didn't see the other man's face?"

"No. I didn't really know anything was wrong, then."

Amos tapped the pencil on his notepad. "Did you notice anything else?"

A light dawned in Kennedy's eyes. "Yes. Yes, I

did. I thought it was strange that he was wearing mukluks and not work boots in the warehouse."

Amos pulled on his mustache. "Thank you, Mr. Kennedy. If you remember anything else, let me know."

"Yes, sir. Terrible business, this." He left as Amos turned to Anders.

"Mr. Anders, along with the note, I want this board as evidence, and don't fix that rail yet."

"Anything you say, Sheriff." Together they wrested the wooden rail off the iron bar.

Amos took leave of Anders and climbed into his patrol car. Heading to the office, he knew he would ask Sarah Lakat to work on the case. His Tlingit woman deputy was a damn good detective. *And if it concerns the Eskimo community, she'll be an asset.* He smiled slightly and warmed at the thought of working closely with her on a case. Then he brought himself up short. *I'm a bachelor, and I like my life the way it is. Anyway, we already work together. Well, in the same office.* Amos shoved his feelings for Sarah into a far corner of his mind.

Chapter 2

Sarah Lakat waved at Deputy Sam Lindsey as she came in. "Anything going on, Sam?" she asked the handsome young man.

"The sheriff was called to the Polar Star Cannery. Seems there was an accident there."

Sarah came through the gate to the rear of the office where Sam sat behind his desk. Sliding into her desk chair, she commented, "Sounds interesting." She flipped her notepad. "At least better than a bicycle theft. That was solved when we discovered the man just forgot which lamp post he had left it shackled to."

Sam chuckled. "Been mighty quiet around here for a few days."

Sarah sighed, lining up her report sheet in the cranky typewriter. "Still have to report it." She stifled a yawn. In the middle of her report, the sheriff banged the door open.

"Lakat, I want to see you in my office as soon as you're finished."

She wrapped up the bicycle report and knocked on the sheriff's door. "You wanted to see me?"

"Come in."

"What is it?" She closed the door.

"Sit. We have trouble brewing." He passed her the bloodstained envelope. "What do you make of that?"

She studied the paper. "Looks like somebody has it

in for the cannery business." She gave it back. "Do you know who the first two victims were?"

Amos shook his head. "That's what I want you to find out. Go to the *Daily Empire* and check their news feed for the past few months on trouble at canneries." Sarah rose to leave. "Wait a moment. The murderer went out of his way to tell us this was number three and why. I wonder if there was a warning that appeared somewhere before it happened."

"There could be, if the purpose was to stop the canneries from using the traps. The personal notices section of the newspaper could have had a veiled message. I've heard of that happening before."

Amos jumped up. "I'll go with you and see if there's anything suspicious in the Personals."

The channel fog was lifting in Juneau as they climbed into the patrol car. The April sun filtered down as though shining through layers of cheesecloth. The temperature was in the fifties, but snow still glistened on Mount Juneau and Roberts Peak. Juneau, the territorial capitol, nestled between the mountains and the ocean waters of Gastineau Channel. Sarah took a deep breath of the familiar salty smell of the sea mingled with the tang of oil from the wharfs. It felt good coming out of winter and into the promise of spring.

Amos parked in front of the newspaper building and together with Sarah strode up the steps into the lobby with its ever-present battery of busy typewriters. The wooden half-wall with a gate separated the public from the reporters. Sarah didn't have any idea how they got work done in such a din.

A man at a large desk in front hurried to the gate.

"Can I help you, Sheriff?"

"Deputy Lakat and I are here on department business. Could she see the territorial news for the last month? And I would like to look over the Personals for the last week."

The man nodded. "Would this happen to do with the Polar Star Cannery?"

Sarah watched Amos' jaw twitch. "How would you know about that?"

"Word gets around fast."

"I'll bet it does, Mr.—?"

"Edwards. Ray Edwards. I'm the news editor." He turned to Sarah. "Miss Lakat, the files are through that door on the left. Mr. Day is the file clerk. He can get the folders you need. Sheriff, the Classified Department is down the hall on the right. Last door on the end."

Sarah slid through the door to the filing room. Wooden cabinets lined the walls and marched down the center. Two small windows let in some dusty light. In front were three tables, and a desk where a mousy man with a pencil-thin mustache looked up. "May I help you with something?"

"You must be Mr. Day." There was something about him, something oily, that made her feel uncomfortable, and she hurried to show him her identification card, using her most authoritative manner. "I'm Deputy Lakat, and I'd like to see files for the territorial news for the past two months."

She must be fresh steak, the way he eyed her. "Just a moment. I'll get the files from the last eight weeks. You may sit." He indicated one of the tables.

Sarah pulled the chain on the old desk lamp on the table, and it gave a yellow glow. He came back in a few minutes with a stack of folders. Standing behind her, he set them down, brushing her arm. He smelled of rancid hair tonic, and she grimaced. "Can you tell me what you're looking for?" The odor of old cheese floated on his breath.

"No. I'll know when I find it." He slunk back to his desk, grumbling something under his breath, while she opened the first folder and took out the stack of papers.

****

Amos came to a door whose frosted glass window held the words, "Classified Department" stenciled in black block letters. Opening it, he stood at a wooden counter where a young man in a blue suit worked at a typewriter. "Excuse me, Mr.—?"

"Perkins." The young man turned and said, crisply, "Do you want to post a classified?"

Amos shook his head. "I'm Sheriff Darcy, and I'm conducting an investigation. May I see the Personals from last week?"

Perkins rose and went to a wooden file cabinet. Shuffling through the drawers, he pulled out one of the folders and brought it over. "We usually keep copies of all our Personals, by the month. You'll find the past week's at the top."

Amos thumbed through the notices of lost pocket watches, lonely hearts, and greetings. A short message caught his eye. *There will be a third at Polar Star, Wednesday next.* "Mr. Perkins, may I see the record of who purchased this message?"

Perkins brought the ledger to the counter and matched the number on the sheet to the one in the ledger. "It was purchased by a Mr. John Smith."

Amos pursed his lips. "John Smith? Really?"

Perkins clattered his fingers on the ledger page. "We aren't required to ask for identification for a Personal, Sheriff."

"Do you think you would recognize him if you saw him again?"

"Perhaps."

"Didn't you think this was an odd post?"

"Sheriff, if I questioned every unusually worded Personal message, I wouldn't get any work done."

"May I take this?"

Perkins nodded. "I don't see why not."

Amos turned on his heel and exited the room. *At least I have a handwriting sample.* He hurried to the filing room to see if Sarah had found anything. As he opened the door, he heard a smack and a howl of dismay. Sarah was glaring at someone—the file clerk, he assumed, who was rubbing a red mark on his cheek. "What happened here?"

Sarah gave a startled, "Oh!" and then, with a contrite look, added, "I'm sorry you had to see that."

"Well?"

"I'd rather not say."

Mr. Day huffed. "You shouldn't send a woman to do a man's work."

Sarah sneered, "If I were a man, you wouldn't be hovering over me like a vulture."

Amos clenched his jaw. "Stop it, both of you. I'm guessing you're Mr. Day. Find something else to do, away from here." Day hesitated. "Now!" Amos barked. For some reason, he wanted to rip Mr. Day's head from his neck.

She waved him off. "You didn't have to come to my rescue. I can take care of myself."

Amos sat across the table. "I know you can. I wanted to see what you found."

Sarah wrinkled her nose as if displeased. "There've been accidents at the North Seas Cannery in Cordova and King Cannery in Soldotna that each resulted in a death, but it doesn't mention if there were notes found with the bodies."

Amos stroked his mustache. "I suppose I could send a wire to their law enforcement to see what I can find out."

"Did you get anything in Personals?"

He showed her the message and related what the clerk told him.

"Well, we do have a few things to go on."

"Come on, Lakat, we can go back to the office to plan our next move."

She called behind her, as she caught up the needed clippings, "You may put the folders away again, Mr. Day. Thank you!" There was a hint of sarcasm in her too-lilting voice.

On the street, Amos turned to her. "Tell me, Lakat, what made you slap him?"

An amused smile tried to come through, but she said, "Mashers get what they deserve."

Amos shook his head as he got into the auto. *Some people make the mistake of thinking Sarah is an ordinary woman. They usually don't make it twice.*

Chapter 3

Back in Amos' office, Sarah sat facing the desk, clutching a coffee mug. She took a sip and watched him pore over the information. "What do you think our next move should be?"

"Whoever this is, he seems to be going in some sort of pattern. If we can figure it out, we may be able to catch him before he strikes again." Amos reached into a lower drawer and pulled out a map of Alaska. Opening it, he studied it for a moment. "If this was the third, he seems to be moving south."

Sarah shook her head and tapped the map with her finger. "Soldotna is farther west than Cordova. How do we know if he'll stay in the southeast? There's a number of towns west of us that have canneries. How would we know which one he'd strike next?"

A knock on the door broke their train of thought. "Come in," Amos called.

Sam leaned in. "Sir, Elmer is here. He says he finished examining the body."

Amos rose from his chair. "Lakat, let's see what he found."

Sarah didn't enjoy this part of the job, but it came with the territory. She followed Amos and Elmer next door and downstairs to the morgue. Elmer opened one of the cold storage rooms to reveal a sheeted body on a metal gurney.

Elmer peeled the sheet down to the shoulders, and Sarah sucked in a quick breath to fight her nausea. The head seemed to have been split in two like a ripe melon. Her stomach threatened to rebel, but she pushed it down and set her mind in business gear. Holding the two pieces together, Elmer pointed to the side of the neck. "I think the initial wound was this bruise here. Then he was hit on the back of the skull, which must have cracked it. I'll bet, when he fell, he landed upside down, which split it open."

Amos steadied himself against the wall, not looking well. "Does it look like he fought back?"

"No. He must have been struck from behind and had no warning." Elmer turned to a shelf and picked up a small corked glass vial. "I found these embedded in the wound."

Amos opened it and shook the contents into his hand, studying them carefully. "Lakat, look at this."

Sarah peered at the items. "Those are splinters of wood. Do you think he was hit with a board of some kind?"

Amos nodded. "It seems like they're from a finished mill board and not raw wood." He was silent for a moment. "Come with me to the cannery, and let's see if we can find anything else." He deposited the wood fragments back in the vial and gave it to Elmer as he guided Sarah out.

They hurried to the patrol car and, as Sarah slid in, Amos started the engine. He glanced at her. "If it was a board that killed him, then given the force needed to crack his skull we should find some wood fragments on the catwalk or down below."

A sea fog was coming in, coating the land with a

gray misty chill. Sarah shivered a bit as they headed into the warehouse. A plant guard stopped them. "Where do you think you're going?"

Amos stepped up. "I'm Sheriff Darcy, and I want to inspect the crime scene."

"Come in. I'll go tell Mr. Anders."

Sarah followed Amos through the huge wooden sliding doors into the drafty building. A few men milled about, away from the crime scene. A couple of them glanced at her and started whispering. One of the larger men strode over. Jabbing a finger toward Sarah, he whirled on Amos. "What's she doing here?"

Amos' eyes flashed. "She's one of my deputies and working on the case. Why?"

"She's one of them Eskimos and, from what I know, one of those people killed Mr. Thornton."

Sarah ground her back teeth, longing to deck this oaf. She also knew she couldn't get anywhere with this type. May as well let Amos deal with the bluster.

Amos was in the man's face. "What, exactly, are you saying?"

The idiot didn't back down. "I'm sayin' they're all savages and cover for each other."

Amos grabbed the straps of the man's overalls and swung him against a wooden crate. "You take care of your business and I'll take care of mine, or you can spend the night in the hoosegow for accosting an officer. You got that?" He hit him against the crate again, as if for emphasis.

Shrugging Amos' hands off him, the man straightened up. "Yeah, I got it."

Peter Anders hurried up from the far door. "Is there trouble here, Sheriff?"

"Taken care of." The bully went back to his buddies. "Mr. Anders, I take it no one has disturbed the warehouse or the catwalk?"

Anders nodded. "I've had people watching it."

"Good. Deputy Lakat and I want to give it a closer look. If I have her search down here, I don't want any of those bulldogs bothering her. Understood?" At Anders' nod, he turned to Sarah. "You search for anything that might have come down from the walk, and I'll look up there."

Sarah skirted the drying bloody pool and checked the floor for anything suspicious that could have fallen from above. In the corner, by a pallet, she spotted something and investigated. Crouching down, she saw it was a splintered piece of rounded, finished wood. It had spots of blood on it. She called, "I've found something down here!"

Amos answered from the catwalk, "Leave it where it is. Is it on the side where he fell?"

"No. It's on the other side."

"Hold on— Yes! Lakat, I'll be right down." Amos strode to where she was waiting and examined the piece of wood. "Looks like a piece of baseball bat, and it sure matches the splinters." He pulled out his handkerchief and wrapped the piece to take with him. "Come and see what I found upstairs."

As they walked out on the catwalk, Sarah studied the area. A faint chalk mark before the cut railing caught her eye. "Looks like someone tried to erase this mark."

Amos nodded. "The murder was planned out, not a random killing. Seems Mr. Thornton came to inspect the warehouse by himself around the same time every morning, using the same route every time."

Sarah took a breath. "So the one that followed him up must have put the chalk mark down to let him know when to strike, so Thornton would fall through the weakened railing."

"The man who was seen following Mr. Thornton up had on mukluks. Probably to muffle any footsteps."

A shock wave shot down her spine. "That's why that worker thought it was a native who killed him!"

"Lakat, don't jump to conclusions. Anyone could put on a pair of mukluks." Amos inspected the railing on the other side. "If the wood piece was found on this side, then...ahh, here it is!"

Sarah ran her finger over a dent in the board. "That must be where he broke the bat." She pointed to a few wood fragments between the wall and the floor of the catwalk. She scooped them into a handkerchief.

Amos wielded an imaginary bat. "The killer was right-handed if he swung like this to the neck. The body would have fallen to the other side when he brought the bat down like this to break his skull. The bat broke when the tip hit the rail."

Sarah moved to the other side. "Then he would have to shove the body this way to make it look like Mr. Thornton fell." As they worked out the details, both Sarah and Amos moved back and forth, their paces becoming almost giddy. A distant "ahem" made them stop in their tracks.

Mr. Anders stood by the door. "Sheriff, when can we clean the warehouse?" A slight irritation colored his tone.

Amos snagged Sarah by the arm and headed toward Anders. When he got to the agitated cannery owner, Amos slapped him on the shoulder. "You can now. I think we have what we need to start on the case."

As they slipped through the door to the outside, Sarah chewed on her lip. "Where do you think the rest of the bat is?"

"He probably hid it under the long coat. I don't know if he chanced disposing of it nearby, but he may not have wanted to be caught with it, either." They took a walk around the plant but turned up nothing.

Disappointed, they returned to the patrol car and started back to the office, but just outside the cannery's gated entrance Sarah noticed a pile of waste wood. "Pull over for a moment. We can take a look there."

Amos nodded. "Good idea." He parked on the road, where the hill sloped to the channel. They picked carefully through the tall grasses to the discarded wood and started inspecting pieces. Sarah heard a shout from Amos. "I found it!" She stepped cautiously around the debris, and he handed her the remains of the bloody bat. "Hold this a moment." He brought out the piece they'd found inside, which he'd wrapped in his handkerchief. Freeing the bit of wood, he aligned the tip with the rest of it. "Swell catch, Lakat! I'd say we had a profitable morning. What do you say? Let's stop at Millie's for lunch. I'm buying."

Sarah's stomach growled. "Perfect." She grinned as Amos carefully put the evidence in the back of the patrol car.

Ilona Fridl

Chapter 4

Amos dropped off the pieces of bat at the coroner's, after lunch, so Elmer could compare it to the splinters he found in the body. Back in the office, he watched Sarah sit with her coffee. He loved having her work with him—hell, he loved having her around. Her eyes were dark and her lips pursed. "Well, what are you thinking?"

Sarah sighed. "I hate to think this was caused by a native. We've been going through so much to convince the American government that we are indeed civilized. Now this has to happen."

"I thought you could put in a form to become a citizen."

She gave a slight snort. "We're trying to let them know we are all civilized, whether we follow the old ways or not."

Amos had come to think of her as an equal, even though she was a native and a woman. He'd learned to respect her judgment as they worked together on case after case. Times like these, he was brought up short. "Do you think you can be objective?"

"Yes, I'm sure I can."

A surge went through his chest, and Amos had a fleeting thought of holding her. "Lakat—Sarah, I respect you and your knowledge as a detective. But if you feel like you can't deal with the killer possibly being a native, tell me now."

She didn't say anything for a moment. "I guess I was worried how you felt about me working on this case."

Hurt, he smacked the desk with the flat of his hand. "I thought you knew me better than that. I've found outlaws in every group of people. I've also found good in all of them, too. I've rounded up many a bad American in my time. You know that."

Sarah studied her shoes. "I'm sorry. I guess I've been stung so much, I never considered it from another point of view."

"I've treated you as an equal and thought of you as such. Never forget that." Amos ran his fingers through his hair. "Now, let's get back to work."

Sarah took out some of the clippings she'd extracted from the news folders and started reading. "Seems like there were a few fights between the cannery fishermen and the natives that live upriver from Cordova. The canneries have what's called fish traps that can snare a full school of fish. The natives upstream complained there weren't enough fish left for them to catch to feed their people."

"Do you think some of them could be angry enough to resort to murder?"

Sarah shrugged. "Anything's possible, I guess."

Amos played with an idea, but he didn't know if she'd agree to it. "You belong to the Alaska Native Sisterhood, don't you?"

"Yes, but why—?"

"Both the Sisterhood and the Brotherhood are geared for helping the natives get citizenship and a fair deal with the Americans. Do you have access to the

Brotherhood?"

She gripped the arms of her chair. "My family belongs to both."

"When's the next get-together?"

"This Saturday night."

"Maybe you could listen in on some scuttlebutt around there. Someone might know something about the murders."

Her face flushed. "You mean spy on my friends and family?"

"Look, if it *is* a native, there might be people who know what's going on. I'm not going to start another Indian war up here. I just want to find whoever's killing these people. You know very well if I went to a meeting they wouldn't tell me anything."

Sarah sighed. "And if it was me, they'd speak more freely. All right, I'll do it."

Amos could sense she didn't like any of this, but she seemed to understand what he was asking. He wasn't so sure he wouldn't feel the same way. "I'm going to fly to Cordova and Soldotna to find out what they know up there. I'll be gone four or five days."

"What if we get anything on the Personals?"

"You can take care of it. Tell the authorities in that area to watch canneries carefully." Amos took a sip of coffee to hide the well of feeling. "I have every kind of faith in your abilities."

Sarah smiled, a brilliant thank-you smile that set his body to tingling. She took her cup and headed for the door.

Chapter 5

Sarah tried to buck herself up as she paced a line on the oriental rug in her parlor. This meeting tonight had her nerves on edge. *I've managed investigations before, but never on my own people.* Then she thought of what Amos had said. *He manages to do it on his people. Why am I having a problem? Maybe I want my people to be too perfect so Americans will see us as civilized. I don't like it that some of us don't measure up.* The doorbell made her jump.

Her cousin, Kata Nikolaevich, stood on the porch. "Are you ready to go?"

Sarah opened the door wider and stepped back. "I will be in a few minutes. Come in for a bit."

Kata studied her face. "Something's bothering you. I can see it. What is it?"

Sarah waved her hand toward a chair. "Sit. I have to get my light coat." She went to the wardrobe and fetched the pale blue spring jacket.

Kata's jaw twitched. "I've grown up with you and know when you're worried. Now tell me."

Sarah sighed and sat next to Kata. "The murder at the Polar Star Cannery is filling my mind right now. I can't discuss it, but there are things about it that I don't like, that's all. Come on, we'll be late."

The late afternoon April sun shone dimly through the sea fog rolling in from the channel. Sarah shivered with the damp cold and pulled her coat tighter. "How is everyone at the Golden North?" Kata worked as head of costumes at the theater where Sarah and Amos had once investigated a murder.

"They're all swell. Business has been good lately, since we've been able to get movies within a few weeks of release."

They soon arrived at the Alaskan Native Brotherhood meeting hall for the social that would include both the Brotherhood and the Sisterhood. Kata's brother-in-law, Will, waved from the door. "I've saved a table for all of us."

Sarah had lost her two brothers and father at sea, so she felt close to her cousins, Mary and Kata. Their family had taken her mother and her in when she was in her early teens. Her mother, Grace, waved to her. "We're about ready to start. I'm glad you two made it." Close to fifty now, her mother still looked like a young girl when she smiled. Sarah waved to Aunt Jane, who was Grace's sister, Kata's and Mary's mother.

Sarah slid into a seat next to her mother. "Sorry we're a little late. It was nice we could get this table."

When it was their turn, the family worked their way to the buffet servings and loaded their plates with the fresh fish, fruits, vegetables, and breads. Sarah gratefully dug into her dinner, and her mother poked Sarah's shoulder. "You look like you're in the middle of a potlatch ceremony. Haven't you eaten today, child?"

"Just some. I've been working on a case and haven't had too much time lately."

Will frowned. "The sheriff expects too much from you. You seem to do most of the work and he gets the glory."

Sarah snapped, "He works as hard as I do. He's north, getting information we need."

Her mother pursed her lips. "That's the first time I've ever heard you defend *them*."

"Maybe it's because I'm tired of the 'us and them' feuds. That's what causes most of the problems in this town."

"You aren't concerned that we're losing our traditions?"

Sarah glanced heavenward. "All cultures grow and change. The white Americans are here to stay, so we may as well adapt."

Her mother shook her head. "Like Kata taking Ivan's name? Will took Mary's name, as it should be."

"Will married Tlingit. Ivan isn't Tlingit."

"I never should have sent you to the missionary school. They fed your mind this poison."

Sarah threw her fork down. "Stop it, Mother! That school prepared me for the changes, and I'm happy you did." She rose from the table. "If you'll excuse me, I need some air."

Sarah stomped outside and leaned against the cold bricks of the building. *Unfortunately, the small minds of either side make it difficult to exist together. I remember in history I read of cultures coming together and becoming stronger. It takes time to sort things out, though. What to keep and what to throw away.* A murmur of voices from around the corner caught her attention. The words "fish traps" and "canneries" hit her ear. She moved to the edge.

"Those damn canneries are setting the traps on the mouths of the rivers, and our village is losing most of the fish," came a gruff voice.

"Something should be done about it," sounded a baritone.

Sarah jammed her fists in her coat pockets and strode purposefully around the corner. She nodded to the men. "I thought I heard someone out here."

Jack, with the rough voice, tipped his hat. "Evening, Miss Lakat." A light on his face dawned. "Say, you're a deputy. Have you heard anything about Polar Star?"

"You know I can't discuss it."

Bobby, the younger man, angrily turned on her. "Word is, the sheriff is going to convict a native."

Sarah fixed her glare. "He's looking at all angles right now."

"And you insist on working for the enemy."

"You know, it's people like you who make it hard to get along with anyone."

Bobby pushed by Sarah, and she leaned against the wall. Jack took his hat off as he walked by. "Sorry, Miss Lakat. Bobby is mad about losing the salmon upstream."

When Sarah saw she was alone, she wrote "Bobby Cusnoo" in her notebook and tucked it back in her pocket. *We should look into some of the upstream villages.* Amos was supposed to be back Monday. She would make that suggestion.

A hand snagged her arm from behind and a glove smacked down on her mouth. Sarah started kicking with her feet and elbowing her assailant, until cold steel landed none too gently on the back of her neck. "Don't move, just listen!" a raspy voice hit her ear. "Have the sheriff call the dogs off. We're doing this for our people's good." She found herself shoved behind several barrels. Before she could jump up, the man ran around the building.

"So much for some air," Sarah murmured to herself as she straightened her hat and inspected a tear in the hem of her skirt. As she went through the door, she brushed as much of the dirt off her clothes as possible and ducked into the women's lavatory. When she was presentable again, she rejoined her family.

Sarah sighed as she pulled out her chair. "I'm sorry, Mother, I know how important tradition is to you."

Her mother opened her mouth like she was going to say something, then smiled. "I'm sorry, too. I hate the changes, but because of your schooling, at least you can make your way through this new world."

Sarah kissed her cheek. "You have to remember you were raised different than your parents were, too. Before the Russians and Americans, our people were living quite primitively."

The social went on for several hours of dining and dancing. Sarah kept watching for anyone suspicious, but all seemed in order. She watched the people Bobby Cusnoo talked to but didn't see anyone she thought was her assailant.

She and Kata left together and, when they were out of earshot, Kata pointed at Sarah's hem. "What happened outside?"

Sarah gathered herself in innocence. "Why do you ask?"

"Your hem wasn't torn when we left your house."

"Takes a seamstress to notice that. I ran into a little trouble outside."

"Job?"

"Seems like some people don't take too kindly to investigations. A man grabbed me from behind and told me in no uncertain terms to call it off."

Kata stopped and faced Sarah. "Please be careful. Tensions are high in this town right now. If you're seen to be a traitor—"

Sarah embraced her cousin. "Don't worry. I'm just out to find who's been killing these people. The person behind this isn't doing anybody any good. Besides, the sheriff is due back on Monday."

They started on their way again. Sarah digested the tidbits from the evening. *Our investigation is making someone nervous.* In a way, that was very satisfying, but she wished it could be an American she was after. She hated that she wasn't impartial. The trouble between the whites and Tlingits made Sarah feel like she was caught in the middle of a culture war.

Chapter 6

Amos tugged at his mustache as he listened to Sheriff Mike Mahoney of Cordova. "Did someone actually hear these threats made?"

The red-haired Irishman nodded. "One of the members of the ANB here was nervous about the murder at our cannery. He thought it was just talk, but when the executive was found in the cutting machine at the factory, he told me what he'd heard."

"Did he know these people?"

"Nope. He said they weren't regulars at the Cordova camp."

Amos extracted an envelope from his jacket pocket. "Did you happen to find one of these?" He showed him the note that was found on the body.

Mahoney glanced at it, then reached for the folder on his desk. He flipped an envelope with a number one emblazoned on the front. "If you look at the note, it's the same."

After a perusal, Amos asked, "Was there anything in the newspaper Personals that could have related to the murder? A warning, perhaps?" A clipping appeared under his nose. "Well, it looks like we're dealing with the same person."

"Or group. Have you heard from any other community about a warning yet?"

"Not yet. We've alerted the coastal canneries to

check the Personals for anything suspicious." Amos put his hat on. "I'm catching the airplane to Soldotna to see what I can find out there."

Mahoney extended his hand. "Keep in touch, Darcy. The more lawmen who know about this, the better the chances of catching the murderers."

Cordova's airfield was on a flat plain that stretched close to the Gulf of Alaska. If anything, it was nippier up here than by the sheltered channel seas of Juneau. Early in May, there were still little patches of stubborn snow in the shadows, patches that would be gone in a week or so. Amos clutched his sheepskin-lined jacket closer around him against the chilly wind as he waited for the airplane.

A small canvas-covered biplane bounced onto the field and Amos waved at the pilot. The machine gave a few sputters as it taxied up to the station, and when it stopped the pilot swung down from the wing. "Are you Sheriff Darcy? The one who wants to go to Soldotna?"

Amos nodded.

"We'll leave in a few minutes. I have to refuel. You can get into the passenger seat." He indicated the front of the airplane.

Amos climbed in as the station manager and pilot wheeled the fuel tank out and hooked up the hose. He was looking forward to getting back to Juneau and comparing notes with Sarah. *Hell, you want to see Sarah again. You hate being away from her. That's the reason you asked her to be a deputy, but you're too scared to give in to your feelings for her.* He cursed himself. He needed to be a confirmed bachelor, because it hurt too much when someone he loved died. A family could be a serious complication to a lawman. He needed to be single-minded.

The pilot climbed in, the station manager gave the propeller a quick turn, and the engine sputtered to life. They picked up speed along the field until the plane soared into the blue. The hour and a half to Soldotna was taken up with the different puzzle pieces Amos had discovered on this trip. Maybe it was a good idea to have Sarah keep her ears open at the Juneau camp, just in case.

The meeting with the sheriff in Soldotna produced the same results, with an envelope emblazoned with a number two in the same handwriting. Amos gave him the lowdown on what had happened in Juneau. "How was the man killed here?"

The sheriff checked his coroner's notes. "Looks like his morning cup of coffee was tainted with rat poison. These people seem to have various ways of getting their point across."

Amos nodded. "Keep me informed on how the investigation is going here, and I'll do the same."

After leaving the sheriff's office, Amos walked to the little airfield. "When is the next flight to Juneau?"

The field manager checked his list. "There's a plane going out at ten in the morning."

"Good. I'll be here. Is there a place nearby where I can stay?"

The man made a motion toward an old wooden structure south of the field. "That's where a lot of the pilots spend the night."

Amos's lip curled as he came up on the rickety porch that protested when he trod on the boards. His room reeked of old sweat and cigars. He couldn't wait to get out of there in the morning.

After a tough two-day flight, the familiar sight of Mt. Juneau came comfortably into view. The snow on the top glowed pink with the late afternoon sun. *Home.* Amos couldn't wait to have a decent dinner at Millie's and crawl into his own bed.

God, it's good to be back in Juneau! I tend to forget how primitive other parts of the territory can be. Millie's was a welcome warm glow to the soul as he strolled in from the gray blanket of sea fog slowly clutching the city in its damp grip. Millie looked up and grinned. "Welcome home, Sheriff!"

"What's good tonight?"

She pulled her pencil from behind her ear. "The chicken is very good. Can I get you some with mashed potatoes and peas?"

"Plenty of gravy on those potatoes, Millie."

"Yes, I know." She hurried to the kitchen.

When she served his dinner, he stopped her. "Anything going on in town?"

"Nothing big." She pursed her lips. "But I did hear there was a bit of a disagreement at the ANB social Saturday. It concerned Sarah."

Amos was instantly alert. "What happened?"

"Well, I happened to hear about Jack Harper talking to Sarah. Seems he and Bobby Cusnoo were discussing the problems with the fish traps while they were taking a breath outside, and Sarah showed up. Bobby asked her to tell how the investigation was going. She refused, and he shoved past her. Jack apologized for Bobby's rudeness."

Anger started to bubble, and Amos ground his teeth. "Thanks for letting me know, Millie."

She patted his shoulder. "Relax, Sarah is fine.

Enjoy your meal." She started on her rounds of the tables.

For some reason, Amos' mind was finding ways of dismembering Bobby Cusnoo. Then his brain hit a slot. *Why was Bobby so interested in the investigation? Is he involved somehow?* Amos was sure Sarah must have thought of that, too.

Amos finished his meal and had started toward his apartment over the drugstore when he had a fleeting thought of visiting Sarah. *No. That can wait until tomorrow.* When he came to the stairwell door between the two retail stores on the street level, Amos took the steps two at a time to his apartment, where he pulled out the folder of the information on the murder, spread it out on his bed, and pored over it until exhaustion dealt him senseless.

Amos greeted Sam the next morning as he arrived early. "Have Lakat come in as soon as she gets here. Any news about Personals from anywhere else?"

"No, sir. Did your trip go well?"

Amos nodded. "At least we know it's the same person writing the notes." He went into his office and stirred the embers in the potbellied stove, adding some kindling. When the branches caught, he put some stove wood in and gingerly closed the iron door, adjusting the damper. After he fetched water from the back, he started the coffee.

As the smell of the fresh brew wafted out, there was a knock and a call at his office door. "It's Sarah!"

"Come in, Lakat!" His breath caught for a moment. Amos was happier to see her than he let on. He wanted to embrace her, but he caught himself up short. She could have gotten herself killed. "Sit, and I'll show you what I found as soon as you explain what in the Sam Hill you were doing at the social. I told you just to keep your ears open."

Sarah sighed, pouring some coffee into her mug. She sat across from Amos. "I knew both Jack and Bobby. I thought they would talk freely with me, so instead of someone catching me eavesdropping, I thought I'd do this aboveboard." She stopped and glanced at him accusingly. "You must have had dinner at Millie's last night. Every story in town seems to end up there."

"Anything else happen?"

Sarah pursed her lips. "Yes. After Jack and Bobby went inside, I was grabbed from behind by a man whose voice I didn't recognize." She went on to tell what happened.

Amos rubbed the stubble on his chin. "Call off the dogs, eh? Are you sure Bobby didn't go around the building?"

"This man was taller than Bobby. I looked to see if there was anyone inside like that, but I didn't see any stranger. From what I heard of the conversation, I think we should look at some of the villages upstream, too. What did you find out?"

Amos told her and showed her what he'd come up with on the trip.

"So we do know that it's one man."

"Well, the one that's writing the notes is. I'm sure with an operation this complex there's more involved."

"Maybe he has allies in the plant."

Amos nodded. "I have a feeling someone was watching Thornton's habits from the inside. Does Bobby work at Polar Star?"

Sarah hesitated. "I can find out. Do you think he had something to do with it?"

"He seemed upset you didn't give him information. There has to be a reason why."

"I know his sister. She works at Millie's. I'll go now." Sarah set down her mug and prepared to sweep out.

"Lakat?"

"Yes, Amos?"

"Be careful." She looked at him strangely, then left.

Amos cursed himself. *She's an experienced deputy. Of course she'll be careful.* It was getting harder to keep his feelings for her under the surface.

Chapter 7

Sarah held her jacket closed against the gray fog that saturated her hair. It was good to have Amos back. *I seem to feel more confident when he's around.* She was aware of her chest tightening when she thought of him. *No. I can't get that deeply involved. He's my boss.*

Sally Cusnoo was working the counter, so Sarah slid onto the cushioned yellow oilcloth stool and greeted her. "Can I speak with you for a moment?"

Sally smiled. "Hello, Sarah! I have to refill the coffeepot. I'll be right with you."

Sarah had gone to school with Sally and hoped that friendship was still there. Sally brought a cup of coffee and set it in front of Sarah. "You need anything to eat?"

"No, thank you. I need to ask you something."

"Sure. What?"

Sarah blew on the coffee and took a sip. "Where is your brother Bobby working now?"

"He works at Polar Star. Why?"

Sarah thought fast. "I was wondering if he spoke to you about the murder. We're trying to get as much information as we can."

She shook her head. "He just told me what was in the paper. I guess he didn't see anything. Why don't you ask him?"

"He didn't seem that sociable to me when I saw him last."

34

Sally chewed on her lip. "I know he's upset that the law is looking to blame a native."

Sarah sighed and rose. She drew a nickel out of her pocket and placed it by the coffee. "We have to check everyone. Thank you, Sally."

Back at the office, Sarah told Amos what she'd found out.

"Well, you did find out he works there. We can keep that in mind." Amos sat back in his chair. "Now, we wait for any of the traps we've set up to spring."

Later that day, a courier came in with a telegram. Sarah watched from her desk as he disappeared into Amos' office. Sam glanced at her. "Wonder if one of the departments found something?"

Sarah shrugged. "I'll guess we'll know in a few minutes."

When the courier reappeared, Amos was right behind him. "Lakat, come in here."

Sarah hurried in and sat across from Amos. "What did you get?"

He showed her the telegram. "It's from Mike Mahoney of Cordova. He got word from a relative in Sitka that a suspicious Personal was posted in their newspaper similar to the ones we have. He said since we're closer, we should alert the law there and help investigate it. He'll come down to help, if anything happens."

"When do you want to leave?"

"We can take a rented flight from the airfield. Go home and pack clothes for a few days' stay, and I'll arrange for a plane and pilot. I'll pick you up at your house in an hour."

"I'll be waiting!" she shot back, closing the door

behind her. Sarah rushed to her small house, only three blocks from the station, and grabbed a bag. Forty-five minutes later, packed and with the house closed down, she waited for the patrol car as she sat in a rocker on her porch, her bag at her feet.

The auto pulled to the side of the street in front of the house, and Amos swung her bag into the back with his as Sarah climbed into the passenger seat. "Any trouble getting a plane?" she ventured.

"Not when you tell them it's business. We're off when we get there." He concentrated on the winding road to the airfield. When they arrived, there was a little transport plane warming up and a young pilot waving to them.

Amos parked the patrol car near the airfield's office and carried his bag and Sarah's to the young man. "Lakat, this is our pilot, Bill Wright. Bill, this is my deputy, Sarah Lakat."

Sarah held out her hand to the blonde-haired, blue-eyed pilot. "Nice to meet you."

Bill acknowledged her and took their bags to store in a compartment of the plane. He waved them to the back. "There's seats back there for passengers. You can strap yourselves in, and we'll be off in five minutes."

The seats proved to be little more than cushioned metal frames bolted to the floor. Sarah and Amos found the ends of the safety belts that would hold them in the contraption. Finally, the craft started bumping along the grassy field. Sarah swallowed hard and closed her eyes. This was the first time she had flown, but she knew this was the fastest way to get to Sitka, so she didn't tell Amos.

About ten minutes into the flight, Sarah heard,

"Lakat, are you all right?"

She hesitated a moment. "Yes. Why do you ask?" She opened her eyes and peered at Amos.

Amos tugged at his mustache with an amused glint. "You're as pale as death. Is this the first time you've flown?"

"Yes. But I can take it."

Amos broke out into a grin. "Swell. I hope I don't have nursemaid duty when we get to Sitka."

She gave him an evil-eyed glare. "You won't. Now, if you don't mind, I'll handle this myself." She closed her eyes again and rested her head against the metal bulkhead just as the little plane gave a jerk. Amos snorted as she rubbed the bump on the back of her head. "Not a word, Sheriff." She glared at him.

They arrived at Sitka without further incident, and the plane bumped along the grassy airfield there. When the craft stopped, Amos undid his safety belt and moved to help Sarah.

She felt like her stomach was still up in the air, but she gathered her dignity about her as a shield. "I can handle my own belt, thank you!" To her dismay, as she rose her knees promptly buckled, and Amos caught her. It was disconcerting to have his arms around her, and an unwanted tingling went through her body. "I'm all right now."

Amos hesitated. "You sure?"

She pressed her lips together. "I'm sure. You can let go of me now." Willing her legs to hold her up, she straightened her clothing. "Come on."

Bill had their bags off the plane and waiting at the bottom of the steps. When they exited the plane, he held out his hand to Amos. "I hope the trip was smooth enough."

Amos nodded as he shook Bill's hand. "It went swell. I'll wire when we're ready to come back."

"Good. I'll see you then." Bill turned and tipped his cap to Sarah. "Miss Lakat."

"Thank you, Bill."

Bill climbed back into the plane, and Sarah saw Amos loading their bags into a Ford truck, assisted by a burly man in a khaki jacket. She hurried over as Amos turned.

"Sarah, this is Sheriff Ray Tunny of Sitka. Ray, this is my deputy, Sarah Lakat."

Ray Tunny regarded her without speaking. "Your deputy is a woman Eskimo?"

The hairs on the back of Sarah's neck prickled. She held out her hand. "Yes, I am a woman deputy, but I'm a Tlingit."

He ignored the hand. "Get in the truck. I'll drive to the hotel. We can speak during dinner." He directed the information to Amos.

Sarah glanced at Amos. He blew out a breath and shrugged. "Come on." He helped Sarah into the truck cab and slid in beside her. She ended up sandwiched between them, and it was mighty silent on the way. They stopped by the Seaside Hotel, and Tunny pulled the brake back.

"This is it, Darcy. You can register, and I'll unload the bags."

Sarah followed Amos inside the marine blue building, past its wide white porch where wicker rocking chairs bobbed back and forth in the breeze. A distinguished-looking man with salt-and-pepper hair was behind the registration desk. "May I help you, sir?"

Amos leaned on the desk. "Yes. I'd like two rooms for a couple of days."

"For—?"

"Myself and Miss Lakat."

The man's eyes turned to her for the first time. "I'm sorry. We don't rent to Eskimos."

Through his teeth, Amos growled, "I'm Sheriff Amos Darcy from Juneau and she's my deputy. We're here on official business."

"I'm sorry. That's our policy. No exceptions."

Before Amos exploded, Sarah put a hand on his arm. "Let's go someplace else."

Amos stalked out of the hotel and confronted Tunny. "Are there any other hotels in this town?"

With a half-smile, he ventured, "Something wrong, Darcy?"

"Yes, there's something wrong! Take us to a place where they don't have brainless people working for them!"

"You're not going to find many who will take *her*. There's an inn near the docks who will rent to anyone."

"Take us there."

Tunny shrugged. "All right."

They reloaded the bags and mashed together again in the front seat. In a few minutes, they were in the seedy harbor section with a bunch of ramshackle buildings leaning crazily along a dirt road. Tunny stopped in front of a place called The Harpoon just as a couple of rummys reeled down the street and started to fight. Tunny slid out and grabbed them by their collars. "Go home and sleep it off, or I'll throw you in a cell."

They turned their unfocused eyes on him and straightened up. "Sure, Shurff!" Then Tunny pushed them in another direction.

He went back to the truck. "We're here. The Harpoon has rooms upstairs that anyone can rent for a price."

Amos exploded. "Where did the sots get the booze from? Shouldn't you be looking for that?"

"Darcy, the speakeasies around here change from day to day. It's hard to keep up with them."

Sarah sighed. "Amos, I'll stay here. You go back to Seaside."

Amos gave her an angry glare. "The hell I will! You're not staying here!" He bellowed, "Tunny!" Then he jumped out of the truck. "What in the name of all that's unholy do you think you're pulling?"

Tunny spit on the ground. "I can't help it if you have a poor choice of deputies."

Amos grabbed both the man's lapels and shook him. "She's a deputy, and a damn good one. Now you find a place for us to stay that isn't Skid Row!"

Sarah was sure the two men were going to engage in a fistfight in the middle of the street. They seemed like two bull moose, each trying to stare the other down.

Tunny jerked away from Amos and straightened his jacket. "We're not getting anywhere like this. Look, Darcy, my wife and I have a cabin on our property we can lend you. How's that?"

Sarah could tell the adrenaline was pumping through Amos. Certainly his chest was heaving. Amos blew out a breath and stepped back. "You'd do that for us?"

"Darcy, the Tlingits have a bad reputation in Sitka, but if you think that much of her, she must be okay."

Both men got into the truck like nothing happened. Sarah knew it was prudent to keep her mouth shut. Tunny pointed the truck inland, and after ten minutes they found themselves at a little cottage at the edge of town. Tunny pointed to a small road. "The cabin is at the end of that lane. That was the home here before the cottage was built. We use it for guests, so it's clean." He stopped by the cottage. "Wait here a moment, and I'll take you." He got out and went in the side door.

Sarah glanced at Amos. "My, he had a turnaround. What was that all about?"

Amos shook his head. "The hell if I know. He seems to have a Jekyll-and-Hyde streak."

"Oh, well, at least we don't have to stay at that dive. I think women would be viewed as *working* if they stayed there, and I don't need the extra money," she added with a smirk.

Amos opened his mouth as if to say something but apparently changed his mind. Tunny came back out with a woman of equally solid build behind him, wiping her hands on a dish towel.

Tunny opened the driver's door and introduced them by their first names to his wife, Flo.

Flo leaned into the truck. "I'm sorry you had to see the bad side of the community. I want both of you to come in for dinner tonight and breakfast tomorrow. I insist!" She waved away any protests.

As his wife went back into the house, Tunny slid into the driver's seat. "I'll take you to the cabin." They bounced along the dirt road until a log structure came into view. "Well, this is it."

The picturesque building was set next to several hemlock trees, and a trellis of climbing roses arched over the path to the door. "This is beautiful," Sarah observed.

"I thought you'd like it. Come on, I'll help you with your bags." He opened the door and they followed him inside. Ecru lace curtains hung from the windows, and the whole place was modestly furnished in clean, half-century-old furniture. Only one thing was wrong—it was a one-room cabin. "I had to tell the wife you were married or she wouldn't have let you stay here."

Amos whirled on him. "Tunny—!"

"Something wrong, Darcy?"

Amos took a fistful of Tunny's shirt. "You've had it in for us since we got here. I'm not about to lie to your wife, no matter what you say. Now, I'm telling you to treat us like fellow officers, or you can deal with this killing spree on your own!"

Tunny put his hands up. "Okay! I'll bring your meals out. We'll start to the cannery first thing after breakfast."

Amos still cursed under his breath after Tunny banged the door behind him. "Lakat, I'm sorry I got you into this. You don't deserve this treatment."

Sarah shrugged. "I'm a victim of birth. The reputation Tunny referred to was the Tlingits burning down the town of Sitka. Even though that was in the last century. Some people have trouble letting go."

Amos lit one of the kerosene lamps and hung it over the table. "I'll have to be honest with you. I didn't realize what your people were going through until now. Oh, I saw the Indian sections of restaurants and theaters in Juneau, but this goes much deeper."

Sarah sat in one of the chairs, and Amos settled

across from her. She rested her chin on her cupped hand. "And Juneau isn't as bad as some of the towns in the Territory."

"For tonight, we can fashion a room divider of some sort, so you can have some privacy."

Sarah smiled. "Thank you, Amos." She was very grateful that he thought about her comfort and her feelings. A few minutes later there was a knock. Amos got up.

Tunny brought in two trays, then went out again and returned with a coffeepot and mugs. "Here you are. The alarm clock is by the bed. I figured we could leave by six. That way we'll be there when the executives arrive at the plant."

Amos nodded. "We'll be ready by five-thirty for breakfast, then."

Tunny gave a short cough. "Ah, yes. 'Night." The door closed with a bang.

"Bastard," Amos said under his breath.

"Amos, let's make the best of a bad situation. The chicken and dumplings smell delicious." Sarah lifted the covers off. Fresh peas were swimming in a thick sauce, and rolls with butter were on the side. A slab of apple pie rounded things out. Amos poured the coffee while Sarah set up the meal. She paused before picking up a mouthful. "Really, this isn't so bad. We could have been stuck in that heap of a waterfront building."

Amos shook his head. "I'm sorry. I guess I didn't understand what this was all about. The Indians, I mean. I grew up on a ranch in Idaho, where there wasn't anybody but white Americans. The Indians were put on reservations before I was born."

"Don't apologize. Probably because of that you're

more accepting of me." She smiled. "It's nice to find an American who doesn't care what you are as long as you can do the job."

He raised his mug of coffee in a salute, and she did the same. After dinner, Amos rigged a blanket across the small cabin between the bed and the couch. "There. You can have the bed, and I'll sleep on the couch."

"Amos, you're taller than I am. I can manage with the couch."

"Sarah, humor me. Set the clock for four-thirty."

She took her turn at the outhouse, then retreated to her side of the cabin. She lit the hurricane lamp on the wall by the bed and set the alarm clock. The steady tick-tick comforted her. She changed into her flannel pajamas, blew out the lamp, and wriggled under the sheet that smelled like bleach and lavender. Hearing the door open and close, she called out, "Good night, Amos!"

A gruff "Good night, Lakat" came from the other side of the divider blanket. Sleep came quickly.

****

Amos shook out another blanket he'd found, then removed his outer clothing and fluffed a down pillow next to one of the arms. After he turned out the light on the kerosene lamp on the table, he groped his way back to the couch, managing to stub three of his toes on a chair. Cursing under his breath, he found his makeshift bed.

When he swung his feet up, Amos discovered he was about five inches longer than the furniture and had to bend his knees to fit. Silently condemning Tunny to hell without a fan, he lay back—and cracked his head on the arm. He rubbed his head, propped the pillow on the couch's arm, and scrunched up on his side.

Tick-tick-tick drilled into his brain. *Damn clock!* He shoved the edges of the pillows around his ears and screwed his eyes shut. He could still hear Sarah shifting around in her sleep. Being that close to her was doing things to him he'd rather not think about. He tried to push down his erection, and that made it worse. He knew there was going to be unrequited pain tomorrow. After hours of tossing and leg cramps, the alarm's little brass bell dragged his senses out, unprepared for morning.

He heard Sarah out of bed, busily doing things back there. "Good morning, Amos!"

"Lakat, just get to the outhouse and back in here!" Amos wasn't putting up with a chirpy female.

"Ohh, somebody's grumpy."

"Now!"

Sarah hurried from around the blanket, buttoning up her shirt. She eyed him as she opened the cabin door. "Bad night?"

Amos growled, "Women!" As she closed the door, he got up and pulled on his clothes. The sun was peeking through the trees when she returned and it was his turn to slog through the wet pine needles. The chill in the early morning air added to his mood. Tunny was delivering the breakfast trays when Amos returned. Sarah had tidied up the cabin while he was out.

Tunny turned a questioning glance at Amos. "Slept well?"

Amos glared. "It was livable. That's all I'm going to say."

Tunny grinned. "You had the couch, eh?"

Amos said evenly, "We'll be ready to go at five-thirty."

"All right. You'll probably be happier with some breakfast and coffee in you." He picked up the dinner trays and left.

Sarah poured the coffee as he sat at the table. "I told you to take the bed."

"There's some things I won't do. One of them is not being a gentleman." He dug into his flapjacks without another word.

At five-thirty, they were on their way to Alaska King Cannery. The filtered sun sparkled on the waters as they drove along the coast. Amos looked at the Personal from Sitka's newspaper. Yes, it said something was going to happen at the cannery today. Now, maybe, between the three of them, they could prevent another tragedy and catch whoever was doing this.

Tunny pulled into the grassy lot that served as a parking area. "The executives should be arriving soon. We can corral them and have them work with us."

Amos frowned. "Did you let any of them know?"

"I told the owner, Travis Johnson, that there was a strange message in the paper for the cannery and that we would watch for any funny business. All of them are going to be here at the same time, so we can talk to them."

One by one the men arrived over the next fifteen minutes. Tunny gathered them around. "Sheriff Darcy is here from Juneau to talk to you about the Personal in the newspaper two days ago."

Amos faced the men and explained the situation, adding, "I've checked in Cordova and Soldatna, and the warnings were the same as the one in Juneau. So far these criminals have taken the lives of three executives. Tunny and I, along with Deputy Lakat here, will stay at the plant all day. We suggest that if you have a daily routine, break it. Don't go anywhere alone, and be aware of everyone around you."

Tunny nodded. "If you see anyone suspicious, find one of us and let us know."

The men dispersed, and Tunny turned to Amos. "Why don't you take the warehouse, I'll take the canning area, and Miss Lakat, you can handle administration."

Amos agreed. "I think we should take lunches in shifts, so there will be at least two on the beat." He pointed at Sarah. "Lakat, take your break from eleven-thirty to noon. Tunny, noon to twelve-thirty, and I'll take the last."

Amos walked into the cavernous building that looked similar to Polar Star's. Workers hurried about, putting boxes of cans on great pallets to be picked up by trucks and ships that moved the stock every day.

After eight hours, the executives were ready to leave. Three of the plant guards were with them. They joined with Amos, Tunny, and Sarah by the administration building, so they could be escorted to their automobiles. Tunny pointed along the fence line. "We'd better keep careful watch in all directions."

Amos put his fingers on the handle of his revolver. "All right, let's go." Amos' stomach knotted. Something wasn't right. He could feel it in his bones. Suddenly, something whizzed past him from behind and he heard a thud. Mr. Orville Jensen went down with a cry, an arrow stuck in his lower back. Everyone hit the dirt at the same time. Amos pulled out his gun and took off toward a patch of trees to the rear of the fenced area. He heard a rustle in the bushes and took the chain link fence in a step and leap. Landing on his feet on the other side, Amos took off to where the noise had come from. Footprints were visible in the soft mud.

Concentrating on the tracking, Amos felt himself ensnared by something from above. As he cursed and struggled, he became tightly tangled in whatever it was. Tunny and Sarah ran up, and Tunny continued the way the assailant had gone.

Sarah dropped beside Amos. "Stop moving around. You're caught in a fishing net." She pulled a pocket knife out of her jacket. "I'll have to cut you out." She stood and cut two trailing lines that were attached to the bushes on either side. "Looks like they planned for anyone chasing them."

Amos was beyond angry. "God damn it! I fell for it like an ignorant school boy! Ouch!"

"Hold still! This net is hard enough to cut without you flailing your arms around."

Amos took to muttering curses to himself as Sarah finished cutting the entwined strands. "Lakat, we failed. All that planning for nothing. I really thought we had outsmarted them."

Sarah sat back on her heels. "Tunny took off after them. Maybe he can catch whoever it is." She gathered the bits of net and put them in her jacket pocket. "I suppose we should keep this in case it helps our case." She snapped the blade back into its groove and the knife followed the net into her jacket.

"Who's taking care of the injured man?"

"The plant guards are handling that. Tunny and I came as soon as we saw you were in trouble."

Amos sat and steamed for a few moments. "Let's go tail Tunny." They set off following the footprints. Arriving at a small stream, they found Tunny examining the shore.

Tunny glanced up. "Must have had a craft waiting for him. It was gone by the time I trailed him here." He pointed to where the tracks disappeared by the water. "With it being springtime, the stream is at its deepest now. Other times it's a trickle."

The three studied the area around the tracks to see if anything had been dropped, but they found nothing. Sarah pointed to the ground where the tracks ended. "It may mean nothing, but there are some animal tracks here, too."

Tunny looked closer. "Looks like there may have been a wolf here."

Sarah shook her head. "They look more like a domestic dog. See, where the man's prints are? It seems a dog pranced around him. They go in a circle, then disappear again."

Amos made a note. "So we think he might have acted alone, but he had a dog with him."

She pointed downstream. "The current is strong. He's probably quite a ways by now."

Tunny nodded. "Let's see what's happening at the plant." They climbed the bank and tramped back through the woods.

One of the plant guards greeted them. He turned to Tunny. "The doc is here. He said to give you this." He handed the sheriff the broken arrow.

"Darcy, look at this." Tunny untied a piece of paper that had been wrapped around the shaft. He glanced at it and gave it to Amos.

Number four. Will the traps come down before another dies?

Amos pulled out the envelope from Polar Star and compared the handwriting. "We're dealing with the same man." He put his hand on the guard's shoulder. "How's Mr. Jensen?"

The man ran his fingers through his hair. "The doc broke the shaft off and took Jensen to the hospital to remove the rest of it."

Amos turned back to Tunny. "Let's go back into town. I want to wire for an airplane to take us to Juneau."

Tunny looked surprised. "But don't you—?"

"You can take care of it. I have my own fish to fry in Juneau, so to speak. We can keep each other informed on anything else that happens. I'll tell the offices in Cordova and Soldotna."

Sarah took a step forward. "We should stop by the hospital to see about Mr. Jensen before we leave."

Amos patted her shoulder. "Good idea, Lakat. Tunny, wire us with any developments. We'll see if we can help in any way."

After they took care of the communications, Tunny pulled up in front of a large white clapboard building. "Here's the hospital."

The three made their way to the reception desk, where Tunny removed his hat. "I'm Sheriff Tunny, ma'am," he said to the nurse. "I would like to find out about Mr. Orville Jensen, who was brought in here earlier."

She consulted a ledger. "Ah, yes. Dr. Harper is still in surgery with him. Would you like to wait?"

Amos cut in. "Since we can't leave until tomorrow

morning, we'll wait for word on Jensen. I'm Sheriff Amos Darcy from Juneau, and this is my Deputy, Sarah Lakat."

The nurse nodded, then went back to her work.

Tunny turned to leave. "I have to make a report. I'll check with you later and get more details."

When he left, Amos and Sarah settled on two of the padded chairs in the waiting room. Sarah had concern in her eyes. "Amos, don't take this so hard. We tried our best to keep the man safe and catch our murderer."

Amos ground his teeth. "I probably would have caught him if I'd seen that net."

"You weren't expecting a trap. Any of us would have been caught. I can find out, at least, what tribe he's from. Every group has their own way of making nets. That's why I kept the pieces."

"Good thinking, Lakat." Amos put his head back and closed his eyes. Between last night's miserable sleeping arrangements and the long day he'd just had, he was exhausted.

"Amos—Amos!" The words were accompanied by a gentle patting on his shoulder. "Tunny is back, and we have a report from Dr. Harper about Mr. Jensen." Sarah's voice was a sweet thing to wake up to.

Amos slowly stretched his stiff neck. "Thank you, Lakat. How is he?"

Tunny took up the report. "The doc said he came through surgery, but it's going to be touch and go for a while. His liver was damaged, but they were able to remove the rest of the arrow safely and repair the damage."

Amos rubbed his eyes. "Well, here's one the murderer wasn't able to pull off. I wonder if the stakeout had anything to do with it."

Tunny nodded. "He might have had something else planned, but we got in the way."

"We'd better alert the other coastal law offices to do this if there's a suspicious Personal ad in the paper."

Sarah sat on the other chair. "Hopefully, they won't quit posting them because of this."

Tunny turned to her. "This is a way they can get their message out. I think there should be a tighter identification system for the Personals, but I don't know if the papers will change their policy."

Amos jabbed his thumb southward. "The problem is, we don't know where he will strike next."

"Darcy, do you want to go back to the cabin to wait for morning?"

Amos winced at the thought of that couch from the nether regions. "No. Can you think of anything else?"

Tunny hesitated a moment. "We have a couple of cots at the office, in the back room, for when we have to be there overnight. You're welcome to use those."

Amos glanced at Sarah. "I don't—"

"We'll take them," Sarah interjected. "I know you didn't sleep well on that couch. I don't care who wags tongues in this town. We'll be gone tomorrow."

Tunny nodded. "I'll treat you to supper and then get you set up. There are pillows and blankets at the office."

After they'd eaten at one of the diners, Tunny brought what they needed for the room at the office. "I'll bring in some breakfast on trays in the morning before I take you to the airfield." He removed his hat and turned to Sarah. "Miss Lakat, I want to apologize to you for your reception in Sitka. I think you are as good a deputy as any of my men here. I was impressed with your work today."

Sarah looked surprised, but shook the offered hand. "Thank you, Sheriff Tunny. I accept your apology."

With a smile to them both, he took his leave.

Sarah picked up one of the pillows and a blanket and made up one of the cots. "I'll sleep in my clothes, so you won't feel uncomfortable."

Amos followed suit. "You're a classy lady, Lakat."

Sarah grinned as she stretched out on the cot. "You're quite the gentleman, Amos, when you want to be."

Amos grunted as he turned out the desk light. "Go to sleep." He was out in seconds.

Chapter 8

Sarah awoke to a pounding on the door. At first, she didn't know where she was, until she heard Sheriff Tunny's voice ring out, "Breakfast!" She swung her feet to the floor as Amos opened the door. Tunny balanced two trays in his hands and set them on the desk. "There you are. You have an hour before we leave for the airfield."

She went into the station's lavatory to freshen up a bit. When she returned, Amos already was digging into his ham and eggs. She picked up her knife and fork and cut some of the fragrant smoked ham, savoring it.

When they'd finished eating, Amos took his turn in the lav and came out a little less disheveled than when he went in. "Ready to go home?"

"More than. This has been quite a trip. I trust you slept better on the cot?"

Amos' face had a strange, amused glint to it. "As well as could be expected."

Sarah cocked an eyebrow at him but didn't offer anything, as Tunny came in and hustled them out of the office. She slid into the back seat of the patrol car while Tunny and Amos stored the bags in the trunk.

The sea air had cleared the night fog away and the sky was a deep Alaskan blue as they turned into the airfield and bounced along the gravel path to the waiting plane, where Bill Wright waved to them as they stepped out.

Amos went over and shook his hand. "Mr. Wright, I'm glad you could make it here so early."

Bill nodded. "With the daylight getting longer, I can get an earlier start." He juggled their bags and started up the steps. "Come on in when you're ready."

Tunny gave Amos' shoulder a clap. "Thanks for your help. If you need anything in Juneau, let me know."

"What we need is to get the word out and catch whoever is doing this. Keep in touch, Tunny."

Tunny tipped his hat to Sarah. "Thank you, as well, Miss Lakat."

Sarah expressed her goodbye and joined Amos on the airplane. They strapped themselves into their seats, and Amos called to Bill that they were ready. Sarah was a little more comfortable this time, knowing what was going to happen. She broke out of her reverie and found Amos watching her with a small smile as they started moving.

She chuckled. "Before you say anything, yes, I'm better about this now."

"I know. You seem to overcome things that bother you. I think I understand you more than I did before." He grinned.

Amos was an attractive man, hidden under all that scruffiness. She'd seen him one time shaved and polished and had been astonished. *I can't let myself fall for him.* She admonished herself for such foolishness.

The small plane bounced along the airfield until it was airborne. Bill Wright had to be an A-one pilot, because he took pains to keep the plane steady on their way to Juneau. They arrived in time to have lunch at

Millie's.

As Millie served their soup and sandwiches, Amos glanced up. "Anything happening here the last two days?"

She shook her head. "No, it's been quiet." She glanced at Sarah. "I almost forgot. There was a man asking about you yesterday."

Surprised, Sarah asked, "Did he say what he wanted?"

"No. I never saw him before."

"Thank you, Millie. I'll keep an eye out." When Millie left, she found Amos staring at her. "What do you think?"

His jaw twitched. "That doesn't seem to be any of my business."

Sarah swallowed a bite of sandwich. "As far as I know, I wasn't expecting a man to be looking for me. Especially a stranger."

Amos cocked an eyebrow at her. "Wonder if it had anything to do with that incident at the ANB?"

A bolt of concern burned through her mind. "I hope I didn't stir up the wasps' nest too much."

"Be careful. Whoever it is may not like you continuing to work on the case. No telling what he'll do."

After lunch, Amos gave Sarah the afternoon off, so she headed the three blocks to her small house. Everything looked the same as when she'd left, but she hesitated when she put the key in the lock. She opened the parlor window a bit to let the stuffiness out of the ground floor. Because of the warning, she cautiously checked every nook and cranny. There didn't seem to be anything amiss or out of place, so she slowly relaxed. She lit the gas range and put the water kettle on to boil.

Hurrying upstairs to her bedroom, Sarah changed out of her uniform and into one of her house dresses, then scurried down to the porch to gather up the delivered newspapers and mail. By then, the water was whistling urgently, and she put some hot water and tea into the ceramic pot to steep.

With yesterday's newspaper spread in front of her, she settled down. The sound of someone turning her doorbell brought her up short. "Just a minute!" she called, throwing a shawl across her shoulders. Sarah peeked out the parlor window, and when she saw a large man standing at her front door, she reached deftly into her desk drawer and palmed her Derringer.

Behind the fringed curtain on her door, she called out, "Who is it?"

"An old friend," came a voice from out of the past.

"George?" She opened the door. "George!" A choking weight gripped her chest. *George!?* Slipping the small gun into the sash of her dress, she stepped out onto the porch and put her fists on her hips. "Where in God's name have you been for six years?"

The handsome Tlingit man grinned, and the outer corners of his dark eyes crinkled. "You missed me?"

She laid her hand in a smart smack across his cheek. "You left me a week before our marriage! Not a word except a note saying, 'See you sometime. Be well.' "

"And I meant every word of it," he remarked, rubbing his cheek. "Here I am, and you look well. May I come in?"

Sarah was tempted to use the small gun, but she

swallowed her anger. She was curious what kind of story she was going to get. "Yes, but I wouldn't try anything funny if I were you. I am armed."

"Really? Come here and greet me with a hug." He reached out for her, and she ducked away.

"Don't you dare touch me!" She pointed at a chair. "Sit here, I'll pour some tea, if you'd like."

"Thank you." He settled onto the seat.

Sarah banged the cups and saucers down. *What on earth is he doing here, and why? Breaking my heart, then showing up on my doorstep years later... Well, I'll let him have his say and then show him out the door!* She poured tea into the cups when she had put down the serving tray on the small table in front of George's chair. "Cream or sugar?"

"Two sugars, please. You should remember how I like it."

She restrained herself from throwing the tea in his lap. "You have the gall to come in here and tell me I should remember, when you lit out on me? I'm trying to be civil, because I want an explanation, but I *will* show you out the door."

He laid his hand on her arm as she set the cup down. "I had a good reason. Sarah, sit and listen. You won't need to use that gun tucked into your sash."

"At least you realize I told you the truth."

"My mother sent me out before I was ready to find a woman. I know the tradition is to find a wife in another village and settle there. You would own everything and I would just be your protector and provider. I couldn't do that. There was so much I wanted to experience, and having a family was far down on the list." He sighed. "I wanted a business of

58

my own, and I joined the Americans in their world."

Sarah was silent a few moments. "As you can see, I don't hold to the Tlingit traditions, either. If you had bothered to tell me then, I would have understood. You hurt me."

"I'm sorry. I was too young to think about anyone else, but I've changed." His fingers caressed her cheek. "Will you take me back? Please?"

Strangely she wasn't moved by him anymore. "I've changed, too. I'm not the wide-eyed child you left. I've made my own way in the American world."

"That's what makes us so right for each other. We know how to take care of ourselves. Is there anyone else courting you?"

Sarah's mind flashed to Amos for some reason. "Not really. I've married my job."

"Then let me try to win you back. Dinner tonight?"

"George, no—"

"I'll pick you up at seven."

Sarah hesitated. "All right, but I want to be home early. I just got back from a trip."

"I promise I'll have you here before ten." She'd forgotten how wonderful his smile made him look. She walked him to the door and watched him go down the street. *What the hell have I done? I don't want anything to do with him. Well, I'll go tonight and tell him I'm not interested.*

Later, she readied herself for the outing she was dreading. She slipped her new dropped-waist silk dress on, adjusted her new cloche hat, and slipped on her white gloves. Just as she put on her pumps, the doorbell rang. When she opened the door, Sarah took in the handsome man, clean and fresh-shaved.

"Are you ready? I thought we'd go to Golden North for dinner and a movie." He made a motion to come in.

"I've got my coat right here." She slipped it on as she came out. "I want you to know right now I'm only going because I want some answers."

He tipped his hat and offered his arm. "Shall we?"

They were silent as they walked to the theater. Sarah was trying to come up with explanations in case anyone happened to ask tomorrow. The brightly lit theater marquee advertised *The Sheik,* with Rudolph Valentino, as the main feature. *Wonderful. A passionate movie, to boot.*

George nodded to the young girl in the ticket booth. "Dinner and a movie for two, please."

"That will be thirty cents for the tickets, and the feature will start at eight-thirty."

He gave her the money and picked up the tickets. "Thank you." After checking their coats, they hurried through the lobby doors and into the adjoining restaurant. The hostess at the door seated them and slipped the menus into their hands. After she left, George leaned in. "How's the food here?"

"The cook here is exceptional. Anything will be good." Sarah was secretly hoping that no one she knew would see her. After George ordered two Swiss steaks, she glanced at him. "I want more of an explanation than I got earlier. Why did you choose now to have a change of heart?"

He lifted his glass of ginger ale toward her in a toast. "You're such a fascinating woman."

"This isn't getting you very far with this woman." She raised her glass. "You didn't answer my question."

"A detective to the end. Okay, I started a business I could make a king's ransom on. I lead expeditions into the back country for rich scientists and explorers. Also, I have been hired by bored rich people who want a fashionable outdoor experience."

She glared at him. "Why didn't you tell me this in the first place? I would have understood. You chose to disappear without a word."

"I thought you would lean more to the traditional life."

She rapped her fist on the table. "Then you didn't understand me at all. Maybe it's better that way. You should have left it as it was."

As soon as the waiter had served their food. George patted her arm. "Calm down. Let's enjoy our meal."

She picked at her food. "I think this was a big mistake. I thought you cared for me. I gave myself to you because I thought we would be married." She felt her cheeks burn. "I guess you got what you wanted."

George sighed. "Do you think so little of me? Let's start fresh. Please give me another chance."

She sat silent for a few moments. "After this outing, I'll think about it. Don't press the issue."

"All right. I won't push you into anything tonight."

Sarah nodded. Later, in the theater, she found it hard to concentrate on the dashing sheik trying to lure the innocent maiden into his ridiculously lavish tent in the desert. The young woman she was years ago had adored George, but now time and wisdom had come into play. Something about him troubled her, but she couldn't quite figure out what it was. Were her detective instincts simply working overtime?

The sun hung low on the horizon as they strolled back to her house, and shafts of red-gold rays cut between the buildings. George came up onto the porch with her, and she offered him her hand. "Thank you for the outing. I enjoyed the dinner and movie."

George cupped her chin. "I enjoyed the company. I forgot how enchanting you are." He leaned down and kissed her. Sarah didn't stop him. It had been a long time since anyone had kissed her.

She stepped back and took a quick breath. "Goodnight, George."

He smiled. "Goodnight, Sarah." She opened the door, then turned back to watch the figure disappearing down the street. Her feelings were in a turmoil. On the surface, she knew he had treated her like dirt and she shouldn't give him the time of day. Then there was that breathless young woman who had fallen in love with him. She wanted one more chance.

****

Sarah hummed to herself as she stepped into Millie's for a fast breakfast early the next morning. She chose one of the stools at the counter, and Sally gave her a menu.

"I'll have a doughnut and coffee."

When Sally served her, she thrust a folded paper into Sarah's hand. "I found this on the side table by Billy's coat at home. I thought you might be interested."

When Sally moved down the counter to refresh the customer's coffee, Sarah unfolded the sheet. It read:

Men of the ANB
We can't trust the Americans to fix the problem of the canneries trying to starve us

out. A group, Revenge Ravens, needs members to either fight for our fishing rights upstream or to eliminate the problem ourselves, once and for all. Able-bodied men are encouraged to join. Ask for the members in each ANB camp.

Sarah refolded the paper and slipped it into her coat pocket. *Amos is going to want to see this!* She put fifteen cents down by her plate and waved to Sally. "Thank you for everything!"

Sally acknowledged her and went back to work as Sarah exited the restaurant.

She hurried to the sheriff's office and ducked in the door. "Sam, is Amos in yet?"

He nodded and waved his hand toward the door. "Got here a few minutes ago."

She knocked at the door. "May I come in?"

"You've got something?"

She opened the door. "Yes." Closing it behind her, she gave Amos the notice. "Sally found this on the table by Bobby's coat this morning."

Amos took a look at it. "This might be quite a network of saboteurs. Is there any way you could question some of these people?"

"Just men are allowed at the meetings." Sarah hesitated a moment. "Maybe I could go undercover."

"Trouble is, the men at the camp know you. They could see through any disguise."

"My cousin, Will, lives in Angoon. I'm not well-known there. Maybe I could go as his guest and take a look around. Most of the people there are Tlingits, so there isn't as much suspicion."

Amos paused and rubbed his forehead. "Think you

could pull off going as a man?"

"I had two older brothers and a father. I think so."

"No, that isn't what I meant. Physically." He flushed a bit.

Sarah laughed. "There are things I can do to become more masculine. I won't stay very long, so the lav won't be a problem."

"Do you think you can get your cousin to go along with this?"

"I think so. If he gives me any reason to doubt, then I won't go through with it."

Amos seemed resigned. "All right. I'll let you set it up."

****

Sarah headed to the family home where her mother and Aunt Jane lived. As she reached the modest log cabin she'd grown up in, she saw her mother working in the kitchen garden and hailed her.

Her mother hurried over and hugged Sarah. Sarah breathed in the warm earth smell before her mother pulled back. "Well, child, I wasn't expecting to see you. This is a pleasant surprise."

"Is Aunt Jane here? I need to ask her a favor."

"She's in the house. Come, I'll get some refreshments."

The wood plank door squeaked on its hinges, and the aroma of smoked salmon and seaweed cooking on the stove caressed her nose. Sarah called out, "Aunt Jane?"

Her aunt came out of their small kitchen, wiping her hands on a dish towel. "Sarah! How good it is to see you!"

Her mother nodded toward the kitchen. "Is the tea

still in the pot?"

"Yes. And I still have some berry bread in the cupboard."

They settled around the dropleaf table with the snack, and Sarah laid her hand on her aunt's arm. "I have a favor to ask. When are Will and Mary coming from Angoon again?"

Aunt Jane hesitated. "I believe they're going to be here on Friday."

"I need to talk to him. Is it all right if I come over then?"

"You know you're welcome here any time."

Sarah thanked her, and they spent the hour chatting until Sarah bade them goodbye. She had to make her plans on the undercover work, and next on her list for that was a visit to Kata.

****

Sarah grinned as Kata studied her skeptically. "You want me to help you look like a man?"

"I want to go to the meeting of the ANB in Angoon with Will. It's undercover. I can't tell you anything else."

"Has Will agreed to this? You know how he was at the social."

Sarah shrugged. "I can use my powers of persuasion on him. He's the only male family member I can go to, since your father passed on."

Sitting in the parlor of Kata and Ivan's home on the edge of downtown, Sarah looked at her cousin with a plea in her eyes. "I don't know—" Kata began.

"You're the head of costumes at Golden North. Surely you know something about make-up, as well."

Kata shook her head. "This won't be playacting. If

it's not convincing, you could get hurt. The sheriff wants you to do this?"

"I twisted his arm."

Kata sighed. "Well, if Will says yes, I'll see what I can come up with." Just then, Kata's infant son, Joe, put up a squall in the back room. Kata disappeared and came back with the baby.

Sarah chucked him under the chin. "My, he's getting big. He's going to take after his poppa, I'm sure." She collected her things. "I have to go. Plans to make. Thank you for your help."

Chapter 9

Friday, as her shoes squished through the damp soil on the way to her aunt's house, Sarah carefully thought what she could say to convince Will to get her into the meeting at the ANB. Will's truck sat on the level ground next to the house. She swallowed nervously and sucked up her courage.

As she rapped on the door, calling out, "It's Sarah!" Mary's two-year-old girls ran up, giggling. Soon, she was surrounded by her family. Sarah hoisted the two girls in her arms. "Oh, Mary, they seem to have grown an inch every time I see them!"

Mary laughed and plucked one of the girls from her, then gave Sarah a hug. "It's so good to see you!"

Aunt Jane took the other girl. "Go sit at the table. We were just getting tea ready." Sarah's mother hustled her to a chair.

Will sat across from her at the round dinner table. "Will, after tea, could I speak to you in private? I need to ask a favor."

He nodded. "They said you wanted to talk to me."

After tea, Sarah joined him on the porch, where he was filling his pipe. "What favor do you want to ask?"

She explained what she wanted to do, while Will puffed the smoke. When she was finished, she waited for an answer.

He took a long draw and blew out the smoke

slowly. "Was this your sheriff's idea?"

"No. It was mine. He wasn't too keen on it."

"It seems like spying to me."

"Will, I wouldn't ask you to do this for me if I didn't think it was important. Whoever is doing this is causing more harm than good. We should be proving we can be upstanding citizens, not acting like the savages some people think we are. I, for one, would like to have some say in our government."

He sat for a long moment gazing out over the horizon. "The next meeting is Tuesday evening at seven. I'll get you in, but after that you're on your own. Come to our house at six-thirty."

She put her hand on his arm. "Thank you. I won't get you in trouble, I promise."

He gripped her shoulder. "I worry about you working for the Americans, but I do agree with you about wanting to have a say in the government."

****

Early Tuesday morning, Sarah rapped on the stage door at Golden North. Kata opened it and bid Sarah to come in. "Are you sure this is all right with the Shafers?"

Kata nodded. "I explained I was helping you in undercover work, and they agreed to anything you needed."

"Be sure to thank them for me. And thank Ivan for the use of his truck."

Kata led her to one of the dressing rooms, then picked up some items. "Take everything off. I've got all male clothes for you, right down to the underwear."

Sarah inspected the drawers. "I hope these aren't Ivan's. He's quite a bit bigger than I."

Kata giggled. "No. I went on a special shopping trip for you."

Sarah finished removing her clothing and slipped on the drawers. She pointed to her breasts. "What have you got for these?"

Kata handed her a heavy linen corset. "I've modified this to become a binder." She put it over Sarah's head and pulled it tight against her chest, then started tightening the laces in back.

The flattened linen material squeezed Sarah's breasts against her chest. "Should it be that tight?"

"If you want to look like a fellow, it does."

When Kata finished, Sarah had a flat chest with just enough of a roundness to suggest muscular pecs. Sarah pulled on work socks and a man's undershirt. Kata brought in a wrapped parcel and a pair of worn boots.

As she unwrapped the package, Kata explained, "I got these from the church charity basement, because it won't look like a new outfit. That would raise suspicion. You can probably stuff the boots with this tissue."

Sarah nodded. "Good idea." With the Levis, flannel shirt, and boots on, she turned to Kata. "Well—?"

"Something's wrong. Too flat in the pants."

"What?"

"Here. Roll a sock up and put it in the front of the drawers."

Sarah's cheeks burned as she did so.

Kata gave her the critical eye. "Looks right. Now, sit in the make-up chair." As Sarah did so, Kata stretched a large sheet over her clothes. "I'll fix your hair. Since you have a bob, it can grow out fast."

Sarah stared in the mirror, while Kata brought out the comb and scissors. Kata parted Sarah's hair on one side and proceeded to cut it very short. The vain woman in her gasped in horror, but this had to be done.

Kata cleaned off the cut hair when she was finished. "Luckily, our men aren't very hairy like the Americans, but we have enough to give you some finishing touches. I'm going to use spirit gum to attach some of the hair to the back of your hands and wrists, and some on your face."

Afterwards, Sarah stood and gazed with horror and fascination at the man in the full-length mirror. "Kata, this is unbelievable! Thank you!" Sarah pulled on a stocking cap.

Kata hurried her out to the stage door. "You'd better be going if you're going to make Angoon by six-thirty."

Sarah climbed into the truck and hit the ignition button. She'd learned to drive a truck before she went into law enforcement, because it might be needed. Now it was. She headed over the bridge that crossed the channel and caught the road to the west side of the island. She'd have enough gas to get to Angoon but would have to fill up when she arrived at the docks there.

Avoiding the deep ruts in the ancient road bed, Sarah saw the harbor village of Angoon in the distance. A quick check of her watch let her know she had an hour to spare. She turned in at the main fishing pier, where gas was sold to people with autos. *Well, time to tell if this masquerade is going to work.*

Sarah swung into a masculine stride as she

approached the man at the gas tanks. "Say, fella, what's the going rate for gas here?" she said in a raspy voice.

He spit into the dirt. "Fifteen cents a gallon."

"Fill it up."

He hauled the tank to the truck and proceeded to pump gas into the vehicle. "Haven't seen you around here before."

"Visiting a friend."

The man shut off the tank and turned to Sarah. "Dollar thirty." And he spit in the dirt again.

Sarah dug into her jeans pocket and counted out the change. "Thanks, fella. Keep the change."

He grunted as she climbed into the driver's seat. *It seems like I passed that test.* Soon, the neat little clapboard house of Will and Mary appeared around the bend in the road. She pulled into the front yard and hopped out. For the neighbors' sake, she took the long strides again.

Mary came onto the porch and stared, wide-eyed. "I don't believe it."

Sarah took the steps two at a time. "Surprised to see your cousin Seth? I thought you'd be happy."

Sarah hugged Mary and swung her around before letting her say, "It's done so well. You really do look like a man. Kata did a wonderful job!"

Will came out with the twins and stared at her, slack-jawed. "I never would have known. I think this will work. Did I hear your name is Seth?"

"Yes." Sarah made a move to hug the twins, but they clung shyly to their father. "Looks like they don't remember their cousin."

Mary laughed. "Come in for something to eat before you go."

Sarah checked in the mirror before she left with Will. "You can tell your friends that I'm an acquaintance of yours from Juneau."

He nodded as he slid into the driver's seat of his truck. "I meant what I said. I'm letting you go around on your own."

Sarah patted the pocket that held the notice. "I won't get you in trouble." She pushed down the trembling that threatened her as they arrived at the Angoon Camp. She drew a deep breath. "Wish me luck, Will."

He hesitated a moment after he turned off the engine. "You know I'm not agreeable with this, but I do care about you. Be careful."

She strode to the door with him, and he signed her in. "Thanks."

"Was nothing." Then he went over to a group of his friends.

Sarah saw an open seat at a plank table, where men were engaging in arguments over coffee. "Hey, fellas."

"Hey, yourself. Who are you? I've never seen you before."

"Came in from Juneau with a friend." She turned to the dark-eyed, middle-aged man who had spoken. "I'm Seth Jones. I own a fishing boat in Juneau."

He squinted at her. "I'm Paul Thomas. You look too young to own a boat."

"I got it from my father when he was washed overboard last year."

"Ah. Good legacy when you go looking for a wife."

"As long as there's any salmon left. The cannery has one of those damn traps." Sarah reached into her shirt pocket and pulled out the notice. "Do you know anything about this?"

He hesitated as he read it. "Why didn't you ask about this at the Juneau camp?"

"I was given this a couple of days ago. This is the first meeting I've gone to since then."

Some of the other men chimed in with, "He could be a spy for the canneries," and, "We shouldn't trust a stranger."

Sarah's fist came down on the table. "I don't care where I join. These bastards are starving us out. Especially the villages upstream, who rely on the spawning season to feed their families."

Paul Thomas studied Sarah carefully. "I could give you the name of our contact in Juneau. But you better be who you say you are. Revenge can come swiftly to those who choose to betray us."

"I accept that. I will not betray you."

Paul gave a short nod and took out a pencil and paper. He wrote something and thrust it into her hand. "This is our Juneau contact. See him."

Sarah tried not to gasp when she read the name. *Bobby Cusnoo. Of course, he works in the factory.* She did feel guilty for lying to Mr. Thomas, but this group seemed to be in support of the killings. She tucked the paper in her pocket along with the notice.

A while later, the men assembled in the hall for the meeting. She sat in back and observed the conversations around her. She caught Will eying her several times. Nothing else of any importance came out in the meeting or asides, as far as she could tell.

The meeting adjourned, and she made her way out to Will's truck. The sea fog was heavy and gray in the twilight. She couldn't make out if Will was back at the truck yet. Then instinct told her there was someone behind her. She felt a large hand clamp on her shoulder.

A voice rasped in her ear, "We don't like troublemakers coming here from other camps."

Sarah whirled around. Two other forms in coats stood behind the one who had grabbed her. "Hey, I don't want no trouble. I'm leaving." A fist shot out and connected with her jaw. Pain skimmed across her skull and down her neck. As she hit the ground, she noticed two other forms running toward her, and they flattened two of the men. The third had turned at the sound and was pulled into the fray. Sarah's foot shot out and tripped up one of the men who had risen to rejoin the fight. She jumped up and put a well-placed boot toe in his gut.

The two who had given her a hand finished dispatching the other combatants, and the three troublemakers disappeared into the fog. She recognized Will as he took her arm to guide her to the truck. "Thank you for giving me a hand with those three, but who was that with you?" She turned at the footsteps behind her. Will didn't need to answer. "Amos? What are you doing here?" She was angry he hadn't let her do this on her own, but she was glad to see him, just the same.

Amos helped her into the truck, then said in a lowered voice, "You may learn to walk and talk like a man, but you don't understand male society. They challenge any outsider."

Will nodded as he swung into the driver's seat. "Your sheriff is right. It was a good thing he decided to come down here to keep an eye on you."

Sarah had an urge to hug Amos, but in her present disguise, that would be awkward. "How did you know which one of the men was me?"

Amos hesitated a beat longer than he should have. "A woman's hips move differently than a man's when you're walking."

Sarah felt her cheeks heat. "Oh."

Amos straightened up. "I'll see you back at the office tomorrow?"

"I'm spending the night at Will and Mary's house. I'll be in around noon to give you my report."

He put both hands on her shoulders and gripped her for a moment. "Take care coming back." He released her and disappeared into the fog as Will started the engine.

"Your sheriff seems to care a lot about you."

Sarah's face warmed again. "We're partners working on crime. We work together well."

Will was silent for a few minutes. "I was wrong about Sheriff Darcy. He's a good man, for an American."

Sarah studied Will's profile as he drove. "Thank you for saying so. I trust him with my life."

Sarah leaned back in the seat and dealt with the intense tingling that she always experienced when she thought about Amos. *I don't know how long I can keep these feelings down.* Something inside was bothered a little bit about Amos coming down here to keep an eye on her. Would he do that with any of the other deputies?

Chapter 10

Amos glanced up from his desk as Sarah strode into the office. "Hell of a bruise. Well, sit and give me your report."

Sarah rubbed her jaw. "I'll live." She told Amos what she'd learned at the meeting.

Amos nodded. "Bobby Cusnoo, huh? That confirms some of my suspicions. We'd better look into him and his friends."

Sarah rose to pour herself a cup of coffee. She sat across the desk from Amos. "May I ask you why you traveled to Angoon?"

Amos tugged on his mustache. "I told you why."

"You wouldn't have done that for any of the other deputies."

Amos shifted uncomfortably. "I was worried you might get in over your head, and I was right." He knew that wasn't the whole truth and wondered if she could read that, too. "We should go to the cannery to see if Cusnoo was at work the day of the murder. Personnel should have a record of that."

Sarah rose. "I'm ready."

As Amos was driving to the cannery, he glanced at Sarah. "Your hair is very short."

She put her hand up and touched it. "Kata fixed it so I could comb it over into more of a bob, but it has to grow out a little."

"Good. I don't like it that short."

Sarah smirked. "You're giving fashion advice now?"

"No." He let it go there. So much for thinking out loud.

Amos sat at the desk in the Personnel Department with Sarah peering over his shoulder. He thumbed through the pages of the ledger the timekeeper had given them until he found the date of the murder, and then he ran his finger down the column of names. "I don't find an entry for Cusnoo. He doesn't seem to have been here that day. Hmm, that could be significant."

Sarah patted his shoulder. "You mean he could have been free to commit the murder. Should we get a search warrant to look in his home?"

Amos nodded. "I think now would be a good time. Let's see if we can find anything that would link him to the crime. Got your notes, Lakat?"

She pulled them out of her pocket and showed him. "Let's go."

They made a stop at the courthouse to pick up the warrant before they arrived at the Cusnoo home. Bobby was coming off the porch in his work clothes. He saw Amos and scowled.

"What do you want, Sheriff?" he spat out.

"Cusnoo, I have a search warrant here for your house."

"What's this all about?"

Amos stepped in front of him. "This is about the murder of Mr. Thornton at the cannery."

"Since when am I under suspicion? I wasn't even working that day."

"I know, but you are also the liaison for the Revenge Ravens at the Juneau camp."

"Who told you—?" He noticed Sarah. "Ah, our little turncoat."

Amos gripped his shoulder. "Never mind that. We're going in." Bobby continued to glare at Sarah as they went into the house. Amos pointed to Bobby's room as he said to Sarah, "I'll see if any of the clothes match the descriptions. Why don't you check if you can find anything on that desk."

Amos yanked open the wardrobe and went through the clothes without finding a long coat or mukluks. Nothing looked blood-stained, but there had been time to clean up.

Sarah rapped on the door frame. "I found something on this calendar." She handed him a desk organizer and pointed to the day before the murder.

Amos read it. "Meet R. R. at Millie's for lunch?" He took the calendar outside and showed it to Bobby. "Who is R. R.?"

Bobby frowned. "A friend of mine, why?"

"Are you sure it doesn't stand for Revenge Ravens?"

"Ray Robertson. You didn't find anything, did you, Sheriff?" A shade of triumph colored his face.

"No. But I'd advise you to stay in Juneau." Amos knew he was guilty of something, but Bobby seemed to have covered his tracks well. "One other thing. Have you been out of town for any reason in the past month?"

"No. You can ask anyone. May I go to work now?"

Amos nodded.

As Bobby left, the sheriff glanced at Sarah. "Care

for an early lunch? I want to check a few things with Millie."

Sarah smiled. "You want to check about Ray Robertson."

He glowed. "You know me too well."

Millie's was warm and welcoming in its little niche by the street. A few men were lingering over coffee at the counter, but the tables were deserted after the breakfast crowd had departed. The cooks in the back were busily getting ready for lunch in about an hour. Amos and Sarah took one of the tables on the far side.

Millie hurried over. "You two are here before everything is finished."

Amos shook his head. "All I want is a ham on rye."

Millie glanced at Sarah. "And you?"

"Do you have the chicken noodle soup?"

"Yes. Coming right up."

When the items were delivered to the table with a cup of Millie's finest coffee for each, Amos put a hand on Millie's arm. "I need to ask you a few questions."

"Shoot."

"A couple of weeks ago, Bobby Cusnoo said he was here with a man named Ray Robertson. Now you know most of the people who come in here regularly. Do you know a Mr. Robertson?"

Millie pressed her lips together and tapped her pencil on her pad. "No. But I did see Bobby with a man I didn't know. He looked familiar to me, though. I don't think his name was Ray."

"If you remember his name, let me know."

"Sure thing, Sheriff." She gave them their bills and went back to the counter.

Sarah stirred her soup. "Do you think Bobby is the

one who killed Thornton?"

"If he didn't, I'd lay a million smackers that he knows who did. Possibly the one he was in here with the day before."

After lunch, they headed back to the office, where they found Sam with an amused look on his face. "Sarah, you received a delivery while you two were out." He pointed to a long cardboard box on her desk.

She had a puzzled look, while Amos' suspicions peaked. Sarah opened the box and gasped. "A dozen red roses?" She glanced at the card and colored as she quickly put it back and closed the box.

Amos pointed at it. "Who in Sam Hill is that from?"

Sarah shook her head. "I'd rather not say. Please, don't ask."

"But, why—?"

"I don't know why it came here. It's personal."

Anger threatened to spout, but Amos bit his tongue. "I'll be in my office." He banged the door a little harder than he intended to. *When did she start seeing someone?* He hit the desk with his fist, then pulled back. *What right do I have, butting into her private life? I feel like a green-eyed jackass.* His fingers drummed on the ink blotter. *Amos, you'd better keep your feelings to yourself.*

****

Sarah trimmed the stems of the roses as she carefully put them in the vase on the table in the parlor. *Do I really want to see George again? He was the one who broke my heart.* She hadn't let any man in her life since then, although feelings for Amos came unbidden often. *I know my mother despairs that her daughter is a hopeless spinster.*

The late evening sun made patterns on the floor of the room. Split by the lace curtains flowing back and forth with the sea breeze, the rays had a life of their own. A turn of the doorbell stopped her train of thought.

As she opened the door, George stood in front of her, hat in hand. "Good evening, Sarah. May I come in?"

She took a step back and relieved him of his hat and coat. "Come. Thank you for the roses. That was very thoughtful." As he entered the house, she waved her hand toward the parlor. "Have a seat. I'll get some tea."

He grasped her hand and pulled her to him. "You mean a lot to me. I want to show you how much."

A small streak of anger colored her mood. "You could have done that six years ago."

"How many times do I have to apologize?"

"Until you understand what you did to me." She disengaged her hand and went into the kitchen. *Why do I keep seeing him? Maybe I need the attention of a man.* Putting a serving tray together, she went back into the parlor.

George stood in front of her family picture, taken nine years ago at a clan gathering. He turned as she entered the room. "That was the year I first saw you. Do you remember?"

She set the tray on the table and poured the tea. "Yes, I do." She sat on the couch.

He strolled over and sat beside her. "My mother told me to pay attention to you. That you had a strong jaw." He glanced at her face. "Where did you get that bruise?"

Sarah put her hand to her face. "I almost forgot about it. The investigation got a little rough. It's complicated to explain."

"I think this line of work you're in is too dangerous. A woman should not work in law enforcement."

Her spine straightened. "I knew the risks going in. This is who I am. It's not your decision to make."

He cupped her chin. "It will be if we get married."

"Hold it! You're making some fast moves. Who said anything about marriage?" She pulled back from him. Resentment grew, and her stomach tightened up.

He softened. "We don't have to talk about that now."

Sarah rose. "No, we don't. Or ever, as far as I'm concerned." She retrieved his hat and coat. "I think the evening is over. Goodnight, George."

"If you would let us work this out..."

"Goodbye, George. May you have luck with your business."

He put on his hat. "Sarah?" She glared at him. "Never mind. Good evening."

She closed the door firmly behind him and slumped against it. *How dare he, trying to tell me what to do!*

Chapter 11

Amos was especially grumpy that morning. Seeing those flowers Sarah received the day before had stuck in his craw all night, and it was getting harder to reason away his feelings. Now, he was ready to draw and quarter any man who got close to her. A knock on his office door brought him back to reality.

"Amos?"

"Come in, Lakat."

She poured some coffee and sat before him with inquisitive eyes. "Well, are you going to arrest Bobby?"

He slammed his hand on the desk. "You know as well as I do we don't have enough on him to justify bringing him in." He ran his fingers through his hair. "Could you speak to Sally Cusnoo again to see if she knows where he was the day of the murder?"

"All right. She's off from work today, so we'll have time to talk." She put the coffee down. "Amos, is something else bothering you? Or is not being able to find enough on Bobby rubbing you the wrong way?"

Amos glared at her. "Flowers."

"What?"

"Flowers. There will be no more delivery of flowers to this office. We're not a goddamn lonely hearts club. Keep your private life at home. You got that?"

"Loud and clear, Sheriff." She rose. "I'm off to

speak to Sally."

Amos ruffled the papers on his desk and turned his back on her until he heard the door close. *Maybe I should have gone with her. No, Sally is her friend and wouldn't feel comfortable if I was around. Sarah can handle it.*

With a knock at the door, Sam called out, "You have a telegram from Sheriff Mahoney in Cordova."

"Bring it in."

Sam handed him the yellow envelope, and Amos tore it open. "Sam, there was another warning for a cannery near him. He says he'll take care of it and let me know what happens."

Sam shook his head. "It seems like this group has quite a network of people involved."

Amos nodded. "I, for one, will never suspect the natives to be merely dumb savages. Not after this."

As Sam went back to work, Amos started planning his next move. He had to keep his mind on something other than Sarah's love life.

****

Sarah was glad Bobby's truck wasn't at the house as she went up the porch steps. Sally greeted her at the door. "Sarah, what brings you here?"

"I need to ask you a few questions."

"On the investigation?"

"Yes. Can you remember what Bobby did the day of the murder?"

"Well, he left for work at the usual time—"

"Wait a minute. You say he went to work that day?"

Sally's eyes darkened. "He did. Is something wrong?"

"We checked the personnel list, and his name wasn't on it."

Sally put a hand to her mouth. "Oh, no. You don't think he—"

"We don't know, yet. That's why we keep checking things. What did he do later that day?"

"Well, when I got home from my shift, all he was doing was burning spring brush."

"Burning spring brush," Sarah repeated. Then an alarm sounded in her head. "Where is your burn pile? And do you have a shovel?"

Sally hurried to a small shed and came back with a garden shovel. "Our burn pile is this way."

In the rear of the property, a circle of stones marked the fireplace, and an ash hill rose like a small volcano in the middle. Sarah carefully scooped a layer at a time and sifted through it.

Sally raised her eyebrows. "What are you looking for?"

"Anything suspicious," Sarah shot back.

Most of the layers on top held charred bits of twigs. Sarah continued working her way down to the base of the soot, when she spotted a burnt disk and picked it up. Wiping it off on her sleeve, she noticed it had four small holes in the center. "This is a button! Maybe a coat button." Digging further, she found some fragments of material and the broken blade of a saw. She collected as much of the material as she could find and deposited it in her jacket pocket. "Thank you, Sally. You've been a great help."

Sally's eyes overflowed. "I don't want to believe my brother is mixed up in this."

Sarah put her hand on Sally's shoulder. "We can't

jump to conclusions, but we have to check everything."

As Sarah strode into town, she knocked as much of the soot off her clothes as she could. *I must seem like a cloud going down Front Street.* She chuckled to herself. Sam glanced up as she banged through the door.

He laughed. "Look who the cat dragged in!"

"At least someone's working around here," she retorted.

She laid the side of her fist to the sheriff's door. "I've got something!"

"Come in."

Sarah went like a shot to the desk and emptied her pocket onto Amos' desk, ashes and all. "This is what I discovered in the Cusnoos' fire pit."

Amos picked up the button and bits of burnt material. "What—?"

"Sally said he went to work that day and that he was burning spring brush when she got off her shift later."

"Hmm." Amos opened one of the desk drawers, pulled out a magnifying glass, and studied some of the cloth under his desk lamp. "Ha! Take a look at this." He gave her one of the scraps with the glass. He set aside the saw blade. "This could be what he used to saw through the rail board."

Sarah peered at the cloth scrap, then saw it. "There's a stain that looks like blood."

Amos nodded. "I'll send this over to Elmer, so he can test it. If it is, we have Bobby. Good work, Lakat!" He paused a moment. "Did you say he went to work that day?"

"That's what Sally believed. She became concerned when I told her about the personnel list."

Amos handed her the telegram. "This came in while you were out."

Sarah shook her head. "Oh, no. Not another one. I hope Sheriff Mahoney can keep anything from happening."

As he put the scrap of material and note to the coroner into a sealed envelope, Amos called to Sam.

"Yes, Sheriff?"

"Get this next door to Elmer, and tell him to give me a written report on it."

Sam took the envelope. "Right away." He hurried out.

Amos scraped together the bits and pieces Sarah had deposited on his desk and put them in a separate envelope. "This is the most important evidence we've had so far." He put it in a bag next to the broken bat.

Sarah sighed. "It's too bad we can't get fingerprints off wood."

"Yes, but this should work."

"You seem in a better mood than you were earlier."

Amos gave her a contrite expression. "Sorry for barking at you. That wasn't your fault. Just let your suitor know to send flowers to your home."

"I don't have a suitor. It's someone who's trying to make up for a wrong he did me. I'm not interested."

A look of relief came over Amos' face. "Well, I'm glad. You don't have time for such foolishness."

A glow went through her. *He seems like he's jealous. Does he care that much about me?* "You know, there may be a time when one of us will want to settle down."

"We'll deal with that then. Right now, we'll go get a warrant for Bobby's arrest as soon as we get the report from Elmer."

Sarah was a little perturbed at the reaction to the feeler she put out, but she also knew how stubborn Amos was. He didn't have to be so short with her, though.

Chapter 12

Amos responded to a knock on the office door. "Sheriff?" came Elmer's voice, "I've got that report you wanted."

"Come in. And have Lakat come in, too."

He heard Elmer call to Sarah, and she followed him into Amos' office. Elmer laid a sheet of paper on the desk. "Here's the report you wanted. I tell you, that was a tough assignment. The stain had gone through a fire, but I managed to get enough to make a positive ID on the blood."

Sarah distractingly leaned over Amos' chair to read the report over his shoulder. "Good work, Elmer." He turned to Sarah. "Shall we go get an arrest warrant for Bobby?"

"Ready when you are." She strode out the door.

After a trip to the courthouse, they headed to the Cusnoo home. "Bobby should be off his shift by now," Amos observed. "Look, there's his truck in front." He parked on the road. "Have your gun handy, just in case, and stay behind me."

Sarah took a shallow breath as she patted her thirty-eight in the shoulder holster. "Let's get this over with."

Every nerve in Amos' body was alert with a flood of adrenaline. He hated putting Sarah in danger, but she was a deputy and a good shot, so he couldn't tell her not to do her job. Halfway to the porch steps, the door banged open and Bobby stepped out with a double-barreled shotgun that he leveled at Amos. "And what would you like, Sheriff? I don't remember inviting you over."

"I have a warrant for your arrest in the killing of Mr. Thornton at the cannery. Now, we can do this easy. Just pass the shotgun to me and come along peacefully."

"The hell I will! Get off my property!"

Amos dropped and rolled as the shotgun fired, then heard answering fire and saw Bobby fold to the porch, clutching his knee. Amos ran up the steps and grabbed the abandoned shotgun while Sarah holstered her weapon and hurried to help.

Amos leaned the shotgun against the railing and slapped the handcuffs on Bobby almost simultaneously, and then he set to work cutting the knee of Bobby's trousers to check the wound.

Bobby yelled at Sarah at the top of his lungs. "You god-damned traitor! I'm shot by a turncoat woman who won't defend her own kind!"

"Who's my own kind, Bobby? A band of murderous animals who kill for what they want? No, that's not my kind." She picked up the shotgun and pointed it at Bobby. "I prefer to be on the law-abiding side."

Amos finished securing a strip of trouser material over the wound and yanked Bobby to his feet. "Now we'll take a trip to the doc to fix your leg. Then you can cool off your carcass in a jail cell for a while."

When Bobby was safely behind bars, Amos and Sarah sat facing each other in Amos' office. He let his guard down a little as he smiled. "I'm grateful for your quick thinking. I could have been blown away by the second shot."

"I must be getting better. You didn't add, 'for a woman.' " She hid a grin behind a sip of coffee. "You realize we got the puppet and not the puppet master."

Amos nodded. "But maybe we can make the puppet sing. Usually, these people don't want to go down alone."

Sarah bit her lip. "Unless there's a fierce loyalty there. Some of the members of this group may suffer from a martyr complex."

Amos snorted. "You're beginning to sound like a female Freud. Don't tell me you go in for that psycho horse shit."

"They introduced it in my police training. I didn't go deep into it. It seems as popular as the spiritualism that has been in fashion the last twenty years."

"I swear, I'll quit if I have to get dead Aunt Bertha to solve crimes."

Sarah started laughing so hard Amos was sucked into the hilarity. It felt good to laugh, and to do it with Sarah. He enjoyed being with her. No one had ever filled that void in his life since— Well, he put that dark thought where it belonged.

Sarah wiped her eyes. "That's the first time I ever heard you crack a joke." She added, with great warmth in her smile, "Don't let it be the last."

Amos rose and came around the desk to put a hand on her shoulder. Sarah saw a welling of emotion in his face. "Let's go question Mr. Cusnoo."

Bobby lay glowering on the jail cot as they opened the cell. The iron door clanged shut behind them. Amos slapped Bobby's boots off the cot. "Sit up and face us."

Bobby spit on the floor. "Why do you have me here? You've got nothing on me."

Amos shot back, "Then why were you burning a coat in the fire pit behind your house?"

"It was old. I wanted to get rid of it."

"Most people either give old things away or use them as rags. I never heard of anyone burning a coat. Were you trying to hide the fact it was bloodstained?"

"Aren't I supposed to have a lawyer present?"

"Sure, Bobby, what's the name of your lawyer?"

"I don't have one yet."

"Well, it looks like you stay here as our guest until you do."

Bobby glared at both of them, then pointed an accusing finger at Sarah. "Why were you poking around on my property?"

Sarah smiled. "According to our people's laws, the property belongs to Sally. I asked her permission."

An angry grunt escaped his lips. "I'm not telling you anything else!" He swung his feet onto the cot again.

Amos let Sarah out of the cell door, followed her, and locked it behind him. They made their way out to the lobby, where he leaned toward Sam. "Lindsey, see that the court provides a legal counsel for Mr. Cusnoo first thing in the morning. Who's on night duty?"

"Luke Ayers, sir."

"Tell him to keep an eye on Mr. Cusnoo and report if there's anything suspicious going on outside. I think there are more in this gang, and they might try to spring him." He turned to Sarah. "Feel up to a meal at Millie's?"

"Sounds good."

"We're officially off until tomorrow."

Sam bid them a good evening, and they went to Millie's. They slipped into the cheerful little restaurant and ordered the special, meatloaf and gravy. As they were digging in, Amos heard a female voice call Sarah's name.

Sarah dropped her fork on the plate. "Mother? What are you doing here?"

Grace nodded to Amos. "Hello, Sheriff."

"Evening, Mrs. Lakat."

"Sarah, are you going to be home in an hour or two? I must talk to you."

"I can be home by seven. Anything I should know?"

"No. I wouldn't want to bother the sheriff with details, but it is important."

Amos didn't know why, but it seemed Grace was upset to find him with her daughter. She kept frowning at him.

Sarah sighed. "All right, Mother, I'll see you later." Grace gave a nod and left. "I know that look. I'm going to be lectured about something."

"Have you argued lately?"

"Constantly. Mainly about my unmarried status. Being a spinster hurts the passing of inheritance. Right now, it's just Mary who will receive the Lakat property. Kata forfeited by marrying Ivan, and I don't have any prospects."

"If you do, will you and Mary split it or have to own it together?"

"Together. My mother and Aunt Jane live on it now."

"What about your house?"

Sarah paused. "That would have to be sold. It's a shame. I love that little house."

They topped off their dinner with a slice of coconut custard pie before they headed for her home. Amos contemplated what had been said. Sarah was distressed about her situation, and it made him want to help her somehow, but he had no idea what he should do.

As they arrived at her porch, Sarah turned to him. "You didn't have to walk me home."

Amos cleared his throat. This did look like a suitor's outing. He clasped her shoulders. "I—it's just with the gang—the murders—hmm..."

Sarah smiled. "Amos, you do care." She kissed him on the cheek, and his body set to warming.

He stepped back and tipped his hat. "Evening, Lakat." He started off toward his apartment, knowing it would be another sleepless night. Damn it, he wished she wouldn't—stimulate him like she did.

Chapter 13

Sarah was putting the tea in the pot to steep when she heard a knock at the door. *Mother.* "Come in. I just put the tea in the pot."

Her mother removed her coat and handed it to Sarah. "I need to talk to you. I saw George Ignot yesterday." She swept over to a chair in the parlor and sat.

Sarah stood there, stunned, holding the coat. "You saw George?"

"Dear, don't stand there with your eyes bugged out. He told me all about your outing."

Sarah put the coat on one of the hooks. "Did he also tell you I didn't want to see him again?"

"Now, now, I wouldn't dismiss him so fast. He's made a lot of money on expeditions. He would be a wonderful provider."

"Mother, I want more to life than to be provided for. I have a job, too."

"Oh, there you go with that modern nonsense. Mary seems to be the only normal person in this family. It's easier to just take care of the property and children than it is to work outside the home."

Sarah's chest tightened. "Excuse me a minute. I have to check on the tea." She strode into the kitchen and slammed together the necesssary items on a serving tray. Taking a deep breath, she calmed herself before she confronted her mother again. She re-entered the parlor the soul of reason. "Would you like some lemon with your tea?"

"No, thank you." Her mother's smile was more like a grimace.

Sarah poured the tea and gave it to her. "You have to understand that I love my work. There's a satisfaction in bringing criminals to justice. I read mysteries and true-life crime when I was in school. This was all I ever wanted to do."

"That awful missionary school again."

"Not awful. I needed to find my purpose in life, and I'm very good at it. If that means I forfeit being a wife and mother, that's all right with me."

"Humph! At this point I'd even be happy if you settled for the sheriff."

Sarah's teacup slid on the saucer and sloshed on the table. "Why did you say that?"

"My dear, darling daughter, I noticed how he was looking at you when I talked to you at Millie's. That upset me at the time, but I see your face when I mention him."

Sarah's cheeks heated as she mopped up the spilled tea with a towel. "He's my boss and a friend. Neither one of us has gone past that."

"Two very stubborn people." Her mother's lips curled slightly at the corners as she raised the cup to her mouth.

"Mother, quit trying to marry me off to anyone in pants!"

"I'm getting old. I'd like to see my blood passed along, and you are the only one of my children left. Make an elder happy."

Sarah made an incomprehensible sound as she took another sip of her tea. *And what did she mean, how Amos was looking at her?*

She thought about what her mother had said as she headed to the office the next morning. *Could Amos really feel the way I do? Is he hiding his feelings for me?* Her mind went to little things he'd said and done for her these past few weeks. Especially, when she went to the ANB meeting in Angoon. At the time, it hurt that he seemingly didn't have enough faith in her to let her carry out an undercover job by herself. Could he have been worried about her?

The sheriff's office loomed ahead. Suddenly she heard, "Good morning, Sarah."

Glancing up, she took an angry breath. "What do you want?"

He was standing beside her with a Husky on a leash, the dog's tail waving slowly. The animal was beautiful, different shades of gray and white, its ice-blue eyes steady on her. "This is Shadow. He's my lead sled dog, and a friend." He paused. "I spoke to your mother."

"I know. She told me," she snapped. "Why can't you leave me and my family alone?" She moved to go into the office, and he gripped her arm.

"I mean to change your mind."

"Let go of me, or I'll bring you in for accosting a woman," she growled through her teeth. Shadow started barking and prancing on his leash.

He swung her against the rough boards of the building. "You were promised to me."

A hand came and yanked his shoulder. With a cry of surprise, George let go of both Sarah and the dog leash as he was pulled away, his arm twisted behind him, by Amos. Shadow barked savagely, and Sarah managed to snag the leash before the dog attacked.

Amos pushed George's face into the wall. "What the hell is going on here?"

Sarah's relief at seeing Amos come to her rescue was overwhelming. "This is the man who believes he can get me interested in him again." She managed to calm the dog while she gazed at Amos' angry expression.

"That isn't any of your business, Sheriff!" George hissed.

"Roughing up one of my deputies is." He glanced at Sarah. "Do you want to bring charges?"

She hesitated. "If he promises not to bother me or my family again, I won't."

Amos whipped him around. "Well?"

With an angry glare at Sarah, George spat out, "I'll leave her and her family alone." He grabbed Shadow's leash and took off.

Sarah started trembling, and Amos threw an arm of support around her. "Let's go into my office."

She maintained control until she sat in her customary chair across from Amos, and then she burst into tears.

Amos finished pouring coffee for them and set her cup in front of her. He gripped her shoulder. "Talk to me. And I don't want the bullshit that it's none of my business." His hand remained where it was.

"George and I were engaged to be married six years ago, but he disappeared." Sarah sniffed. "He came back a couple of weeks ago, and I agreed to an outing, but I didn't feel anything for him anymore. He's been trying to make me change my mind, and, yes, he's the one who sent the roses. He even talked to my mother and tried to get her on his side."

"Did he?" he asked gently.

"At first. I explained to her how I felt about the whole thing." As she related what was said, Sarah carefully omitted the discussion about Amos.

After she was finished, he was silent for a minute. "He's a jackass."

"That's what I've been telling you." His hand felt so warm on her. A comfort. She looked into his gray eyes and saw a spark of something else. She glanced down. "Thank you."

Amos circled the desk and sat in his chair. "If that varmint comes near you again, you let me know." They were both startled a moment later by the sound of gunfire in the lobby. With their guns drawn, Amos carefully opened the office door. They heard the front door slam and found Sam on the floor, his right arm bleeding. Sarah ran outside to see if the gunman could be caught, but he was out of sight. "What happened?" Amos demanded as he helped the deputy to a chair.

"Food was delivered from Millie's... I took it to the cell... Cusnoo was lying on the floor." Sam took a longer pause and swallowed. "I opened the cell door... He tripped me. From the tray... Was a gun—"

Amos interrupted, "A gun was on the tray?"

Sam nodded. "It was under the cover. He ran out the cell door...me after him. I tried to stop him in the lobby. You know the rest."

"Who brought the tray?"

"It was a dark-haired woman." Sarah got a tightening in her stomach.

Amos waved to one of the other men. "Thomas, help Sam to the doc's."

"Yes, sir." The man helped Sam up.

"Lakat."

Sarah followed Amos to the cell. The contents of the tray were scattered. Amos picked up the plate and cover. "There was never food on the plate. Someone at Millie's set this up. Apparently Cusnoo knew about this and was ready."

"But who—? No! Not Sally! It couldn't be!" Sarah was too stunned to believe Bobby's sister would ever do such a thing.

"Sally would have access to the tray," Amos said quietly. "I'm sorry. I know she's a friend of yours."

"I guess we're going to Millie's."

"Yes. Though I'd be willing to bet she didn't go back."

Sarah sighed. "She probably helped Bobby on the getaway. And I don't think they would have gone home."

"Concentrate, Sarah. Where do you suppose they would escape to?"

She paused, deep in thought. "Possibly the ANB hall. Maybe someone there could get Bobby out of the area."

"Then that's where we're headed. Johnston, you're in charge." Amos was out the door. "I'll get the patrol car."

Sarah slipped into her jacket and jumped into the passenger side. They raced the six blocks to the hall. The two-story public building was situated near the docks of the old Tlingit settlement north of downtown. She hoped her hunch was right as she searched the area around the building. "That's their truck in the lot south of the hall!"

Amos pulled the brake. "I'll check by the pier over there, and you ask in the hall."

Sarah jumped out. "Yes, sir!" She went inside and looked around. Several men were playing pool in the rec center. She recognized Bobby's friend, Jack. "Jack, can I speak to you a moment?"

"Sarah! I guess I can leave the game. What's on your mind?"

"Did you see Bobby come through here a few seconds ago? His truck is in the lot."

"Why, no." He turned to his companions. "Any of you see Bobby?" As everyone in the group responded in the negative, he turned back. "I thought he was behind bars."

"He escaped a few minutes ago, and I thought he might have come here."

"No, sorry. I'll let you know if I see him."

"Thanks." *But I don't believe you,* Sarah added in her head. Something about the way everyone reacted was too rehearsed. She darted out to see what Amos had found.

Amos, red-faced, was hollering at the pier's caretaker. He glanced at Sarah and made his way to her. "They're all covering for each other! I can't get a blasted thing out of these tight-lipped varmints! What did you find out?"

Sarah stung from the venom of his words. "Well, this varmint didn't find anything out either!" she barked out.

Taking a few steps back, Amos seemed stunned. He smacked his forehead with his hand. "I'm sorry. I'm just upset."

Folding her arms across her chest, Sarah said, "I've never heard you talk like that before. You're not any better than any of the other no-brained Americans."

Amos pointed at her. "You're doing it, too!"

She took a short breath and opened her mouth to say something, then shut it again. "All right! We're both asses once in a while, but this isn't getting anything done. Should we get a boat to search for them?"

Amos shook his head. "We don't know which way they went, if they did take a boat. They left the truck here, but I doubt if they'll come back while we're here."

"There's a small restaurant across the way. Maybe we can park the patrol around the block and stake out there."

"Good idea, Lakat." They headed to the auto, and Amos drove to a side street to keep it out of sight.

They strode to the restaurant, and suddenly Amos tore off his hat, slamming it to the ground. "God damn it all to hell! The truck's gone!"

Sarah's eyes locked on the spot the truck had occupied. "They must have seen us leave and moved it immediately."

Amos snagged his hat, grabbed her arm, and together they ran back to the patrol car. He gunned the engine, causing it to backfire, and raced to the lot. He jumped out and checked the tracks in the dirt. "Looks like they turned south." Climbing back in, he turned to her. "Hang on. We're going to try to find them."

The patrol car bounced crazily along the rutted waterfront road. Sarah tried to search in all directions for the errant truck. Not a side street or back alley was left untried.

Finally, Amos parked back at the office lot. "Damn, we should have waited and watched the truck there."

Sarah shook her head. "They wouldn't have done anything until we left, no matter how long we waited."

He gave her a half-smile. "You're probably right. We'd better issue Wanted posters to go up all over town."

In the office lobby, Amos asked Thomas, "How's Sam?"

"Doc says he'll be back at work in a couple of days."

"Good. I want you to write the report."

Johnston came in with the tray and its contents. Amos pointed to a shelf in the back. "Put that over there until we can get it back to Millie's." He turned to Sarah. "Let's get the wording to go on the poster, and I'll take it to the newspaper so they can run off copies. I'll hire a couple of the newsboys to hang them."

As Sarah followed him into the office, she went to the stove and poured each of them a cup of coffee. When she turned, she saw Amos with his elbows on the desk and his face in his hands. She set the cups down. "Amos?"

He raised his head and gazed at her. "Sarah, I'm tired. Something about this case is draining the life out of me. I think I'm close, and then something happens. There are too many people involved."

She came around the desk and started massaging his shoulders. "We'll get them. They're bound to make a misstep, with all the webs they're weaving."

Amos sighed. "I hope so."

They got back to work.

Sarah wanted to believe she was right. This case was wearing on her, too.

Chapter 14

Amos closed the door to the printing office at the newspaper. "Mr. Roberts?"

A jovial balding man glanced up from his desk. "Sheriff! What brings you here?"

"I have information for a Wanted poster. Could I have a hundred run off by tonight?" He handed Roberts a folder.

"Any photographs?" he asked, perusing the paper.

"No. Just a description. I'll pay some of the newsboys to hang these around town."

"They should be done in a couple of hours. When I give the newsboys the papers, I'll give them some of the posters, as well."

"Thanks, Roberts." Amos headed back to the reception area and noticed a stack of newspapers on a table. He motioned to the editor. "Are these today's?"

The news editor nodded. "Hot off the press."

Amos picked the top one off the pile and flipped a nickel on the table. "I'll take one." He folded it over without looking at the front page. Before he reached the door, he ran into Mr. Perkins from Personals.

"Sheriff, I heard you were here and hoped to catch you before you left. I see you have today's copy."

"Perkins, what's this all about?"

"The picture on the front page." He stabbed a finger at it. "That's the man who posted the ad about the cannery."

Amos unfolded the paper and studied the fuzzy black-and-white photo. Then his jaw dropped. "Him? That's the one?"

Perkins nodded. "I'm sure of it."

Amos was staring at a picture of George Ignot, Sarah's former intended. *Damn, I turned him away this morning! I wonder if Sarah knows where he's staying?* He thanked Perkins and hurried to the office.

Sarah was busily banging on the typewriter as he came in. She glanced up. "Anything at the newspaper? You've got that look about you."

"Good and bad. I think you better come in."

Sarah's mouth was in a tight straight line as she sat across from him. "What is it?"

"I ran into Mr. Perkins from the Personals office while I was there. He knows who posted the ad about the cannery. The man's picture is in today's edition." He flipped the front page around so she could see it.

Sarah picked it up. "There's an article about expeditions." She stared at the picture, then gasped. "That's George! Oh, no, that couldn't be right! He's the one who wrote the ad?"

"Mr. Perkins identified him. Do you happen to know where he's staying?"

Sarah hesitated a moment. "No. I didn't even inquire, because I didn't care where he was. He's probably at one of the hotels."

"Let's find the ones who rent to natives. That should narrow it down." He watched her stricken face. "Sarah, are you all right?"

"No. I can't believe George is wrapped up in this. He wasn't like that when I knew him." She slumped in the chair.

"People change. Who really knows why." Amos knew that first hand. He cared how she felt about this. Hell, he cared what this was doing to her.

Sarah seemed lost in her own world. "A distraction. He knew what he meant to me and he used that to distract me from the investigation." She wiped her eyes. "He hurt me when he walked away, and then he comes back and gives me some cock-and-bull story about how he wasn't ready to settle down. That bastard was manipulating me." Tears were rolling down her cheeks.

Amos had a tightening in his chest. He rose and went around the desk to her, drawing her up into an embrace. "Sarah, I'm so sorry." She didn't pull back but cried on his shoulder.

She sniffed. "I don't usually fall apart like that." She straightened and glanced at Amos, embarrassed. He gave her his handkerchief, and she gratefully dried her face.

"If you want to bow out of this investigation, I'll understand."

Sarah sighed. "No. I want to see it through. I hate being played a fool." Her businesslike side returned. "I know of three hotels in the area around the ANB hall that take natives. We can start there."

Going out to the patrol car, Amos imagined several different ways to disembowel George for what he'd done to Sarah, never mind that he was also in on the murder plots. He wanted George's carcass out for the wolves.

The first hotel proved to be fruitless, so they tried the Juneau Gold Hotel. The desk clerk nodded at him.

"Yes, Sheriff, what can I do for you?"

"Do you have a George Ignot staying here?"

The clerk opened up the guest book and ran his finger down the column. "Ah, yes. We did have him here, but he checked out this morning."

"How long was he here?"

"Off and on for three weeks."

"What do you mean, off and on?"

"He said he had business around the area. Sometimes he didn't come back for a couple of days."

"Do you have an address for him?"

"All he put down was Yakutat, Alaska Territory."

"Well, that gives us something. Thank you, Mr.—?"

"Bailey, sir."

Amos and Sarah went back to the office to plan their next step. "Do you know anything about Yakutat?"

Sarah nodded. "It's a mostly Tlingit settlement northwest of here. We could book passage on a ship, but they don't have an airfield yet."

Amos half-smiled. "There's the seaplanes."

Sarah made a face. "I suppose."

Bill Wright was available, so he flew them up to the pier on the cape near Yakutat. Amos helped Sarah onto the pier, and then Bill hopped off the plane and made sure the rope was secure to the dock. He tipped the shore man who had pulled them in before turning to Amos. "You said you wanted me to wait for you?"

Amos nodded. "We shouldn't be more than an hour or two."

Bill jerked a thumb toward a building. "I'll wait for you at the commissary."

Amos glanced at Sarah. "You up for the walk into town?"

She grimaced. "Let's get this over with."

In twenty minutes, they were in the middle of the small settlement. An old whitish-gray clapboard building had Sheriff's Office in large black weathered letters on the side wall. They came into a plain whitewash-walled room with pine plank floors. Two black iron cells stood unoccupied along the back. A young Tlingit deputy stopped sweeping the floor and a graying native looked up from the desk behind a railed divider in the front corner. He stood. "I'm Sheriff Creag. Can I help you?"

Amos and Sarah strode to the divider, and Amos extended his hand. "I'm Sheriff Amos Darcy of Juneau, and this is Deputy Sarah Lakat."

Creag shook Amos' hand and nodded to Sarah. "What brings you to Yakutat?"

"We're seeking information on someone who claims he's from this town." Amos went on to explain about the cannery murder and the investigation so far.

Creag rapped his fingers on the desk. "I did hear about the string of cannery murders. Who is the man you're trying to find?"

"Do you know a George Ignot?"

"George Ignot? No."

Sarah handed him the picture clipped from the newspaper. "This is what he looks like."

He studied the photograph. "That's George Annok! He lives outside of town with his wife, Leigh, and their sons."

Amos watched Sarah blanch. "Could you tell us how to get there?"

Creag pointed out the window. "Go due north from here about a mile and a half. It's the log cabin on the right of the road, with kennels. They raise Huskies."

Sarah stalked out the door, followed closely by Amos, after they took their leave of Creag. She seemed like someone who could commit murder joyfully. "He lied to me! He used me! He *never* cared for me!" She kicked an old rusted can into next week.

Amos' heart went out to her, and he put a gentle but firm hand on her shoulder. "I'll go to the house myself, if you think you can't handle it."

"No. I'll be as professional as ever, but it'll be hard not to kill him."

They came upon the weatherbeaten cabin in a shelter of hemlock trees. A chorus of barks and howls greeted them as they walked up. A young Tlingit woman came out of the door carrying an infant. "Hello! What do you want?"

Amos called out, "Are you Leigh Annok?"

"Yes."

Amos introduced himself and Sarah. "We're looking for your husband. Is he here?"

She shook her head. "Last I knew, he was in Juneau on business. He sometimes stops at his village near the headwaters before he comes home."

Sarah shifted her feet. "Is it off the big river southeast of here, near the Canadian border?"

Leigh stared at her. "Yes. How did you know?"

"It doesn't matter. When do you think he'll be back?"

"It'll be a couple of days. He walks back. Should I tell him you were here?"

Amos glanced at Sarah and shook his head. To

Leigh he said, "Just have him check with Sheriff Creag when he gets home. Thank you, ma'am." He tipped his hat, and Sarah fell into line behind him as he started for the road.

Out of earshot, Sarah asked, "Why are you having him check in with Creag?"

"Because if she mentions us to George, he may bolt. We're going to tell Creag to wire us when he has him."

On the way to the seaplane, they stopped by the sheriff's office to tell him the plan. Amos couldn't put his finger on it, but something bothered him about Creag. On the way to the plane, Amos noticed Sarah had the look of a person ready to explode. She said not a word all the way to the pier. Bill readied the plane, and Amos helped Sarah to board.

They settled into their seats, and Bill took off on the three-hour flight to Juneau. Amos passed Sarah a thermos of coffee. "I brought this with us for a midday meal." He pulled two tinfoil wraps out of his canvas sack and handed one to her. "Have a ham sandwich."

"I'm not hungry," she said quietly, studying the contours of her boots.

"With all the shocks to your system, you need to keep your strength up." He paused. "I realize these past hours have been rough on you, but don't sacrifice your health for it."

She laid the sandwich on her lap and a tear slid down her cheek. "He didn't care what he did to me. The one man I trusted six years ago disappeared and then came back to deceive me."

Amos grasped her hand. "Not all men are like George." He sincerely wanted her to believe it.

She shook her head. "I've been very good on my own. I guess I wasn't cut out to be a wife, and that's going to upset my mother. I'm the only child she has left."

Deep down, Amos was chiding himself. *Damn it, tell her how you feel. She's as low as a bump on an ant's leg. You care about her.* Aloud he said, "If it helps, I care."

She patted his arm with her other hand. "You've been an understanding boss to me, and I am grateful. I guess I have to realize I'm not a desirable woman."

He released her hand and cupped her chin. "What the hell are you talking about? I've been ready to carry you away these past months. It's because of the job that I haven't."

Sarah started to laugh and cry. "You're a good friend, but I don't want your sympathy."

"Sympathy?" he spat out. "Why do you think I slept so bad at the cabin in Sitka? You were in the same room. Why would I go down to Angoon to keep an eye on you? I was worried what would happen. And way back, why do you think I asked you to become a deputy? I like being around you. When you got those flowers from George, jealousy was eating my innards. There, you got it from the horse's mouth."

She stared at him as if he told her he was a three-headed monster. "Well, Amos, this certainly complicates things."

He clenched his teeth. "No. It was about time the truth came out. You don't know how many nights I couldn't sleep because of the way I felt."

Sarah smiled. "I may know more about unspoken truths than you think."

In a way, Amos regretted his confession. "Maybe I shouldn't have said anything. We were a good working team."

"I don't think getting things out in the open is going to change that. I love my job and I love working with you."

They started on the ham sandwiches and coffee, passing the time in light conversation for the rest of the three hours back. Relief flowed through Amos now that he didn't have to hide how he felt. Sarah seemed relaxed and at ease. Maybe the confession was good for her, too.

"I'm coming down to home," Bill called back. Soon they felt the plop of the seaplane into the water of the channel. When the plane was secured to the dock, he helped Amos and Sarah off.

After they took leave of Bill, Amos turned to Sarah. "Why don't you go home and freshen up. I'll stop by in a couple of hours, and we can go to Millie's for dinner."

Sarah grasped his hand. "Instead, why don't I cook something for us? We need to talk, and I don't want the whole town gossiping."

"Good idea. I'll see you then." Amos headed to the office to check up on things, but he walked like a vast weight had lifted.

Chapter 15

Sarah readied the vinegar marinade for the fresh salmon fillet she'd purchased on the way home. She chided herself for being giddy and nervous about tonight. Though Amos assured her nothing had changed, knowing he cared made her feel unsure.

For once, she wasn't thinking about the case or worrying about George. His importance to her had washed away in the revelation from Amos. She had suspected Amos treated her as someone special because she was a woman, but she'd never thought he cared for her to that depth.

After cleaning up and changing her clothes to a fresh spring dress, she added a crisp white apron and heated the gas oven for the salmon. A saucepan of asparagus went on one burner, and on another a skillet of butter, onions, and sliced potatoes sent an incense of cooking through the house. A new pot of coffee was started on a third burner.

The bell at her front door ground out its metallic notes. A flood of happiness and fear washed over her as she hurried to it. Standing on her porch was a man in a suit, with a white shirt that had a clean starched collar. And he was shaved, except for his mustache, which was trimmed.

"Evening, Sarah." Amos removed his hat. "I stopped at the confectioners for some chocolates." He handed her the box of sweets he was holding. "You look beautiful."

She melted and got the tingle that happened every time she thought of Amos. "Thank you for both the compliment and the candy. Let me take your hat and coat." She set the box on the table in the parlor and hung his things on the entrance hooks.

Amos cleared his throat and shuffled his feet. "Dinner smells good."

She waved him to a seat in the parlor. "It's almost ready. Wait for me to bring it to the dining table, and then we can start." She gathered serving dishes of food and fixed the coffee tray. "It's ready!"

Amos pulled out her chair, and when she was seated, he settled across from her.

She indicated with her hand. "You can take what you want from the dishes."

Without a word, he carved some of the salmon fillet and put it on her plate, then took some for himself. After serving the fried onions and potatoes, and the asparagus, and taking a hunk of bread, he set to eating. "Everything tastes swell," he said after a swig of water.

"Thank you. Was there anything going on at the office?"

Amos looked relieved. "Got word from Mahoney that they were able to stop any shenanigans at the cannery in Cordova, but they didn't catch the varmint."

When they had finished the meal, she moved to clear the table. "Go into the parlor. I'll pour the coffee, and we can have some chocolates." As she moved the dishes into the kitchen, she was lost in thought. *Maybe it wasn't wise to change our relationship like this. He seems so uncomfortable with me now. He only relaxed when we talked about work.* When she returned, she expressed her concerns.

"Sarah, no. I'm glad we got this out into the open. I haven't felt this way about a woman for a long time. Although it is dredging up memories."

"Do you want to tell me?"

Amos paused. "Well, I know about your problem with George, so I guess you should know about me." He took a breath. "The reason I left Idaho. My intended died of pneumonia two weeks before we were to be married. I had been in love with her for years, so it was quite a blow. I couldn't stay there where everything reminded me of her."

Sarah grasped his hand. "Oh, I'm sorry."

"I came up here and buried myself in law enforcement, not wanting to be hurt like that again." He sighed. "I hadn't counted on an upstart Indian detective gaining my undying respect and then my heart." He traced his fingers lightly down her cheek.

Sarah was trembling. She released his other hand and they gazed at each other.

He grasped her shoulders and pulled her toward him. "May I kiss you?"

Uncomfortable, but wanting that kiss, she nodded. They both hesitated with their lips inches away. Then he closed the gap, and his mouth attached firmly to hers. Her whole body was ready for that kiss, and she leaned into it. She was aware of the scratchiness of his mustache, the hardness of his body, and the masculine scent. His tongue probed her mouth and both their breaths came in rasps. Sensations she hadn't felt for years flooded her body. She gently pushed on his chest and sat back. "Oh, my."

His eyes were on fire with a beautiful warmth, and he cupped her chin. "I didn't want to mess up our work, but I couldn't help myself. I'm in love with you, woman."

She tenderly laid her hand on his smooth face. "You look so much younger and handsomer when you shave."

He grasped the hand and kissed her fingers. "I think I'll call it a night before we get carried away." He rose, taking her with him.

She brought his coat and hat. "Tonight, I feel renewed. This will work out."

He embraced her, and she welcomed it. Snuggling on his shoulder, she pressed her nose to the rough fabric. It was good in his arms. "Sweet dreams, Sarah. See you tomorrow."

Instigating another kiss at the front door, Sarah smiled. "Same to you. Goodnight, Amos." *Lord, that kiss was as delicious as the first.* She lingered on the porch long after he disappeared around the corner. *Looks like Mother will get her wish after all.*

The next morning, Sarah swallowed nervously as she opened the door to the office. Sam glanced and nodded a hello. She hurried to her desk and checked her report file. A boy with a Western Union uniform came in a few minutes later.

"Is the sheriff in?" he asked Sam. "I have a telegram from Sheriff Creag in Yakutat."

Sam rose and took the envelope. "I'll take it in to him." He flipped the boy a quarter.

"Thank you, sir!" The boy tipped his cap and was off again.

Sam knocked at the door of Amos' office and

disappeared inside for a moment. Amos came to the door as Sam went out. "Lakat, come in!"

Sarah was relieved that Amos was the same as always. She ducked in. "What is it?"

Amos waved the yellow paper. "Creag has detained George."

"Are we going to bring him to Juneau?"

He paused. "Sam and I are."

"What? Why am I not going?"

"Because I need someone strong to help manage him if he gets out of hand."

Sarah slammed her fist on Amos' desk, causing everything to jump. "I helped you bring Bobby in, and he was shooting at us!"

Amos glanced down as if he was caught. "Well, yes—but you weren't ever engaged to Bobby."

"What has that got to do with it? We're bringing in a suspect of murder." Her voice kept rising.

"No, you're not! I'm the sheriff, and I'm saying you aren't!" He stood almost nose to nose with her.

Her chest heaving with anger, she shook her finger in his face. "You said nothing would change in our work. You lied!"

"Lakat, get out of my office!"

She ripped the badge off her shirt. "Gladly. I quit!" She threw the badge at him and rushed out the door, grabbed her things off her desk, and left.

"I knew it," she grumbled as she headed home. "Everything just blew up in my face. He can't let me do my work."

She heard footfalls behind her and her shoulder was grasped. "Sarah, stop."

"Let go of me or I'll break your arm."

"Goddamn it, woman, listen to me!" He whipped her around to face him. "You are the most mule-headed person I know!" He shook her slightly. "All right, you can go with me to Yakutat." He handed her badge to her. "I didn't accept your resignation."

She waited a few moments for her anger to uncoil. Then she pinned the badge to her shirt. "When do we leave?"

"After lunch. We'll stay in Yakutat and bring him back tomorrow." He paused. "Go home and pack. I'll pick you up at eleven-thirty for lunch, and then we'll go."

She grinned. "Thank you for giving in."

"Just don't let me regret it." She caught a flash of amusement as he turned to the office.

After lunch at Millie's, they met Bill at the airfield. Amos shook his hand. "Any problem with you staying overnight?"

"No. This is the first overnight since our daughter was born, but the wife said it was all right." He turned to load the plane. "You can get settled."

It was coming up to four o'clock when the seaplane plopped down near the pier at Yakutat. The three of them walked into the town center and the only hotel, the Raven's Nest. It was a simple clapboard building with a totem pole in the front with a raven watching grimly from its top perch. The inside was bright with its plain whitewashed walls in the afternoon sun. An elderly Tlingit man sat at the old oak reception counter with a case of cubbyholes and key hooks behind him.

Amos went to the desk. "I'd like two rooms next to each other for the night. One for us," he indicated Bill, "and one for her." He pointed at Sarah.

119

The old man nodded. "I'll need all of you to sign." He turned the register book toward them. "The rooms are a dollar a night."

Amos took out two silver dollars and gave them to the proprietor. "We'll be going early in the morning. Where's a good place to eat?"

He thrust his thumb to the left. "Kate's Kitchen is down a block."

Amos tipped his hat. "Thank you."

The native pulled two door keys off the cubbyhole hooks. "You've got Rooms Two and Three, one flight up."

Amos flipped the key for Room Three to Sarah. "Let's get settled, then take care of some business."

Sarah and Bill followed Amos up the creaky stairs. No one can sneak around this hotel, she thought with amusement. Even walking to their rooms was a symphony of creaks and squeals of the old floor.

She opened the door to a reasonably clean room, although it was sparsely furnished and smelled like old wood. A wooden caned chair, a washstand, a chest of drawers, and a bed were the only furniture. Yellowed lace curtains cut the sunlight into geometric shapes, while dust traveled the beam's length. Someone had tried to brighten the place up with braided rugs and framed ancient color advertisements.

Sarah carried a washcloth and towel to the bathroom at the end of the hall to freshen up. Back in her room, she brushed her still-too-short hair to make it look fuller. A knock at the door made her jump. "Who is it?"

"Amos. Are you ready?"

She opened the door. "Yes."

"Good. Bill's going to meet us at the restaurant. I think we should check in with Creag before we eat supper."

A light mist was starting to coat the dirt road as they hurried across to the sheriff's office. Creag sat at his desk, and, out of the corner of her eye, Sarah saw George behind him, in one of the iron cells. Creag stood to greet them.

"Glad to see you again, Darcy. You beat Mahoney. He wants him, too."

Amos shook his head. "If he wants him, Mahoney has to wait until we're done with him in Juneau."

A voice from the cell invaded her ear. "See, Sarah, someone—"

"Shut your mouth!" she yelled back. "I don't want to hear anything you have to say!"

"But—"

"Enough!" Her fingers clenched into fists.

Amos strode to the cell. "Listen, Annok, you're going back to Juneau to face the music. Don't let me have to put a charge of harassment of my deputy on that list."

George opened his mouth for a moment, then shut it again. "All right, Sheriff." His eyes shot daggers at Sarah.

Amos returned to Creag. "We'll be here in the morning after breakfast to take him."

Creag shook Amos' hand. "He'll be ready."

Sarah's emotions were percolating from her stomach to her throat as they left the building. She pushed them down and set her face in stone.

Amos glanced at her. "This is the reason I wanted Sam to come instead of you. George can play off your anger."

"I won't let him get to me. I can do this."

Kate's Kitchen loomed into view. They went into the cheery pine-paneled restaurant with its little tables scattered around. At one sat Bill nursing a cup of coffee. "Everything set for tomorrow?"

Amos nodded. "Creag will have him ready. We'll have to handcuff him inside the plane."

"That won't be a problem. You can use the metal rings by the seats."

They enjoyed the meal of stew and biscuits, but Sarah couldn't get rid of the tension. She had visions of gagging George for the flight, knowing he would taunt her if he could talk.

Back at the hotel, they split to their separate rooms. Sarah bid the fellows a goodnight and, as they went into their room, she unlocked her door, then froze. A scrape came from the other side. The hairs prickled on the back of her neck as she turned the knob and then put her shoulder into it. It swung into the wall and she heard a surprised shout. Her prisoner struggled to push back.

Amos bounded out of his room, his shirt unbuttoned and disheveled. "What the hell was that?"

Sarah had her gun drawn. "I have a visitor."

Amos darted around her. "Let him go." As Sarah eased up, Amos grabbed the arm that was flailing and pulled him out. Not giving up, the thug tried to hit Amos with a club in his other hand.

"I wouldn't do that, if I were you," Sarah said as she leveled the gun.

The man dropped the club, and Amos shoved him against the wall. "Now talk. Who are you, and what do you want?"

"We don't want any out-of-town lawmen messing with our people," he barked.

"Are you with the Revenge Ravens?"

The man stared at Amos, but said nothing.

Amos shook him. "All right. We're going to go to the sheriff's office. I'll let Creag handle this." He turned to Bill, who was standing in the hall. "You two keep an eye open while I take this varmint across the street."

Sarah holstered her gun, then looked around the room. "Nothing seems to be missing."

Bill stood at the door. "How did he get in?"

She noticed the curtains billowing out. "Looks like he came in the window." She glanced out. "This room is right over the porch. It would be easy to climb in here." She noticed a stick in the window to hold the sash open. Closing the window, she jammed the stick into the upper section, thus preventing it from being raised. "Bill, look in your room and see if you have one of those, and do the same."

Bill nodded and disappeared. They waited in the hall until Amos got back. When he came up the stairs, he had the proprietor tagging along.

Amos pointed to Sarah's room. "He was in there, and the door was locked."

Sarah told him about the window.

The man rubbed his hands. "I'm sorry this happened." He turned to Sarah and Bill. "The sheriff's department will keep an eye on things here tonight, so we shouldn't have any more trouble."

At their thanks, the man went downstairs again.

Amos glanced at Bill. "Go on to bed. I'll be in

later. I have to tell Sarah what I found out from Creag."

Bill inclined his head. "Then I'll say goodnight."

Amos hustled her into her room and shut the door. He saw her face and said, "What?"

She gave him an impish smile. "This really isn't proper. Especially with your shirt like that." He hadn't redone the buttons.

Amos actually blushed as he set to straightening his clothes. "Excuse me. Anyway, Creag told me there is a big group of Revenge Ravens in these parts and they don't take kindly to one of their members being arrested."

"Did he have any suggestions for us?" She sat on the edge of the bed when he settled in the chair.

"He said we should leave before breakfast."

She thought for a moment. "That will be a long time before eating."

"Bill told me earlier he had some provisions on the plane for emergencies. We can tide over with that."

Something smacked against the outside wall and Sarah jumped to her feet. "Oh, no!"

Amos hurried to the window. "Nothing out there that I can see." He came back and put his arms around her. "Don't worry, we'll be all right."

His gesture melted her. "I know. Thank you for helping me."

"I wasn't about to let someone skin you alive, but I don't think he was counting on you to squash him, either." He chuckled. "Fast thinking, Lakat. Good work," he said softer. Their faces were inches apart.

Sarah gazed at his gray eyes as they darkened to a steel blue. He looked back at her with a warm fire and the gentle hug grew tighter. "Amos?"

"Sarah," he said with a husk to his voice. He clamped his lips to hers, and she ran her hand over the rough whiskers on his face, and then somehow they were both sitting on the edge of the bed.

Sarah's mind raced. *Oh my! We're on a job, and our pilot is sleeping in the next room.* She pulled back. "We shouldn't do this now."

"This was another part of the reason I didn't want you to come with me. I didn't know if I could control myself. A cheap hotel isn't a good place for a first time."

Sarah's cheeks heated. He may as well know, since he'll find out anyway. "It won't be my first time."

A puzzled expression crossed his face. "But you were never married."

"I was promised and close to the wedding."

He gritted his teeth. "George?"

She nodded. "I was so sure he was going to be my husband. The next day he ran off."

"That damned bastard could have gotten you with child." He drew her back and rested his chin on her head. He kissed her hair. "I'm no better. I was thinking of taking you myself."

"You know, I am a fully functioning woman who can make up her own mind. If you want me, all you have to do is ask."

He shook his head. "I'm not taking a chance on a scandal. If we do this, I want to prevent any accidents."

She gave a half-smile. "I also know a few days after my time is safe." She pulled away and gazed at him.

"Sarah, I—"

She put her fingers on his lips. "Hush. Give me a

kiss." She received one that curled her toes. Then he worked his way down her neck and gently nipped above her collarbone. A low moan escaped her as her body awoke with intense vibration. *Lord, it's been years since I felt this way.*

They rose and clothes fell. Amos moaned when her breasts were bared and her nipples hardened under his touch. He tugged on one with his lips and the heat seemed to come up from her feet. The muscles of his chest were tight, and she marveled how they moved in his skin under her fingertips.

He embraced her, and she pressed her body against his warm one. The reddish-brown hairs of his torso prickled her, further spiraling her into a lustful state she didn't want to come out of. The rest of their clothes were removed, and she gazed in wonder. He was as virile as she'd thought he would be, and her body gave a deep tremor as she ran her hand up the smooth, hardened flesh. She was so ready for him.

"Lay back on the bed," he rasped, following her. He gently stroked the inside of her thighs and she bucked with an erotic jerk.

"Amos, please," she begged as he ran his finger over her wet slit.

He hitched himself over her. "Oh, my sweet Sarah." He took a deep suckle of her breast as he settled on top of her. She felt the head of his shaft rub at her opening, and then he thrust in. His tongue invaded her mouth as he started the rhythmic rock of love. They moaned in tandem with the sensation and motion of their bodies.

Sarah was like a spring over-wound until she snapped and the blessed release came. Wave after wave of ecstasy left her boneless and breathless as Amos started pumping into her. Both collapsed with a satiny glow of sweat.

After what seemed like an eternity, they came back to their senses. Amos took a deep breath. "Sarah, you are magnificent." He kissed her on the forehead. "I love you. I'd better get next door, or Bill will be wondering."

Sarah smiled. "I love you, too. Goodnight."

Amos dressed and paused at her door. "You want to know something? I don't give a damn what Bill thinks." He waggled his eyebrows and left.

Sarah's alarm clock went off, and she heard clumps and bangs coming from next door. She shook her head to stir the cobwebs of sleep out. As she dressed, her mind went back to last night and a deep tingle of memory went through her. *I wonder if Amos is having repercussions this morning? Well, I'll have to force my business side on today.*

As she finished packing, she heard a knock. "Are you ready to go?"

She opened the door to find Amos and Bill standing there. "All set." She studied Amos' face, but he seemed to have put on his business side, as well. Dreading to see George this morning, she clamped her back teeth down.

The little group made its way to the sheriff's office, where Bill waited for them outside. Creag's deputy handcuffed George with his hands behind his back and led him out of the cell. Amos nodded at Sarah. "I'll lead him to the plane and you follow behind with your gun trained on him."

"Yes, Sheriff."

George hadn't said anything, and Sarah hoped it would stay that way. Amos firmly gripped George's arm and turned to Creag. "Thank you for your help."

"Welcome, Darcy, anytime."

They went out the door, and Sarah drew her gun. Bill walked behind Sarah with the overnight bags. They were almost to the pier when Sarah heard a shout, and three men came running toward them from the docks. "What the hell do you think your doing, Darcy?" a burly red-haired man called.

"I'm taking George Annok into Juneau to stand trial, Mahoney." Amos' stance was a challenge.

Mahoney crossed his arms over his chest. "The first murder was in Cordova. I want him first."

"But we have someone who can identify him."

Mahoney paused. "I hate to think we came all this way to go home empty-handed."

"Look at it this way. If we can convict him, that will make it easier to try him in Cordova."

"All right, we'll do it your way. But we get him next."

Everyone went to the docks, and Bill loaded the bags and started warming the engine. Amos handcuffed George to one of the seats, and then he and Sarah strapped themselves in. Bill gave them a thermos of coffee and some packaged biscuits.

Amos held up the package to George. "Do you want some?"

George glared at the both of them. "I don't want anything from either of you."

Amos passed the biscuits to Sarah and poured some coffee for her. "Here, this will tide us over until lunch."

She took the cup, then met his eyes. His gaze was intense, and she inadvertently felt her cheeks heat. *I can't look at Amos and keep up this facade.* The trip back was very quiet. The easy banter between them seemed to have been abandoned with this new revelation regarding their relationship.

Back at the office in Juneau, Sam put George in one of the cells while Sarah joined Amos in his office. She wanted to express her concerns to him before they went to lunch.

He shook his head. "If we're going to work together, we have to adjust. We can't let our private life interfere with the crime work."

"If we can't"—she paused—"maybe it would be better if I quit the department."

Amos hesitated. "I don't want that. You're the best detective I've ever worked with. Take the rest of the day off. We'll talk to George tomorrow morning."

"Thank you, Amos." She gathered her things and walked toward home. She needed to sort out her life before she could continue her work.

She went a block, then turned toward the Golden North theater. Heading around to the back, she met up with Mrs. Cora Hutton, the Golden North's chef. The gray-haired woman was dropping a bundle of trash in the garbage can when Sarah strode up. "Good afternoon, Mrs. Hutton, is Kata in today?"

The large woman smiled. "Hello, Sarah. Yes, she's in the dressing room where she alters the costumes. The stage door is unlocked. Just go right in."

She thanked Mrs. Hutton and slipped inside the theater. From the dim hall she could hear the sewing machine's treadle making humming noises, and she followed her ears to the dressing room.

Kata turned as the door opened. "Sarah! What a pleasant surprise! What brings you here?"

"Personal problem."

"What's wrong?"

Sarah drew a chair next to the machine and told Kata about the changed relationship between her and Amos. "Now, I'm very uncomfortable around him. I was thinking about quitting my job."

Kata looked back at her with a not-so-shocked face. "I've seen this coming for a long time. But why quit? You love your job. Are you going to talk to your mother about this?"

Sarah snorted. "She'd have me married to Amos before you could blink twice."

"Did he ask you?"

"No. Everything is raw right now."

Kata scrunched her nose. "Well, I'd say, don't make any hasty decisions. Sleep on it."

Sarah sighed. "Thanks for the advice and for listening. I think I will let it rest for a while." She rose to go.

"You can come to me anytime. I'll see you."

Sarah left as Kata turned to her sewing. Seagulls were screeching overhead as she arrived home. Setting her overnight bag on a parlor chair, she put the teakettle on to boil. She opened the windows to let the fresh spring breeze in and steeped the tea. When it was ready, she took a cup and a plate of cookies to the porch and enjoyed her repast in her rocking chair, letting the salty air play around her hair.

Chapter 16

Amos had to stop himself several times, after work, from going to Sarah's home. *What is wrong with the woman? Why the hell is she ruminating over this? Women! Who can figure them out?* It didn't help that Millie asked where Sarah was when he went to the restaurant.

"I gave her the afternoon off," he said tersely.

Millie slipped the pencil behind her ear. "Sorry if I stepped on someone's toes."

"Don't go reading something into this that ain't there. I know how stories are spread."

She raised both her hands. "Okay! Just wondering, that's all." She hurried off to get his order, while he steamed.

Back at his apartment, he paced back and forth. *I'm supposed to be coming up with what I'm going to ask Annok, not fretting about Sarah.* Trying to sleep wasn't any better. His thoughts overran with Sarah. He came to the horrifying conclusion that he needed her.

The next morning, he arrived at Millie's for breakfast and saw Sarah giving her order. He strode to the table. "Would you mind some company?" he asked, removing his hat.

Sarah smiled. "Yes. Sit."

"Millie, I'll have the sunny-side-up eggs with bacon and coffee."

"Thanks, Sheriff." Millie left with their orders.

Amos glanced at Sarah. "I've had the whole night to think about this. Like it or not, you mean something to me. I tried to fight it for months, but I can't anymore. Damn it, woman, I'm in love with you, but I also need you on this case."

Sarah paused. "I had a lot to think about, too. We work so well together, there's no reason we can't continue. I was confused about my feelings for you—and yours for me."

He put his hand over hers. "We were both hurt by love before, but there's no reason to deny what we feel. That seems to be getting in the way, and we shouldn't let it."

Their breakfast was delivered, and Sarah gently pulled her hand back. "You're right." She paused before she started eating. "I had no idea you were so sensitive."

"That's something that better not leave this table," he growled, but he believed Sarah saw the small smile that was trying to come through.

On the way to the office, Amos snagged Mr. Perkins from the newspaper building so he could make a positive identification. After picking up the case folder from his desk, Amos and Sarah escorted Mr. Perkins into the cell room. Amos pointed at George. "Is that the man who placed the Personal ad about Polar Star?"

Perkins peered at him over his glasses. "Yes, Sheriff, that's the man."

George scowled at him. "Don't we all look alike to you?"

Perkins ignored that as he turned. "Anything else?"

"No. Thank you." Perkins left as Amos turned the key in the cell door lock with a metallic click. The hinges squealed as he pulled it open. "Stay seated on your cot and don't try anything. You'll have to go through several deputies, and your chances wouldn't be very good."

Sarah tore a sheet off her notepad, handing George that and a pencil. "Write this: There will be a third at Polar Star, Wednesday next."

"Go to hell."

Amos clamped George's shoulder. "A request was made of you. Now, do it!"

George wriggled out of his grasp, then threw the pencil and tore up the paper. "No!"

"Look, Annok, we got a positive identification on you. We know that you were involved in the murder of Mr. Thornton at the cannery. You can take the whole rap for it or you can name the persons who helped you."

Sarah spoke up. "First thing, where is Bobby Cusnoo?"

George spit on the floor. "How the hell should I know?"

Amos frowned. "Was it you who came up with the plan to spring him? You were in town at the time."

"Sally was the one who sprung him."

"How do you know that?" Amos' eyes flashed.

"Well... Naturally, I thought... Hmm..." George slammed the heel of his hand on his forehead.

Sarah folded her arms across her chest. "What else do you know? What about the attempted murder in the Sitka plant?"

"Sitka?"

Amos planted himself solidly in front of George.

"We fended off your planned attack then, and in desperation you shot Mr. Orville Jensen with an arrow. Then you strung a net over the path to the river where your boat was waiting, and took off."

"How do you know it was me?"

Sarah's mouth set in a tight line. "By the river we found tracks of a dog about the size of a Husky. You told me that Shadow goes with you in your travels."

"I'm not saying anything else!"

Amos glowed with success. That little slip about Sally Cusnoo had helped to convince him they had the right man. "We're finished with this session, but you can be assured there will be more." Amos relocked the cell door, and he and Sarah went out to the main room. Amos tossed the keys to Sam. "We'll be in the office."

Sam set the keys on the hook. "Yes, sir."

As soon as he closed the door, Amos grabbed Sarah in an embrace. "We can still work together. That was a swell interrogation. Now, we wait."

Sarah looked puzzled. "Wait for what?"

"I want to see if the Revenge Ravens try to get him out."

"Do you think they were behind Bobby breaking out?"

"From what you told me, Sally doesn't seem like the type to break the law. I think she was talked into it by the gang." Amos became aware he still held Sarah and felt the twinge of lust. He broke away and sat behind the desk.

Sarah picked up their cups. "Coffee?"

Amos nodded and waited until she brought over the steaming brew. "Sit. What we need to do is be ready without looking like we are. They might try anything, from a trick from the outside, like when they sprung Bobby, to an all-out assault."

"For one thing, we'll have to inspect everything and everyone who goes in to see him."

"That's good. The gun came in on the food tray." Amos tapped his fingers on the blotter. "We'll have to keep an eye on the outside cell window, too, in case anyone tries to slip him a message."

"When does the judge have the hearing scheduled?"

"In two weeks. I'll set up a duty chart on outside stakeouts."

Sarah rose. "I'll tell the others the special inspections on visitors."

"Good. Dinner tonight?"

"As long as you don't put me on stakeout." She smirked, then disappeared.

Amos scratched his head. This time they wouldn't be caught with their pants down. Lesson learned. He started drafting the chart to schedule his six deputies.

Later, at Millie's, he and Sarah were waiting for their order. "I have you for the nine-morning-to-three-afternoon watch. If we put the stakeout in the patrol car where its parked, there's a perfect view from there."

Sarah wrinkled her nose. "I know we have to do it, but I hate stakeouts. At least it's during the day."

Amos walked her home, and they stood on the porch. He felt very uncomfortable. "Let me say goodnight."

Sarah smiled. "Come in for a while?"

It disturbed him that desire could be triggered so quickly. "I don't think I should. People will talk."

Her arms snaked around his shoulders. "Oh, they

need some juicy gossip to keep them busy."

He leaned in and found her lips. Lord, she tasted sweet. The heat radiated out to his whole body, and Sarah grew warmer in his arms. He was fast losing himself.

"Well, isn't this something?" came a voice from the street.

Sarah jumped back. "Mother!" she squeaked.

Amos' cheeks heated. "I—um, should be going."

Grace set herself squarely in front of him. "Before you do, may I ask what intentions you have for my daughter?"

Amos quickly went through several scenarios. Then he bit the bullet. "I'm in love with your daughter, madam."

Grace set her fists firmly on her hips and turned to Sarah. "Well?"

Sarah opened and closed her mouth a couple of times. "I love Amos."

Grace's arms went skyward. "Well, glory hallelujah! My prayers were answered!"

"Mother, what are you doing here?"

Grace smiled. "It's the last Tuesday of the month. I usually come for a visit in the evening."

Sarah flushed. "I forgot. I'm sorry, Mother."

With a chuckle, she replied, "I'm not."

Amos tipped his hat to the both of them. "I'll go and leave you two to your visit. Good evening."

He hurried to the sidewalk and turned toward his apartment. *Well, it's officially out in the open now and, to tell the truth, I'm relieved. Grace seems pleased. I guess I owe George a thank you for being such a two-timing bastard.* He hummed tunelessly as he opened the door to his walk-up.

****

Sarah poured the fresh-brewed tea into her mother's cup. "Then you don't mind that Amos isn't a native?"

Her mother reached for the sugar. "I'd prefer he was, but the fact that he cares for you is enough. Kata found a good match in Ivan, so I guess some Americans are all right."

Sarah snorted. "Between Amos and George, Amos is A-one in my book. I found out George has been married for several years. He was diverting my investigation by pretending to court me."

Her mother steamed. "He fooled me, too. I thought he was genuinely sorry for running out on you."

They went on to other topics that evening, but Sarah was happy her mother seemed to be on her side. They parted a couple of hours later and, as Sarah cleaned up, the thought that she and Amos were still able to work together made her night. *We can adjust to this. I know it.* She sang to herself as she got ready for bed.

A spring rain woke her up the next morning. The wet moss in her yard was fragrant, and the breeze was fresh and crisp as she came down the steps of the porch. Opening her umbrella, Sarah strode into the street and on to the bakery, where she stopped to pick up a cruller for a quick breakfast.

She greeted Sam as she went to her desk. "Did you hear of anything happening last night?"

Sam shook his head. "No, but Amos is talking to Luke now. He said you were to go in when you arrived."

"—only thing I saw was an old man walking his dog down the alley," Luke was saying as she sat across from Amos.

"Did he stop by the cell window?" Amos asked.

"No, sir."

Amos nodded. "All right, you can go home now." As Luke left, Amos looked perturbed.

Sarah shrugged. "Well, it has only been two nights. Maybe they don't have a plan yet."

Amos shook his head. "Trouble is, if it goes on too long, the person on stakeout tends to get careless and misses things. If these people are smart, they'll wait."

"Too bad you can't have a bigger staff."

"I'm at my allotment right now. Any more, and the government starts complaining about expenses."

"What next, Amos?"

He tugged his mustache. "Nothing but routine work now."

"Should we look for Bobby?"

"No. I have a feeling he'll come to us."

Sarah rose. "I guess I'll get back to my paperwork. It has been sadly neglected lately. I'll see how much I can get done before I go on stakeout."

Amos glanced up. "Would you like to go with me to Golden North for dinner and a vaudeville show Saturday?"

"Sounds good. What time?"

"I'll stop by your house at five-thirty."

Sarah flashed a smile. "I'll be ready." She headed to her desk to wage war on her typewriter.

Chapter 17

Amos, cleaned and pressed, went up Sarah's porch steps with a lighter-than-air lilt. He had been looking forward to this all week. All work and no play made Amos grumpy. He turned the doorbell. A few moments later, Sarah appeared in her green silk dress. Her still-a-little-too-short hair was hidden under a green cloche hat. She came out throwing on a fringed shawl and clutching her drawstring bag.

"Oh, Sarah, you're a sight for sore eyes." Amos kissed her hand.

"Thank you." She ran her fingers over his smooth cheek. "You're very handsome without the fuzz."

That gentle touch ignited him like a brand-new spark plug. Amos took a deep breath. "Let's go."

The early May sun was still high in the sky, and the channel breezes brought the salty air to his nose. Sea gulls dived overhead as they called to each other. Up the next block, the theater and restaurant stood like a white palace, with its colorful marquee announcing the traveling troupe.

After giving their order at the restaurant, they toasted each other with ginger ale. Amos brandished the glass. "Here's to our first official outing."

Sarah grinned. "And here's to many more." They clinked their glasses and drank of the bubbly liquid.

Their order of prime rib with roasted potatoes and

gravy kept them busy eating until it was time to file into the theater for the show. The evening was filled with music, comedy, and dramatic readings. Amos held Sarah's hand during most of the performance. They joined the crowd for the enthusiastic applause at the final curtain, then filed out the lobby doors with everyone else.

Back at Sarah's house, the late evening sun made long shadows on the grass as they walked to the porch. Sarah turned and gazed into his eyes. "Thank you for the wonderful time. Would you like to come in for a few minutes?"

He touched her cheek. "You're welcome. I'd love to." He glanced around. "Your mother isn't going to pop up anywhere, is she?"

Sarah laughed and punched his arm. "No. Now come in!" Inside the door, she tried to go into the kitchen.

Amos grasped her hand. "Not so fast." He pulled her back into an embrace. His lips found hers in a thorough kiss. As she relaxed into his arms, he could feel the throb and tightening of his groin. His body knew hers and wanted her again.

Sarah pulled back and wobbled a bit. "You sure know how to sweep a girl off her feet."

Amos stopped a moment. "I can't seem to help myself." He cupped her face in his hands and leaned in for another kiss. Suddenly, an explosion rocked them both. "What the hell was that?"

Sarah ran to a window. "I see flames coming from a couple of blocks away."

Amos joined her. "That's the direction of the office! We'd better get over there." He dashed out the door with Sarah close behind. They raced up the hill, then turned on the side street, and Amos gasped. There was a twisted pile of metal heaped at a broken wall of the office, with fire licking up the side.

"Oh, my dear God!" Sarah choked out. "I hope no one's hurt!" The bell of the fire truck clanged out as it came to a screeching halt in front of the building. The firemen scrambled off and a few moments later had a steady stream of water roaring out the length of hose.

Amos worked his way through the spectators that gathered, gaping. He was stopped by a red-faced policeman. "Halt! You can't go any farther!"

"I'm Sheriff Darcy! Let me through!"

"I'm sorry, Sheriff. I didn't recognize you." The man stepped aside and let Amos go by. Looking around, he spotted Luke, who was in charge.

"Did you get everyone out of the building?"

"Thomas was supposed to get Annok out. I haven't seen them, though."

Amos raced around to the back, where he caught a glimpse of an old man and his dog disappearing between the buildings across the alley from the jail. A form was lying next to the patrol car. It was Thomas, and he groaned as his hand cradled his forehead, blood trickling between his fingers. An empty handcuff dangled at his wrist. Amos knelt beside him. "What happened?"

It took time for Thomas to get his wits about him. "I—I got the prisoner handcuffed and out here. Then I was hit on the head."

"Did you see who did it?"

"No, sir."

"Son of a bitch! He must have had a handcuff key."

Sarah came running around the building in her stocking feet, high heels in one hand. "Are you both all right?"

Amos told her what had happened. "What about the fire?"

"A hole was burned in the front wall of your office," she said, "but the damage inside wasn't too bad, thanks to the fire department's quick arrival."

Amos glanced at Thomas. "I want the doc to take a look at you." He helped Thomas to stand.

Thomas nodded. "Yes, sir." The three of them returned to the street where the firemen were finishing up.

Amos strode to the fire chief, who was inspecting the exploded vehicle. "Abner, was there anyone in the auto when it blew?"

The chief shook his head. "No. It seemed to be deliberately parked here. I want to show you something." They walked around to the gas tank. "The cap was removed before it exploded."

Amos scratched his head. "Are you sure the blast didn't catapult it?"

"If you examine the tank, the only damage is around the top. If the cap had been on, the whole tank would be in pieces. We are seeing the work of an arsonist."

"Or someone who wanted to create a diversion. Our prisoner escaped."

Sarah appeared beside Amos. "Thomas is being checked over." Sarah paused. "I heard the last of your conversation. Do you think the Revenge Ravens had a hand in this?"

"I'd bet my paycheck on it." Amos turned to the

fire chief. "Thanks for your input, Abner. I guess it's our work now."

The chief slapped Amos on the back. "Happy to be of service." He started helping his men load up.

Amos glanced around. "Luke!"

The deputy strode to him. "Yes, sir?"

"Did you question any of the witnesses to see if they noticed who left that auto there?"

"Yes, I did. No one remembered anything."

Amos sighed. "Let's all go in to see how much damage there is."

Sarah's mouth was a tight line. "What about George?"

"I think he was alerted somehow. We can start in the cell, then search out back." He turned to Luke. "Go through the outer office and mine to see how much is salvageable."

They found Thomas standing near the front door. "The doc gave me a clean bill of health, but he said I should rest."

Amos clapped him on the shoulder. "Go home. We can take care of this."

Amos grabbed a flashlight on the way into the cell room, and Sarah swung the iron door open. "What are we looking for?" she asked.

"Anything." Amos took the side with the cot, and Sarah scanned the wall under the window.

"Amos, hand me your penknife." She studied the floor. She used the knife in the cracks between the boards until a little wedge of paper popped out. Amos held the light over as she unrolled it. "It says, 'Tonight. Be ready.'" She started working on a couple more white flecks as Amos sat on the cot. "This one says,

'Escape being planned.' Then this one, 'This is the way we'll message you.' "

Amos put his face in his hands, a dark cloud descending. "What's the city going to say? This is the second jailbreak in a month. I should have seen this coming."

Sarah rose and patted his shoulder. "You did everything you could."

"No, I missed something. How did he get these messages?"

"We all went through anything he received. As far as going by the cell window, nobody stopped. The only person we saw regularly was the old man and his dog."

Amos gripped her arm. "Sarah! I saw him going between the buildings on the far side of the alley just before I found Thomas. He could have been flipping the small pieces of paper through the window bars as he went by. Damn it, I should have caught that!" He sank to the cot, and Sarah sat beside him.

"We're not perfect, even though we try to be. None of us suspected the old man. Don't be so hard on yourself."

"I'm the sheriff. I need to be on top of everything." He felt Sarah's arms go around him, and the warmth flowed. He sighed. "Let's see if we can find out about the old man." He glanced out the window. "It's dark now. Bring the flashlight."

They stopped to talk to Luke before going out. He was going through the papers Amos had left on his desk, most of them wet but salvageable. Luke opened one of the drawers. "Looks like the papers that were inside the desk are dry."

Amos pointed at the broken front wall. "See what

you can do about boarding up that wall until we can get it fixed. Call someone to help you."

"Yes, sir."

Amos headed for the back. "We can look for footprints. I doubt if we'll get any clear impressions around the burned auto, though."

Sarah held the flashlight over the area where Thomas' scuffle had taken place. "I see three different prints in the dirt. And over here, a dog's paw prints."

Amos nodded. "I know where they went after the escape, but I only saw the old man and his dog." He took the flashlight from Sarah and went to the buildings where he'd last seen the old man. The prints disappeared when they reached the sidewalk. "Damn! With all the people passing by, I doubt if any of them were here when he got to this point."

"Maybe one of the shopkeepers saw something."

"Trouble is, at this hour, most of these shops are closed." Amos glanced at his pocket watch. "It's almost midnight. Come on, I'll walk you home."

Standing on her porch, Amos noticed Sarah's dress was dirty and torn. "I guess we shouldn't have gone to a fire dressed in our best duds."

Sarah grinned. "You're pretty shabby yourself."

Amos pulled her into an embrace. "Come here, beautiful." She smelled like smoke, and he kissed her thoroughly. "We've got our work cut out for us tomorrow. Sleep tight."

She caressed his cheek. "You too. Goodnight, and thanks for an evening of excitement. You really know how to keep a girl interested." Her melodic laugh echoed in his mind as he strode home.

****

Sarah sat on the corner stool at Millie's counter. "I'll have toast and jelly with coffee, please. Millie, have you heard anything about Sally Cusnoo?"

Millie hesitated a moment. "Only hearsay, but I heard that she and Bobby were in Angoon. I'd be willing to bet that's where George Annok escaped to."

Sarah nodded. "That makes sense. Thank you for the tip."

At the office, Sarah told Amos what Millie had said. "Angoon would be the perfect place. The native community would close around them. I'd be the perfect one to snoop around there."

Amos' eyes went dark. "Not after your last episode. People may recognize you even without your disguise."

A canvas tarp waved back and forth, dividing Amos' office in half, while sawing and hammering raised a din as the carpenters worked on the front wall. Sarah sighed. "Can we talk in the cell room?"

After giving the high sign to Sam, they opened one of the iron doors and sat on the cot. Amos turned to her. "How do you know the hearsay was correct?"

"We should check out any leads. I could even ask Will if he's heard anything around town."

"All right, but stay with your cousins. You don't know what the others would do if they knew you were there. Meanwhile, I'll find out about the old man." He gave her a kiss, and then she got her things and took off.

She decided to borrow Ivan's truck, but before that she'd stop at her mother's and ask Aunt Jane if Will was at home. Sarah packed a small bag and headed to the family property. She brightened when she saw

Will's truck in the front. He was on the porch with Aunt Jane and Mother. "Good morning, all! Will, I need to talk to you."

He tapped his pipe out on the side of the railing. "What is it?"

"How long are you going to be here?"

"I was just getting ready to go home."

"Could I ride to Angoon with you? Something has come up in the investigation, and it would be better not to alert certain people."

"How will you get back?"

"I can catch a boat to Juneau."

Will paused in thought. "All right. As long as it doesn't endanger the family."

"You can let me off in town." She greeted and hugged her mother and her aunt and chatted a moment before requesting, "Aunt Jane, could you tell Ivan I won't need his truck after all? He can come pick it up." Sarah hopped into the passenger side of Will's vehicle for the three-hour drive.

Will glanced at her. "I heard about the jailbreak and fire at the sheriff's office last night. Were you there when it happened?"

Sarah related to him what took place.

Will frowned. "These people are giving all the natives a bad name. I thought at first they were really looking out for the villages upstream, but now they're getting power mad."

Sarah nodded. "Killing like that doesn't make allies. I know American fishermen aren't happy with the canneries, either, but they're not murdering the people who work there, as far as I know."

When they reached the outskirts of Angoon, Sarah

had Will stop the truck. "It would be better for you if I walk the rest of the way. No one knows me here."

"One of the men from the ANB might recognize you."

"I'm in female clothes now. I doubt if they'll even look at me." Sarah kissed Will on the cheek. "Thanks for the lift, and give my best to Mary and the children."

Will's eyes were shaded with concern. "I will. If you get in trouble, you know where we are."

Gulls screeched and dived into the waters of the harbor as she came into the village. Men hustled around the boats getting the netting fixed for tomorrow morning's fishing trip. Sarah stopped to breathe in the salty air. *I wonder where I should start looking for Sally. She was a waitress. Maybe the café here in town would be a good place to start.*

A small shack by the wharf proclaimed itself Fisherman's Rest in weatherbeaten blue letters on its side. Underneath was the word Eat. She headed over the uneven path to the door and was hit with a noseful of heavy grease. In the dark interior, a bewhiskered man in a stained white apron served a few sad-looking seamen. There wasn't room for tables—the whole place was a long counter. Sarah sat on a wobbly wooden stool that threatened to throw her at the first sneeze.

The man behind the counter sidled up to her, and his pungent body odor followed. "May I help you, doll?"

Just coffee, please. Black." A steaming mug of questionable cleanliness was set before her. "Do you employ waitresses here?"

"You looking for a job?"

"No. Looking for a friend of mine from Juneau

who worked as one there."

One of the seamen spoke up, "There's a new gal over to the general store."

"Where is it?"

"Next to the town hall. Two-story green building."

Sarah put a quarter beside her cup and rose. "Thank you for the information." She gratefully opened the door to get out of the aromatic tomb and took the road into the heart of the village. She spotted the Dry Goods sign on a green clapboard building with black shutters. From the wooden sidewalk, she climbed the steps into the store.

The smell of dried fish and roasted coffee was strong inside. Two long counters lined the walls on either side in front of the shelves of goods. Larger tools and implements stood along the back wall, and a potbellied stove graced the center of the room where a couple of old men played a game of checkers. A woman with a shopping basket on her arm leaned across the counter, pointing to the items she wanted. The one filling the order was Sally Cusnoo.

Sarah busied herself with a newspaper on the other side of the room until Sally was finished with her customer. Then she put the paper back on the rack and turned to Sally. "Hello."

Sally gave a squeal and her eyes got large. "Sarah! How did you find me?"

Sarah lowered her voice. "That doesn't matter now. Can we talk?"

Sally glanced at the two men. "Yes, we have one of those out back. Follow me." She led Sarah to an unattached storeroom that was little more than a wooden shed. "You're going to arrest me, aren't you?"

"No, I want information from you. If you cooperate, it will definitely help you." At Sally's nod, she continued. "Where are Bobby and George?"

Sally closed her eyes for a moment. "They're on their way to Canada. They plan to meet George's wife in Gustavus and hike their way through the interior to the Chilkoot Trail, where they'll end up in the Yukon."

"When did they leave?"

"This morning."

Sarah worked over in her mind what should be her next move. It would take time for George's wife to make it down from Yakutat. She knew she couldn't try to find them by herself. Instead of taking a boat back to Juneau, maybe she should rent a seaplane. To Sally she said, "Stay here in Angoon. We'll need you to testify."

Sally chewed on her lower lip. "Please don't let them know it was me that told you. They didn't realize I was listening at the door."

Sarah put a reassuring hand on Sally's shoulder. "I won't until I know you're safe."

Sally slipped back into the store. "Thank you."

Writing down the information in her notebook, Sarah hurried to the pier where the seaplanes were docked. A young man was wiping the wing of one of them. "Excuse me, sir. Is this plane for hire?"

His dark eyes appraised her. "Who wants to know?"

"I'm Deputy Sarah Lakat of the Juneau Sheriff's Department, and I need to get there as soon as possible." She showed him her identification.

"All right, ma'am, you got a ten-spot?"

"Yes. How soon can we leave?" She handed him the bill.

"Get in and strap up. Name's Kip Baker."

"Thank you, Mr. Baker." As she strapped herself in, Kip warmed up the engine. "Could you put down at the harbor in Juneau?"

"Sure thing."

The forty-five minutes went fast as Sarah marveled over the wildness of the island that was her birthplace. Kootznahoo, or "bear fort," was a perfect name in the Tlingit language. She lost count of the number of bears she saw from above on this flight as they got up from their long winter nap. Soon Mount Juneau and Roberts Peak came into view by the channel, their peaks floating on top of the gray mist, and she was almost home.

Kip landed the plane with a soft plop into the harbor and guided it to one of the tie-ups. He helped Sarah onto the pier, and she thanked him with a one-dollar tip.

"I'll be at your service anytime." He grinned as he tipped his hat.

A glance at the clock tower let her know it was three o'clock as she strode to the office. "Sam, is Amos in?"

"Yes, he is."

Sarah knocked on the door. "May I come in?"

Amos opened it. "I didn't expect you back today. What happened?"

Sarah told Amos everything she'd learned in Angoon. "I decided to fly back so I could let you know."

"Why didn't you go to Gustavus?"

"I didn't know how many besides Bobby and George would be there. I don't think I could take on an army by myself."

"I wouldn't be so sure."

"What?"

"You can be quite formidable when you want to be." Amos leaned back in his chair, his brows wrinkled in thought. "Was Sally sure of what she heard?"

"As far as I know. She said they didn't know she was listening."

"We know they want to get to the Chilkoot Trail from Gustavus, so maybe we should have someone follow them and at the same time have someone wait at the trail's head near Skagway." He pulled a map from his desk. "Here's a terrain map. We can find the best route to Skagway in the interior. How are you at backpacking and camping?"

"I haven't done it since my father and brothers died, but I still have my pack."

"Good. I'm going to wire Creag, Mahoney, and Tunny to see if they could take the Skagway stake with a couple of their deputies."

Sarah chewed her lip. "Do you think that will be enough? We don't know how many are in this troop."

Amos paused. "You're right. Maybe I should ask them to meet us at Gustavus with their deputies, and alert the Skagway sheriff to watch the trail's head. Why didn't you bring Sally in?"

"I don't think she wants to get into any more trouble. I told her it would go easier on her if she cooperated. I told her to stay in Angoon. Don't worry, I trust her. I think she was forced to help Bobby escape."

"Well, she did give you that information. As long as it's the truth. I hope she's not sending us on a wild goose chase."

Sarah tapped her fingers on the desk. "It's the only lead we have right now. We can find out in Gustavus if anyone has seen them. By the way, what did you find out about the old man?"

"He hasn't shown after the jailbreak. I assume he was a member of the gang." Amos checked his watch. "It's almost four. I'll go to Western Union and send the telegrams out and then pick up my backpack. You go home and pick up yours. We should be able to get a plane to Gustavus before dark. That's only a fifteen-minute flight. I'll be at your house in a half hour."

Sarah hurried home and ransacked her storeroom in the back until she found her old backpack. It smelled musty, but it would have to do. Packing a change of clothes and a few cans of food, she made sure the tent, blanket, and light cooking equipment were still all there. Then she sat in the rocker on the porch to wait for Amos and promptly fell asleep from exhaustion.

Next thing she knew, she was being shaken gently. "Sarah, are you ready?"

She shook her head. "I'm sorry, Amos, I must have fallen asleep."

"I hate to do this to you, but we have to leave." He took her pack and put it in the patrol car while she climbed into the passenger side. "If they're still there, this may be a short trip."

She leaned back on the seat and her eyes kept closing. It was that way on the flight, too. Amos helped her off the plane and put his arm around her shoulder. The familiar tingling woke her somewhat, but she let him lead her to the sheriff's office in Gustavus and set her down on a bench in front of it.

"You sit here. I'll go in and see what I can find

out." He patted her shoulder and disappeared through the door. Deep down, Sarah knew she should have gone in too, but she was at the end of her strength. The next thing she was aware of was Amos beside her again. "I showed them the picture of George, and one of the deputies remembered seeing him with a party leaving for the back country around one o'clock. There were four men, one woman, and a couple of dogs. I'm guessing they are going to travel over the glaciers. They can't move as fast as two people, so we can rest here until three in the morning and take off at first light. If any of the posse is here by then, all the better. Otherwise, they can catch up with us."

Sarah yawned. "At least they aren't aware they're being followed. That's where we have the advantage."

They went to the trailhead campsite, and Amos set up. "We'll put one tent up tonight. It'll be faster to clean up in the morning." He started a small fire, and they opened a can of beans and shared it, with some crackers from Sarah's backpack.

Amos slung the packs over the branch of a tree, just in case there were bears around, while Sarah crawled into the small tent, still fully dressed, and promptly fell asleep.

Chapter 18

Amos set the coffeepot on a flat rock in the fire and checked his watch. It was two-thirty, and the dusky streaks of dawn were beginning behind the mountains. Already the forest had begun to stir. The hoots of the great horned owl were being replaced by the raspy cries of the ravens. Heavy dew gave a wet chill to the early morning.

The tent flap opened and Sarah appeared. "Good morning, Amos!" She took off toward the small stream. To wash up, he supposed. Amos rummaged in his pack for the hard biscuits they could eat with the coffee before they went on their way.

Amos had acted the perfect gentleman during the night, although, during the time he was awake, he had wanted to take her. It was going to be difficult on this journey to control his feelings. He poured the coffee into two mugs as Sarah came to sit by him on a fallen log. She sure smelled fresh and sweet.

She took one of the mugs, and Amos passed her a biscuit. "I'll help you strike the campsite. Then we can be on our way." She took a deep breath. "I love the morning air in the woods."

"Sounds like you miss camping. Been a while, eh?"

"Too long." They finished their small repast and packed up. Amos put out the fire and scattered the ashes before they left. A light rain was just beginning, so they put on raincoats and started following the trail of the escapees. Sarah fell silent as they made their way through the long grasses between the patches of spruce and hemlock trees that appeared like phantoms out of the gray mist. With the soil damp, they could easily make out the footprints of the fugitives.

A couple of hours into their quest, Amos spoke up. "I think we should take a break every two hours. That way we can continue as long as there's light."

Sarah nodded. "Good idea. I see an alcove below that cliff. That would be a good rest stop."

While Sarah took care of necessities, Amos climbed partway up the cliff and had a look around with his binoculars, since the mist was lifting. The land would get hillier, and he saw the first of the glaciers in the distance. He knew it wouldn't be an easy trek, but he was sure that's what the fugitives were banking on, that no one would suspect they would go that route. They probably didn't know they were being followed, and if he and Sarah stayed quiet and inconspicuous, they might have a chance of taking them by surprise.

He told Sarah what he thought before they took off again. Four hours later, they came upon a campsite. Amos felt the ashes of the fire pit. "There's still a little warmth. At least we know we're on the right track."

Sarah sat on a boulder nearby. "Let's see. It's almost nine o'clock. If they left at one yesterday, they camped here around six."

Amos nodded. "And if the ashes are still warm, they left around six this morning. They don't seem to be in any all-fired hurry. They're only three hours ahead of us."

Sarah rubbed her legs. "Shall we take a meal break? I'm starving."

Amos swung his backpack off and started rummaging through it. "Another can of pork and beans. I'll see if I can get a fire going." He found a few pieces of relatively dry wood and soon had a small fire snapping happily in the pit. Opening the can with his utility knife, he set the can close enough to the fire to heat it.

Meanwhile, Sarah put the coffeepot on the fire. "The mist is clearing. I can see the sun coming through. Maybe we could try to spot them after the meal. There's a rise up ahead."

When they had finished, they climbed the rise and Amos removed the binoculars from around his neck. Scanning the land, he handed Sarah the lenses. "Look at the glacier ahead."

Sarah focused on the vast white strip. "I see some movement at the center of it. Seems like we found them."

Amos nodded. "If we keep up this pace, we should catch up with them in a day or so. I hope the rest of our party shows up."

They eased their way down the ridge and into the valley between the hills. Several eagles screeched and circled overhead, dipping down to the stream. Amos envied them their fishing ability and made a mental note to camp near a stream tonight. He could take only so much pork and beans.

The valley part of their trek was easy, and Sarah started singing, "Green grow the lilacs all sparkling with dew. I'm lonely, my darlin', since parting with you..." and Amos joined in. They both were careful to keep their voices light so they wouldn't carry, but they went through several songs before they decided to stop for the evening.

Due to Amos' hankering for some fresh fish, they set up camp by a feeder stream to a lake. He rigged up a makeshift pole from a straight fallen branch, using his utility knife. He didn't have to dig far in the damp soil to find bait for the hook and line he kept in his pack. Within a half hour he had two fine cutthroat trout that he scaled and gutted.

Sarah had the fire going and the small frying pan heating up. "Any luck?"

Amos held up the two trout carcasses as he laid down the two canteens he'd filled with fresh water. "All ready for the fire."

Sarah smiled. "I found a patch of chocolate lilies and cut pellets off several bulbs. We can have the trout with that."

Amos handed her the fish. "That's what they call Indian rice, isn't it?"

"Yes." Sarah squeezed the trout over the pan to get some of the fish oil into it. Then she added the meat and browned it. Carefully putting in water, she dumped her handkerchief full of pellets into the pan. With a finishing touch of salt and pepper from their supplies, the feast was ready.

As Sarah cleaned up the dishes afterward, Amos set up their tents. He thought about just putting up one, but he didn't know if the rest of their party would show up, and that could be embarrassing.

Sitting side by side on a fallen log in front of the fire, Amos watched the mountain snow turn pink as the sun moved to the horizon. His arm snaked around

Sarah's shoulders, and she gave an involuntary shudder. "You cold?"

Her dark brown eyes burned into his. "No." An impish smile played around her lips. "Are you?"

Amos found he was shaking, as well. "You look so wild and beautiful out here."

"Oh, Amos, you do go on." Her lips parted seductively and his latched onto them. She smelled so fresh in this mountain air. Desire pumped through him like a hammer.

"Hello, Darcy!" came a shout from behind.

Amos shot off the log so fast he almost took a header into the fire. When he regained his balance and dignity, he turned. "Mahoney, is that you?"

Four figures came out of the woods and into the clearing. "Sorry, if we startled you. We figured if we went farther this evening, we could catch up. We saw you when you started through the valley."

Sarah rose and stood next to Amos. He made a gesture toward her. "This is my deputy, Sarah Lakat. You know Mahoney and Tunny." Sarah nodded.

Mahoney turned to his party. "This is my deputy, Abner Stewart, and this is Tunny's, Max Cartwright."

Sarah didn't like the way Cartwright was eying her. He had an angry, dark expression. "You have an Indian woman deputy?" he growled.

Amos narrowed his eyes. "Tunny, did you have to bring a troublemaker with you?"

Tunny shrugged. "Sitka is full of them."

Amos turned his wrath on Cartwright. "We don't have time for this kind of damned prejudice. She's been on the case from the first. If you don't like it, leave." He whirled on Tunny. "I expect you to keep your deputy in line!"

Tunny glared at Cartwright. "There won't be any trouble, Darcy. Will there, Cartwright?"

The deputy cringed. "No, sir."

Amos looked around. "I know the sheriff in Soldatna was busy, but did Creag show up?"

Mahoney shook his head. "Not that I know of. Tunny and I arrived about the same time and were told you went on ahead. So we've been tracking you."

Amos jerked his thumb in the direction opposite their tents. "You can set up over there. The stream is northeast of here. We're planning to leave at three in the morning."

Mahoney nodded. "Sounds good, Darcy. We'll be ready."

Amos watched as Sarah crawled into her tent. *This is a hell of a fix. I guess I should have known there would be a reaction like that to her. I keep hoping she will be accepted, but I guess I'm beating a dead horse with the men around here.* Amos was beginning to understand what she must have gone through all her life, and he admired her even more.

****

Sarah removed her hiking boots and rubbed her feet as she sat on her bedroll. *Why do these men have to be this way? I just want to do my job.* She heard them setting up their tents. Loosening her belt, she undid her Levis and unbuttoned her shirt while snuggling under her blanket. She was almost asleep when she heard a light scratching on her tent flap.

"Sarah?" came Amos' voice, "Are you all right?"

She pulled it open. "Yes. I'm used to this. Don't worry about me."

160

Amos sat back on his heels. "Sorry for disturbing you."

She reached for his hand and drew him to her. "Thank you for thinking about me." She caressed his face and gave him a warm kiss.

When he pulled back, he blew out a slow breath. "You keep that up, and you won't get rid of me."

She laughed. "We better not give them more to talk about. Goodnight, Amos." She replaced the flap and settled back into her bedroll. The kiss had given her an electric charge, and her skin tingled. *I wish he could have stayed.* She thrilled at the memory of his body as she drifted off.

Sarah awoke with a start. *What did I hear?* A rustling noise and a snort came from the other side of the camp. *That snort didn't sound human.* She carefully opened her tent flap. Amos, who must have heard it too, was crawling past.

"Stay there!" he hissed under his breath.

"What the hell?" yelled one of the men when they heard a roar.

A bear!

Amos snapped on his flashlight and hit the beast in the eyes with the light.

"I'll get my rifle!" called another man.

"No!" Amos shouted. "Do you want to alert the fugitives? Everyone pick up a rock or a branch and throw it at the bear."

The creature first lunged toward the light, but with the stones and wood bouncing off its hide and the light blinding it, it soon took off into the woods in the direction of the stream.

Amos joined the men in front of their tents. "What

was the goddamn bear after?"

Mahoney answered, "It looks like Abner left some of his provisions on the ground." And then to his unfortunate deputy, he chastised, "Haven't you ever been camping before? You never leave food on the ground!"

"Sorry, sir, this is all new to me."

"Don't let it happen again."

"Yes, sir." She heard feet shuffling and the men returning to their tents.

Amos passed by her tent muttering, "Damn fool kids!"

Sarah settled back down to sleep, praying there were no more bears looking for a midnight snack.

The next morning, Sarah slipped out early to clean up at the stream, hoping she would finish before the men got up. All the time she was cleansing herself, she had a feeling someone was watching her. Hurriedly, she adjusted her clothing and turned back to camp. She stifled a gasp and her cheeks burned. In the path was Max Cartwright pissing in full sight, staring at her, his whole organ exposed.

He leered at her. "See anything you like, injin lady?"

Sarah found her voice. "Not anything I'm interested in. Have you no shame?"

He took a step toward her. "You savin' your whoring for Sheriff Amos?"

She marched up to him and slapped him across his face. "I won't take that from anyone. You stay away from me, or I'll defend myself and shoot the first body part I see."

He grabbed her arm. "Tough talk from a girl."

"Let go of me!" Her voice carried and got the desired effect.

Amos dashed down the path and caught Max by the back of his shirt. "What in hell is going on here? Tunny!" he bellowed.

Max let go of Sarah like a hot poker and quickly tried to put himself together. Tunny appeared on the path, wiping his face with a towel. "What is it, Darcy?"

"Teach your goddamn deputy some manners, or I will have to string up his sorry carcass for bear bait!"

Sarah had to stop herself from running into Amos' protective arms. She didn't want to appear weak in front of this jackass, but she was still shaking.

Tunny took the back of Max's collar from Amos and shoved his deputy toward camp. "Don't worry, Amos, I will."

Amos put his arms around Sarah. "Are you all right?"

She buried her face on his shoulder. "I should have Tunny arrest him for lewd behavior. Why do I always run into these types?"

"Fortunately the staff in Juneau treats you with respect."

Sarah pulled back. "I think that's because they respect you. I'm all right now. We'd better strike camp."

Walking back, she had to steel herself for the rest of the job. She and Amos took the point when they started out on the trail. Campfire was spotted across the valley, and they headed in that direction. The fugitives should be overtaken tomorrow, if all went well. The whole time she felt hostile eyes burning into her back, but Cartwright said and did nothing to her during the rest of the journey.

After they'd eaten, Amos took her aside. "Usually, I wouldn't do this, but I don't trust Cartwright around you. You're sleeping in my tent tonight, and I'll sleep in yours."

Sarah mind reeled. "How would that help?"

"We'll switch after everyone has turned in. If he thinks about pulling anything, he won't find you where you're supposed to be."

Despite herself, she suppressed a giggle. "If he does try something, I'd love to see his face to find you there."

Amos smirked. "Remember, after they all go into their tents."

Sarah kept an eye out from behind her tent flap and watched as the men retreated to theirs. As soon as she saw the last one disappear, she made her move. Carrying her boots, she pussyfooted in stocking feet over the damp ground to Amos' tent and crawled noiselessly through his tent flap. "You can go to mine now." She couldn't see him, but she could feel his warmth, and she got that tight-chested tingle.

"The things I do to protect your sorry hide," he whispered.

She found his face and pasted a kiss on his lips. "I'm very grateful," she murmured as she pulled back.

He groaned and yanked her back into his arms. "You're driving me crazy." His voice was getting husky.

"But my tent is—" She was cut off by a passionate kiss. She gave up and melted into his arms. The dark in the tent made the whole experience otherworldly. His hands stroked down her body and underneath her shirt, cupping her breasts while the nipples peaked under his grasp. Losing most of her conscious thought, she ached for more.

"Sarah, you smell like the fresh woods." He showered kisses down her neck and collarbone. Then he groaned as she undid the buttons of his shirt and felt the muscles ripple and become steel beneath her fingertips.

Sarah writhed out of her Levis as Amos undid his. Her hand moved down his stomach and she grasped his shaft as he moved between her thighs. She wanted him with a fierceness she'd never felt before, but she bit her tongue to keep her moans low.

Amos was stifling noises, himself. She guided him to her warm, slick opening, and he thrust in with a sharp intake of breath. He moved back and forth, slow at first, but gradually building speed. Without the visual, the sensations were all in the touch of his hands, his lips, and especially where they were joined.

Finally, an intense orgasm engulfed her body, and her pelvic muscles pulsed around his shaft. Amos groaned into her neck as she felt the hot spasms of his release. He shuddered a couple of times, then lay bonelessly on her. She rubbed his back, and he shuddered again.

"God, Sarah, that was good." He rose and gave her a heartfelt kiss that set her to tingling again.

The chill of the night air brushed her as he pulled back. "I must say you have incredible heating in your tent."

"I'd better get over to yours before I get too comfortable sleeping on top of you." He got his clothes together and crept out of the tent.

Sarah adjusted her garments, then happily snuggled down into the blanket that smelled like Amos.

****

Slipping through the tent flap, Amos crawled onto Sarah's blanket. Not long after, he heard a rustling outside. The tent flap slowly opened, and Amos held his breath. A form eased in beside him, then grabbed him. "Don't scream, injin lady, or I'll—huh?"

Amos wrestled him over. "Cartwright? I thought you were going to try something stupid." He bellowed out the tent, "Tunny!" He heard a quick shuffling from the other side of the camp and footfalls as he pulled the deputy out. "Put a leash on this dirtball deputy of yours, or he's being tied to a tree for the buzzards!"

Tunny shook Cartwright. "That's it! You're packing in the morning and starting back by yourself. You're fired, Max! Turn in your badge in the morning!"

"Fired? For trying to get—" He was cut short by the connection of Amos' fist with his jaw.

"Get out of my sight!" Amos yelled, as he rubbed his hand. "You're lucky I don't make a eunuch out of you!" He glanced around at the gathering. "Show's over. Get back to your tents."

****

Amos awoke from the best sleep he'd had in a long time. As he stretched, his thoughts went back to Sarah, and he felt a strong twitch from his groin. *Not a good time for thoughts like that.* He made his way to the stream to clean up and met Sarah coming back.

He grinned. "Good morning. Hope you slept well."

An impish smile appeared. "Yes, I did. The best was after the fight with Cartwright. You?"

"Very well. You have a comfortable bedroll."

Others of the men were coming down, so they parted on that note. Amos cleaned up and packed his tent. Grabbing his binoculars, he climbed to a rise that looked out over the valley. A campfire several miles away caught his eye. Mahoney joined him. Amos handed him the binoculars. "Looks like we may catch up with them today."

Mahoney pointed. "They'll probably try to cross that glacier. Skagway should be just a day's trek after that."

Amos nodded. "We can take them before they hit Chilkoot."

The men started down to the campsite. Mahoney nudged him. "Good idea about you and Lakat switching tents last night."

Amos moved his hat forward. "I didn't like the way Cartwright was harassing her. To keep her safe, we tried that. Luckily, he was caught going in where he wasn't supposed to be."

"She must be a good deputy, for you to put up with this."

"She's a good deputy and a good person. I'm beginning to understand, somewhat, the things women are hollering about these days."

Sarah greeted them as they came back and gave them each a steaming mug of coffee and a hard biscuit. *My, she is beautiful in the morning.*

Amos and Mahoney briefed the rest as to where their quarry was. "I think we should keep noise to the minimum. Voices carry in this valley. We don't want to tip them off," Amos warned. Everyone checked their glacier spikes to make sure their gear was in working order. They also had their guns at the ready. Amos set the pace, with Sarah beside him.

For a few hours, all they heard was their footsteps. The edge of the glacier glistened in the morning sunlight, and Amos took a scan of the terrain. The fugitives were less than a mile in front of them. They paused to affix the spikes to their boots and put on their heavier jackets.

Tunny spoke up. "You know we'll be out in the open and lose the element of surprise."

Amos nodded. "We have to hope they don't turn around. It would be nice to have the advantage of them. Maybe we could come upon them in a wide semicircle." He pointed to the east. "Sarah, you take that side. Mahoney, you and Abner, then Tunny. I'll take this end."

The cold of the glacier ice cut through their boots although the May sun warmed the air. The spikes made a scrunching sound, but that couldn't be helped. Amos' stomach clutched with nerves on edge. He glanced at Sarah in the distance and hoped they would get through this without too much of a fight. She glanced at him and gave a nod. She seemed to have more confidence.

The breeze over the ice stung his face, but they were almost on top of the fugitives. Then the dogs ahead started barking, and their pursuit was discovered. The sheriffs and deputies had already shed their backpacks and gotten out their sidearms.

Amos brandished his gun. "Stop! We're taking you in!" A shot whistled over his head, and he dropped to the ice, firing back while the others scrambled ahead. The circle of the law swung around and trapped any exit the fugitives might have had.

"Drop your weapons!" Tunny bellowed.

The fugitives glanced around at the encircling law officers, who stood with guns trained. As the villains slowly lowered their weapons, sheriffs and deputies advanced. Sarah had circled to a point behind George when he suddenly whirled and fired at her feet, sending up a spray of ice. She stepped back, then wobbled and, with a cry, disappeared.

"Sarah!" Amos yelled, the anguish clear in his voice. Mahoney fired and caught the rifle in George's hand, skittering it over the terrain.

Mahoney motioned to Amos. "We can take care of securing this lot, if you want to check on Lakat."

Amos hurried to the place he last saw Sarah, dread making holes in his insides.

Chapter 19

Sarah stood rigid, afraid to even breathe. She carefully assessed her situation. Her left shoulder was jammed in a fissure crack and her feet were precariously placed on a ledge next to a blue ravine she couldn't see the bottom of. She carefully looked up. In her judgment, she was five feet from the top, with bits of ice raining down.

She leaned to her left to keep herself from sliding farther. Her ears caught shouts and more gunfire from above, and she prayed things would turn out all right. Shivering from cold and shock, she knew she had to get out of there soon.

She heard her name called and, without moving, glanced up to see Amos' face peering at her from the top. "Amos, I'm down here. Help me!"

For what seemed like hours, he disappeared, then showed up again with a rope. "Sarah, we looped the rope and are going to lower it to you. Tie the rope around your waist and under your arms, leaving it long enough to step into. When you're ready, put your foot in the loop, then push off the ledge and swing out. We'll haul you up."

Sarah shifted slightly to grab the rope, her foot threatening to slip. She leaned into the crack as far as she dared and snaked the rope around her waist and tied a hitch. Then she wound it under her arms and coiled it around her right wrist for a tight grip. "Amos, I'm ready, but I haven't stepped in the loop yet."

The rope lost slack and she heard Amos say, "Do it! We won't let you go."

She took a deep breath. Lifting one foot from the ledge, she felt her other foot slip. *I'll have to do this in one quick move.* Sweat poured down her face and started to freeze. She moved the rope as close to her boot as she dared. *Now!* The toe of her boot slid into the loop, and she plunged sideways. A hot flash of pain went through the shoulder that had been jammed in the crack, but she held on. "I'm off the ledge. Get me out of here!" she managed to shout.

Every tug of the rope brought a new agony of pain, but she kept pushing back from the face of the ice to help. She was almost to the top when she heard a groan from the rope. Looking up, a piece of it was frayed, and she watched as a couple of the threads snapped. "Amos, hurry! The rope's about ready to break!"

"Grab onto the rim when you get there!" She clawed at the lip of ice until she got a grip and swung herself onto the rim. The men heaved back one more time—and the rope broke. Sarah dug her spikes in to keep from sliding over the side as Amos crawled to her, extending his hand. "Hang on, I've got you!" He pulled her to where the ice was level.

Sarah lay still a few moments, willing her body to stop trembling, before she groaned and rubbed her arm. "I injured my shoulder in the fall."

Amos carefully helped her to her feet and held her. He wordlessly stroked her back, and she realized he was trembling, too. "I almost lost you," he whispered, and she noticed the tears on his cheeks.

The thumbs of her gloves wiped his face and she cupped his jawline. "My hero." She put her forehead to his, and they laughed and cried. She didn't give a damn in hell who was watching or what they thought.

Mahoney appeared beside them. "Miss Lakat, I was trained in first aid. Can I help?"

She pulled back from Amos. "My shoulder. It was jammed in the fissure crack."

"Let's go to my backpack. I've got my kit in there." Amos guided her as they followed Mahoney. She noticed the other two men were guarding the prisoners, whose feet had been shackled together.

Mahoney rummaged through the pack and brought out a hinged metal box, painted white with a red cross. He found a triangular linen cloth and shook out the folds. "Take off your jacket."

Amos helped her out of it, and Mahoney gently moved her shoulder, which made her cry out. "It's really starting to hurt now."

Mahoney nodded. "Being wedged in the ice must have kept it from swelling. Amos, gather some of the loose ice in a handkerchief." When Amos brought him the ice fragments he'd scraped together, Mahoney made a small ice pack, put it on her shoulder, and tied the linen around her arm and waist to keep it immobile. Amos slid the jacket over her good arm and draped it around her other side. Mahoney gave her two white tablets and his canteen. "Here's some aspirin for the pain."

When they had made their way back to the others, Tunny spoke up to ask, "Shall we start hiking back to Gustavus?"

Amos shook his head. "We're less than a day's

walk to Haines. Let's get off this glacier and camp over there in that clearing, then start out tomorrow." They retrieved their packs, and Amos slung both Sarah's bag and his own over his shoulders.

After they ate, Amos and Sarah volunteered to take first watch. Sarah's gun was handy in her holster, and Amos sat with a rifle across his knees. The campfire flickered light across the faces of the fugitives like the effect of a nickelodeon moving picture. George and his wife were a few feet away in their sleeping bags. He studied Sarah for a moment, then turned his head. "Sorry, Sarah."

Sarah snorted. "For anything in particular or everything in general?"

He was silent for a moment. "I used you badly."

"Yes, you did. By the way, what did you do with your children?"

He glanced at his wife. "They're with her parents. They were going to bring them to us when we got to Canada."

Sarah nodded. "I see. Well, they're better off where they are."

"That's enough of the chit-chat," Amos growled.

She opened her mouth to say something, then shut it again. Her shoulder was aching again, so she took out two of the aspirin from the supply Mahoney had given her and washed them down with water from her canteen.

Amos leaned toward her. "If you want to get some rest, I can do the watch myself."

"No. I can do it." The swell of love for this man almost overwhelmed her. She studied his face in the firelight—almost boyish, even with the mustache and

173

scruffy beard. The dim light can take years off, she thought.

Later, when Mahoney and Abner came to relieve them, Amos helped her to her tent. He kissed her forehead. "I love you."

"I love you, too. Goodnight." She curled up in her bedroll for a few hours of blessed sleep.

The next morning, Amos assisted her with taking down her tent and packing. He again carried both their backpacks as he guided her through the trail to Haines. The small military base came into view a few hours later.

Portage Cove, home of the Chilkoot Docks, was besieged by sea birds, all screeching and diving in the gray mist. The travelers gathered at the liner ticket office in a weatherbeaten wooden building near the water. Amos set down the backpacks. "I should only need two others to help get these varmints to Juneau. I'll let each of you know when the trial is finished, and you can barter between yourselves about who gets them next. You can send your people to Juneau and I'll transfer them. Agreed?" Everyone did.

Mahoney returned from the ticket office. "The next liner to Juneau is tomorrow morning at eight o'clock. Why don't you take Miss Lakat to the doctor's office in town while we're waiting?"

Amos glanced at Sarah, and she nodded. "All right. Could you pick up our passage?" At Mahoney's nod, Amos gave him the fare for them and for the prisoners. "We'll be back as soon as we can."

Walking up a rise to the main street, they found the doctor's shingle. The office was up an outside stairway to a whitewashed wooden door that led into a small waiting room with a nurse at a reception desk. She looked up and smiled. "May I help you?"

Amos released Sarah. "I'd like for the doctor to check Miss Lakat's shoulder. She took a tumble into a glacial fissure and injured it."

"And you are?"

"Sheriff Darcy from Juneau. We're bringing in some fugitives for trial."

The nurse hurried into a back room. She returned a few moments later. "You may go in, Miss Lakat."

Sarah slipped through the door and came face to face with a jovial gray-haired man who stuck out his hand. "I'm Dr. Reynolds. I hear you have an injured shoulder."

Sarah explained to him what had happened.

The doctor tsked. "You're very lucky you're here to tell about it. Well, let's see the shoulder. Sit on the table and undo your shirt." He removed the linen and her shirt, then examined her shoulder. "It seems to be badly bruised, but nothing's broken or out of place. I'll tape it for you and give you medicine for the pain. Your doctor at home should check it again in a few days."

After he ministered to her, he helped her get dressed, for which she was grateful.

"Thank you, Doctor." Amos paid for the services, and she leaned on him gratefully. As they went down the stairs, he glanced at her. "You look like death warmed over. Let's get a hotel room for you tonight."

"Don't you need—?"

"We have more than enough lawmen to watch the prisoners. You need a good night's sleep. The rest of us will set up camp near the docks."

She stopped and gazed at him. "At least, have

dinner with me. Then I'll meet you down there at seven-thirty tomorrow morning." He smiled and put his arm around her as they continued on.

The small hotel near the docks was cheerful with its whitewashed porch and blue shutters. Amos went in with Sarah and greeted the man at the front desk. Mingled with the salty water and oily smell of the docks was the delightful smell coming from their dining room overlooking the channel.

The young man at the desk opened his register book. "May I help you, sir?"

"I'd like a room for my deputy tonight. She was injured today, and I want her to get a good rest."

The clerk glanced at Sarah. "But she's—"

Amos slammed his hand on the desk. "I don't want to hear the rest of that sentence. You put her up, and I'll pay for it!"

The man backed down in the presence of Amos' wrath. "Yes, sir. She can have Room Number Five. That's up the stairs and to your right. That will be six dollars." He handed Amos the key as soon as Sarah had signed the register, and Amos paid for the room.

The rest of the lawmen were setting up camp not far from the hotel. Amos excused himself and went to get Sarah's backpack and to tell the others of the plans. Meanwhile, Sarah secured them a table in the dining room.

After a wonderful baked salmon dinner, Amos walked her up to her room, unlocked the door, and set her backpack inside. "Sleep well, Sarah." He took her in his arms and planted a kiss on her lips.

Sarah melted into his embrace and kissed him thoroughly. She felt a hard erection next to her belly and loved that he wanted her as much as she wanted him. "Goodnight, Amos."

"See you in the morning." He pulled back and, with a reluctant expression, headed toward the stairs.

****

Amos folded up his tent while the others were getting ready to leave. He arranged with the sheriff in Haines for three deputies to help transport the prisoners to Juneau, since Mahoney, Tunny, and Abner were going to take seaplanes to Cordova and Sitka. The three Haines deputies handcuffed the prisoners together. George turned to Amos. "What's going to happen to the dogs?"

Amos glanced at Mahoney. "You're the closest to Yakutat. Could you take them back with you?"

He gave a nod. "Yes. I'll make sure they're all looked after."

George seemed relieved. Amos wished George cared about human beings as much as he did his dogs. *I'll never understand how some people can kill so easily. Well, I guess that's what they need me for.*

Sarah appeared over the rise. Her arm was in a sling, but she looked well-rested and bright as a new penny. She set down the backpack she had carried slung around her good shoulder. "Are we all set to board the liner?"

"Now we are." Amos picked up her pack and carried it over his shoulder along with his own, following the Haines men as they marched the prisoners up the gangway. The eight-hour voyage went by without any trouble, and the docks of home came into view later in the afternoon as an eagle sailed over the liner as if to welcome them.

The lawmen from Haines walked the prisoners down the gangplank and up to the street. Amos turned to Sarah. "Why don't you go on home, since it's only a couple of blocks? Change and go see Doc about your shoulder, then take the rest of the day off. We can take care of giving these guests a room."

"Thank you, Amos." She relieved him of her backpack as they reached the others, then waved a goodbye.

He sighed and turned. "Men, follow me. The office is up the hill." Home was going to look so good to him tonight.

Chapter 20

Amos drove the patrol car away from the courthouse, where he had just given their evidence and information on the suspects to Juneau's district attorney. He was taking the rest of the day off, because he had an extra errand to do. He headed to the Lakat property in Douglas. Jane Lakat was tending the garden, hoeing the weeds between cabbage rows. She straightened and shaded her eyes as he got out of the auto. "Evening, Sheriff. What brings you out here?"

"I wanted to speak to Grace. Is she around?"

A worried expression crossed her face. "Is it about Sarah? Is she all right?"

Amos paused for a second. "Yes, she's fine. She did hurt her shoulder in a fall when we were chasing the fugitives, but it's nothing serious. I wanted to talk to Grace on another matter."

Jane made a motion with her hand. "She's around back, feeding the chickens."

He tipped his hat. "Thank you."

He followed the sound of the chitter-chatter and mutterings of the hens and found Grace scattering seed from her apron that she held gathered up so that it formed a pouch. "Good evening, Grace. I'd like to talk to you."

She shook the rest of the seeds over the ground while the hens pushed and shoved like a bunch of unruly children, voicing their greed. "Would you care for some tea on the back porch?"

"That'll do nicely. Thank you."

She disappeared into the house, wiping her hands, and Amos settled on a caned rocker. When she came out with a tea tray and put it on the table that was next to him, she asked, "Is this a social or an official visit?"

"Social. I need to talk to you about Sarah."

Grace poured them each a cup. "What do you want in it?"

"Just a spoonful of sugar."

Grace gave him the cup and set a plate of sugar cookies within his reach, then relaxed in the chair on the other side. "Now, what about Sarah?"

He took a sip of the tea. "I don't know of any way to say this except straight out. I've found myself in love with your daughter and I want to ask for her hand in marriage."

The silence flowed about them for a few moments, and then Grace glanced at him. "Amos, I think you should know a few things about Sarah before I give my answer." She sighed and took a drink of the tea. "How much do you know of the Tlingit traditions?"

He shook his head. "Not a whole lot."

"There were strict rules governing families. The men were in charge of providing for the family and the women were in charge of hearth and home. In fact, the property goes to the female side of the family. Jane and I were the only daughters, so this land is ours. Her husband was crippled at an early age, so she had to take over as a provider. This was during the Gold Rush, and she bought a sewing machine so she could make money as a dressmaker to the wealthy women. He died not long after Kata was born."

"I know Kata works as the costume mistress at the theater."

"Yes, she has the machine now. In the meantime, I was raising two boys and Sarah. My husband was a fisherman and was training the boys to do the same. Sarah was very good at book learning, so we decided she should go to the missionary school, because the public ones for natives were so poor. When her father and brothers died in the accident on the fishing boat, Kata and Sarah had to become the family providers."

"You mean, she gives her earnings to you?"

"Not all of it, of course, but what she and Kata can afford. I was hoping she would find a native who would take care of her. Outside of George, there was no interest. I think she despaired of ever finding anyone."

"I do understand your concern, but if that's the case, she can still give you a percentage of what she earns."

She looked at him with surprise. "You mean, you'll let her work after marriage?"

He grinned. "I've learned a lot about Sarah, and I know if she isn't doing detective work, she won't be happy."

Overwhelmed, Grace put her hand over his. "Then I give you my blessing. You know my daughter well."

"Another thing, Grace. I want a wedding in the Tlingit tradition, as a gift to your family."

An amused little smile played around her lips. "I think Will can teach you the eagle dance. Are you sure?"

"I don't know about dancing, but I'll try."

"Do you have family here?"

"I have no one."

"Then your friends can be your tribe. I'll see what I can do."

Amos kissed her cheek. "Thank you, Grace." He headed back to the auto with a wave to Jane before he left. Driving to Sarah's house, he rehearsed several times what he wanted to say. He sat for minutes in front of her home, until Sarah came out on the porch.

She waved to him. "Is there something you want, Amos?"

He got out of the car. "Will you walk with me?"

She came down the steps. "It's getting a little late. The sun is near the horizon."

"There's a place by the docks that I like to sit at this time of day. Come with me?"

"A moment." She went back into the house and was wearing a shawl when she returned. "The sea breeze is cooling off."

Not many words were spoken as they strolled the two blocks to the harbor. Amos steered her to an iron park bench on a rise that faced Juneau and the mountains. The setting sun cast long shadows, and the seabirds and eagles from the steep cliffs soared overhead. A pink glow colored the glaciers, and everything looked rosy.

Amos held her hand. "I went to talk to your mother this afternoon."

Her eyes widened, then narrowed. "Why?"

"I wanted to ask permission to marry you. Will you?"

Her jaw dropped. "Before I answer, what did my mother say?"

"She agreed to it. I told her we could do it in the

Tlingit tradition."

Sarah suppressed a giggle. "I want to see the eagle dance." Her eyes softened. "You'd do that for me?"

The love in him welled to the surface. "In a minute. Damn it, woman, what's your answer?"

She cupped his face in her hands. "Yes. I love you." They embraced and kissed while the wind played around them. "I can see why you like it here. Juneau looks beautiful."

He gazed into her deep brown eyes. "So do you," he said with a rasp in his voice.

"Let's go back to my house. I'm tired after this long day, but you have made it a wonderful one."

They stood, and he put his arm around her and they walked as one. The twilight deepened as they arrived at the auto. They kissed their goodnight with a bright promise of a happy future.

****

Sarah woke the next morning with a smile on her lips and a song in her heart. Amos not only wanted to marry her, he wanted to blend into her culture and her family. She decided she would take his name like Kata did for Ivan. Word was that the natives should have full citizenship by next year, so she may as well start acting like an American. Thanks to the nuns in the missionary school, it wouldn't be tough.

She went into the office and greeted Sam. "Any word from the DA on the hearings for the prisoners?" Putting her things on her desk, she opened her report forms.

"Not yet. You know things move around here like an ancient turtle."

"Amos in yet?"

"He went to check at the newspaper if there were any threats posted about any other canneries." Sam suppressed a grin.

"Something wrong?"

"Amos had that same look on his face this morning when he talked about you, too."

Sarah's cheeks heated, but she felt a wonderful fuzzy warmth when she thought about Amos. Sliding a report form into her typewriter, she started working on her statement on the chase and capture of the fugitives. She was finishing when Amos got back. "Here's the report." She smartly snapped the paper out.

Amos nodded. "Bring it to my office."

Sarah followed him in and laid the report on his desk, then went to pour herself a cup of coffee. "Well, what did you find out?" she said as she slid into the chair across the desk.

A grin spread across his face. "There have been no more threats against any of the executives of the canneries in southeast Alaska Territory. That means we either got everybody or the others are lying low."

"Did you hear anything from the DA?"

"Nothing yet. I imagine he's still going over the folder full of evidence I plopped on his desk."

"Well, now we wait."

His eyes heated. "We can concentrate on something else. I ran into your Aunt Jane, and she told me we are invited to their house for supper tonight."

She felt her cheeks warm. "Seems like Mother doesn't want to waste any time."

He rose and came around the desk, pulling her up into an ardent embrace. "Neither do I." He planted his lips firmly on hers.

After a few moments, Sarah pushed back. "I don't think we should be doing this here." Her knees wobbled.

A mischievous twinkle sparkled in his eyes. "I know, but wasn't it fun?"

She patted his cheek. "I've got some paperwork I've been sadly neglecting." She winked and sashayed out.

The afternoon sun warmed the patrol car as they stopped by the farmhouse. Sarah's mother hurried off the porch and met her daughter in an embrace. "I'm so happy for you!" Then she turned to Amos and embraced him.

Aunt Jane greeted them warmly inside. "Supper is almost ready. Sit and make yourselves at home."

Sarah watched the whirl of activity and realized her mother had been praying for this day. All of the continued family for her was on Sarah's shoulders. Aunt Jane's daughters had given her three grandchildren so far. The thought of being a mother bounced across her mind. It was something she wanted but had pushed to the back burner long ago. Amos put his arm around her shoulders as they sat on the couch, and the warm fuzzy tingling invaded her thoughts.

"Supper's on!" her mother called from the dining room. The feast spread out for them smelled delicious. Baked salmon was on the platter, with new potatoes and greens. A new loaf of bread, fragrant from the oven, stood ready to accept the summer berry preserves made last year. Amos held Sarah's chair and then sat next to her as the tea was poured.

"Well, when should we plan the wedding?" Mother asked.

Amos glanced at Sarah. "As soon as we can, I suppose. We're not getting any younger."

Sarah's mouth went into a tight line. "We're not that old."

Mother nodded. "We'll need three weeks for the banns to be posted. That would bring us to mid-June. Perfect."

Aunt Jane spoke up. "Will can help Amos on our customs and what we wear. Sarah, do you still have your dress?"

A pang went through her as she remembered being jilted by George. "Yes, I put it in a trunk. It might need some work done on it."

"Kata could help you."

Sarah put her hand on her mother's arm. "I'd like the ceremony at the meeting house at Bear Rock, where Will and Mary had their wedding."

Amos looked up. "Where's that?"

"It's about a mile south. Then we could have the party in the yard here."

Sarah's mother squeezed her hand. "Where are you planning on living?"

Sarah eyed Amos carefully. "I'd like to stay in my house. At least, for a while."

Amos shrugged. "It doesn't matter to me. I don't have a lot. I can move my things in during the week before."

After the plans and the guest list were set, they bid her mother and Aunt Jane their thank-yous and goodnights. The evening twilight was deepening as Amos walked Sarah to her porch. She smiled. "Soon this will be our house. I love you, Amos."

As an answer, he took her in his arms and kissed

her thoroughly. Her head swam and her legs threatened to drop her to the floor. "I love you, too. Goodnight."

She gripped the railing as she waved to the departing patrol car. *I'm counting the days until you can come inside with me to stay.* She sighed and went into the suddenly very empty rooms.

Chapter 21

A week later, Amos called Sarah into his office. Every time she graced his presence, he loved her even more. The waiting for the wedding was interminable. Well, he'd have to bend his mind into a business state. "I need to talk to you. Sit."

"What is it?"

"We got the date for the hearing. It's next Tuesday. I don't think you'll have to testify. Since I'm the senior law official here, I'll take care of it. Oh, and the DA and the judge will give Sally Cusnoo immunity so she can give her testimony."

"I'll send a message to her in Angoon."

With a knock on the office door, Sam came in. "Sorry to bother you, but Assemblyman Walter Hastings is here to see you."

"Send him in."

Sarah rose to leave as Hastings stepped into the room, but he stopped her. "Are you Miss Lakat?" At her nod, he said, "Stay. I want to talk to both of you."

Amos steepled his fingers. "What can we do for you?"

"It's been brought to the Assembly's attention that you intend to marry."

Amos frowned. "What business is that of the Assembly?"

"Rules, Sheriff. A woman cannot work in the city

government if she's married. When you and Miss Lakat do this, she has to turn in her resignation."

Sarah's eyes widened. "What? No!"

Amos put in quickly, "Mr. Hastings, I was able to get the Assembly to change the rules on women being deputies. I'd like to suggest a change here, too."

Hastings shook his head. "I'm sorry, but that's not the same thing. Other women would see that and want the rules changed for them, as well. Can you imagine married teachers?"

Amos checked his calendar. "I see there's an Assembly meeting Friday. I want to talk to all of you and state my side."

Hastings shrugged. "I'll put you on the agenda, but it won't do any good." He turned to go. "Good day, Sheriff, Miss Lakat. Congratulations on your engagement."

Sarah slumped against the desk. "And, of course, they're all men in the Assembly."

Amos pounded the desk. "So am I. Your record in law enforcement is strong. There are a lot of reasons I want to keep you here."

Sarah sighed. "I appreciate your trying. I'll send a wire to Sally to come home."

Amos steamed as he watched her go. *How dare they? She was key to finding out who the murderers were, and they want to toss her over the side. Why? Because she's a woman. It's bad enough she gets no respect for being a Tlingit, they have to throw this in her face.* He picked up the calendar and flung it against the wall.

****

On Friday, at seven o'clock, Amos stalked into the

Assembly and sat himself down on one of the spectator seats in front. He wanted to make sure Hastings could see him, although he didn't look forward to suffering through some dry business discussions before Hastings brought up the topic of their dispute on the marriage. Fortunately, he didn't have to suffer long.

As soon as the minutes of the last meeting had been read, Hastings stood. "Mr. Chairman, as you know we had a discussion of the marriage between Sheriff Amos Darcy and his Deputy Sarah Lakat. On Tuesday last, I delivered the message that Miss Lakat would have to resign the Sheriff's Department when it happens. I told him it was against the rules for a married woman to serve in city government. He wanted to plead his case to the Assembly."

The chairman, Mr. Charles Backus, motioned to Amos. "Stand and state your case, Sheriff."

Amos rose and gazed determinedly at the members. "Men of the Assembly, I have come to you for concerns before, and you were always willing to grant my requests. I stand before you tonight to ask an exclusion to the rules for Sarah Lakat. She has served as a deputy for over a year now and is one of the best detectives I have ever worked with. In this past murder case, she went over and above her duty to solve it, and we wouldn't have done it without her. I see absolutely no reason for her to resign. A man who worked that well would never be asked to resign on his marriage."

Hastings and Backus glanced at each other. Backus mopped his forehead with his handkerchief. "Sheriff, we will take up this matter next week at our closed session, and Hastings will inform you what we decide. Satisfactory?"

Amos nodded. "Fair enough. Thank you, sirs." He left the meeting not entirely confident of the outcome. These were men who fought women's suffrage, saying a woman in the home had no knowledge of government. How wrong they were. His mother had been the one who read the paper to his father, who never set foot inside a school. Yet his father was the one who was allowed to vote. *Times keep changing, but it seems some want to stagnate.*

****

Sarah enjoyed being on the porch at her mother's home in Douglas. Sometimes she just needed to be home. "I'm having Kata alter my dress. I've lost some weight in the past six years. I know Will has talked to Amos, but neither has said how things are going."

Her mother smiled. "Knowing both of them, they won't say anything until they're ready. Since Amos doesn't have family here, we can do away with the ceremonial coming ashore of the canoes."

"He has plenty of friends for his party. They will function as his family." Sarah paused. "Thank you for doing this, Mother."

Her mother gazed out over the farm. "Amos surprised me, asking for a traditional Tlingit wedding. Ivan and Kata married at the courthouse."

Sarah smiled. "He may be gruff and demanding, but Amos is a very good man. That's what made me fall in love with him." Sarah wondered if she should bring up the subject of her job.

Mother studied her face. "It looks like something's bothering you. What is it?"

"The other day, Mr. Hastings came over from the Assembly and informed us that a married woman can't

191

work for the city. Amos attended a meeting last night and argued to let me keep my job."

"I was afraid this was going to happen. Seems like the Americans don't believe a married woman can work."

"Kata is still working at the theater."

"The owners of Golden North are fair-minded people. Kata doesn't have to deal with the government."

They were interrupted by the rumble of Will's truck turning into the yard. Will and Sally climbed out as Sarah and her mother went to greet them. Sally pulled her suitcase out of the back of the truck.

Sarah hugged Will. "Thank you for bringing Sally this far. Did you run into any trouble?"

Will shook his head. "I don't think word about Sally had reached Angoon yet. There's some anger at the ANB about the capture, but I don't think anyone wants to take on the law."

"Sally, I think you should stay with me until the hearing is over. It might be risky living at your house alone. But first, I want you to go to the jail cell and tell me if we got everyone."

She nodded. "I understand. I'll do what I can."

Sarah took leave of her mother and Will and then put the suitcase in the back seat of the patrol car. Once Sally slid in on the passenger side, Sarah started it up and glanced at Sally. "The hearing starts tomorrow. I'll escort you to and from the courthouse when you are needed to testify."

Sally put her face in her hands. "I'm scared. I wish I'd never got involved in this mess in the first place. I blame Bobby for doing this."

Sarah shook her head. "Bobby is angry because he feels slighted by the narrow-minded people in Juneau. I know how that feels. I'm going to lose my job."

Sally looked surprised. "What happened?"

"Amos and I are going to get married, and the Assembly told us I would have to resign. They won't have married women working for the city."

"What are you going to do?"

Sarah sighed. "Amos is pushing to get the law changed, but I have a feeling they're not going to do what he wants this time."

Fifteen minutes later, Sarah turned the patrol car in at the back of the sheriff's office. "Leave your suitcase there. I'll ask Amos to drive us to my house."

Sally was trembling as they went in the back door. Sarah made a motion to Sam, and he called Amos into the reception area.

Amos nodded a greeting to Sally. "Thank you for coming, Miss Cusnoo. I want you to make an identification of the prisoners." When Sarah put her arm around Sally's shoulders, Amos added, "We have a window in the door. You don't have to go in there."

Sally peered intently through the glass. "You have them all except the leader."

Amos' jaw dropped. "I thought George was the leader."

She shook her head. "Everybody thinks he is, but while I was in Angoon the first night, a tall man with black hair and dark brown eyes showed up. He said he wanted to give everyone last-minute instructions. Then they went into the back room. I never heard his name." Sarah's stomach knotted.

"Would you know him if you saw him again?"

"Yes." She looked at her feet. "I wish I could be of more help."

Sarah turned to Amos. "Would you drive us to my house? I want to get Sally settled."

"No. You two aren't going to your house. I'm putting you up in a hotel room."

Sarah opened her mouth to protest, but saw the wisdom in what he said. "Do you think there will be an attempt to silence her?"

"I'd bet a month's pay on it. Sally's testimony is critical and we have to protect her, especially with this new information about the leader still being out there somewhere."

Sarah put a hand on his arm. "What about the rooms upstairs at the Golden North? Everyone has moved out who used to lived there, and I don't think anyone would look for us at the theater."

Dawn came to Amos' eyes as he stroked his mustache. "You may have something. Go in the back through the kitchen. Don't go to your house at all. I'll check with you in the morning."

The women made their way through the alleys to the back of Golden North. The delicious aromas of cooking meat, sauces, and bread wafted out of the building. They must be getting ready for dinners at the restaurant. Sarah took a scan of the alley before she went into the kitchen, Sally in tow.

Mrs. Cora Hutton, the head cook, was inspecting her helpers' dishes when she saw Sarah. "Sarah Lakat, what brings you here?"

"Mrs. Hutton, I need to ask a favor of the Shafers."

She patted Sarah on the shoulder. "Wait here. I saw Zeke in the restaurant a moment ago." She hurried out, then came back with a handsome dark-haired man.

He grinned and came over. "Sarah! It's good to see you again. What can I do for you?"

Sarah nodded at Sally. "This is Sally Cusnoo. She is a key witness for the murder trial that's coming up. There is some danger to her. Could we use one of the rooms upstairs overnight to keep her safe?"

Zeke's mouth went into a tight line. "That's the trial for the Thornton murder at the cannery, isn't it?"

"Yes. They probably wouldn't think of looking for her here."

"All right, but go up the back steps from the dressing rooms. Nobody will see you that way. I'll send one of the girls up to help you."

Sarah shook his hand. "Thank you, Zeke." She went to the kitchen door and peered out to see if anyone would observe them, but there was no one out back. She and Sally slipped out and entered again through the stage door. There, in the dim light, were the stairs.

Sarah's eyes adjusted to the light as she and Sally climbed to the second floor. She heard activity in one of the front rooms. Sarah motioned Sally to follow her to the open door. A short dark-haired woman was pulling a cover sheet off an iron double bed.

The woman greeted Sarah. "I'm sorry we don't have fresh linens here. These will have to do."

Sarah nodded. "That's all right, Addy, we're only going to be here tonight. This is Sally Cusnoo. Sally, this is Zeke's wife, Addy."

"Zeke told me you were keeping a witness safe, so I'll have Cora send up some supper for you, and some breakfast in the morning."

"How much should I pay you?"

Addy waved it off. "It's our contribution to the community."

"Thank you, and thank Zeke for me, too."

Addy disappeared out the door.

Sally, her eyes closed, was curled up on a corner of the bed, trembling so much it threatened to shake her body apart. "I shouldn't have done this. I shouldn't have—" She started to cry. "Oh, why did I listen to Bobby?"

Sitting next to her, Sarah put her arms around the terrified girl. "We'll be all right. I've got my gun with me. Now you relax and get some rest."

Sally stretched out, and Sarah shifted a chair to the door so she could watch the hall, fingering her gun. Now she had time to digest how much danger they all were in. Was this man planning a jailbreak for the suspects before the trial? Was Amos in peril? Her heart dropped to think Amos could be hurt—or worse.

Chapter 22

Amos fidgeted at his desk, pretending to be busy and failing miserably. Finding out only the night before the hearing that there was someone else out there ate at his gut. He desperately wanted to go to Golden North to see that Sarah and Sally were all right, but that might be a tipoff for anyone who was watching. Sarah was armed and an excellent shot, but she was also his life.

A knock made him jump. "Who is it?"

"It's Dan, the night chief. Are you planning to stay here tonight?" The door opened and Dan peered in.

"With the hearing tomorrow and the news that there's someone still out there, yes. Have you been briefed?"

"Yes. Sam told me. He's staying, too. Sir, there's a native out here, Will Lakat, to see you."

Amos slapped his forehead. "Damn, I forgot. Send him in."

Will appeared as Dan went out. "I thought since I was up here, we could talk about the ceremony, but if it's a bad time—"

"Some news has come up to complicate things for the hearing. You may be in danger if you stay here. Can you stay somewhere in the area until tomorrow? Once we get this bunch to the courthouse, I can breathe a little easier."

"I can go back and stay with Mother and Aunt

Grace. Maybe I can meet you at Millie's at noon?"

Amos nodded. "Swell. Things should be on simmer by then."

Will hesitated a moment, then came around the desk and put his hand on Amos' shoulder. "Watch out for yourself. You're almost family, and I don't want my cousin to lose you."

A warmth spread through Amos, and he had to swallow a couple of times before he could speak. "I appreciate that, Will." Will gave a quick nod, then was gone.

It was hard waiting for something that might or might not come. At any rate, Amos had a hell of a lot to live for, and he wasn't about to let an outlaw group take that away. Sure he had chosen the right thing for the women, he hoped Sarah could get Sally back alive. His eyelids started to droop, and he put his head on his arms, supported by the desk. That was the last thing he remembered before he was awakened by Sam shaking him.

"Sir, there's a Sheriff Creag outside with a couple of deputies. He says he wanted to help you transport the prisoners to the courthouse."

Amos worked at clearing the cobwebs out of his brain and absorbed the information he'd just heard. "What time is it, Sam?"

"A quarter to six. You said you wanted to get them over there early."

Something nagged at Amos' insides. How did Creag know when they were going to transport the prisoners to the courthouse? Why did he come clear from Yakutat just for a morning stroll? "Keep them outside. I'll be there in a few minutes."

Amos went to the staff rest area to freshen up and slap himself awake. Checking his revolver, he snapped off the safety and put it in his holster, giving it a pat. He strode outside and greeted Creag.

"Sheriff Creag, this is a surprise. What brings you to Juneau?"

Creag gave him a cautious grin. "I was here on business and thought I'd give you a hand."

"How did you know when the hearing was set?"

Creag hesitated. "I saw it in the newspaper."

Amos' danger flag flashed in his head. "There was nothing about when we were going to transport them." His hand rested on the holster. Suddenly, a shout startled him and Creag's gun was trained at Amos' nose.

****

Early in the morning, Sarah and Sally left the theater, heading to the sheriff's office, retracing their way through the alleys. As they approached the building, Sarah noticed a few men standing outside the door and recognized Sheriff Creag. *I wonder what he's doing here?*

Sally grabbed Sarah's arm. "That's him!" she hissed.

"Him?"

"The leader. The one in the sheriff's uniform."

Sarah pushed her behind some barrels. "Stay there until I come for you." She pulled out her gun and snapped the safety off. Amos was already out with Creag as she made her way along the buildings, and she saw his hand move to his gun. "Creag's the leader!" she shouted. And her heart dropped to the pavement when Creag drew his revolver. In less than a heartbeat, she fired at Creag's hand and he yelped as his gun went flying.

Amos and his deputies flew at the other men, scuffling with them until they were subdued. Soon Creag and his two men were sporting handcuffs. Amos pulled up Creag by his collar as Sarah arrived. "Good work, Sarah!" Sam and Luke brought over their two charges.

Sam had four guns in his hands. "We found these on the other two fellows."

Amos frisked Creag and found another pistol. "This is quite an arsenal. Let me guess. You were going to let us bring out the prisoners for our little walk, and you'd arm them."

Creag glared at Amos but said nothing.

"Luke, take these three and put them in one of the cells. The guns can go in the locked bin. Sam, get the doc to check out Creag's hand."

Both deputies acknowledged their orders and set to their tasks.

Amos turned to Sarah. "Where is Sally?"

"She's in the alley. I told her to hide until I came back. She fingered Creag as soon as she saw him."

"I figured as much. Go get her."

Sarah reached for his hand. "Are you all right?"

He squeezed it and grinned. "No extra holes in my hide, thanks to you."

She took out her handkerchief and daubed his lower lip. "You're bleeding."

"Just a split in the fight. I'm fine." His eyes softened and he cupped her chin. "You're magnificent, my love." His kiss was strong and heartfelt.

Sarah could feel all the stares around them. She

gently pushed back. "We're causing quite a scene."

"Ask me if I give a tinker's dam."

"I've got to get Sally, and I'll meet you at the courthouse."

The paddy wagon pulled up, and Sam hopped out and snapped a salute. "Ready to load the prisoners, sir."

Sarah waved. "See you there." She crossed the street and found Sally still behind the barrels, white-knuckled.

"What happened?" Sally asked as Sarah helped her up. Sarah related what had taken place in the last few minutes, and Sally seemed to relax.

"Is that all the people you remember seeing?"

Sally nodded. "You have them all."

Sarah started up the street with Sally and arrived at the courthouse as Amos and Sam were unloading the last of the prisoners, who went in with their court-appointed advocates. Sam drove the paddy wagon back to the office while Amos and Sarah escorted Sally to the gallery behind District Attorney Clifton Roberts.

Amos leaned over the wooden barrier and told Roberts of the attempted jailbreak and that three more members of the gang were being held.

Roberts whirled around in his chair. "You say that the ringleader is the sheriff of Yakutat? Remarkable. I'll set a date for the other three. Do you think that's all of them?"

Amos nodded. "I believe that's all the principals. There have been no other killings or threats at any other cannery."

The bailiff came to the center of the room. "All rise!"

Judge Henry Ott strode regally out of his chambers,

took his seat behind the bench, and banged his gavel. "The court will come to order. This hearing is convened to sort out which of the fugitives captured will stand trial here for the death of Mr. Edward Thornton at North Star Cannery." He shuffled through his papers. The thin, graying man with a goatee had a presence that belied his size. "Please rise with your advocate when I call your name. "Mr. John Jameson?"

One of the men in the party rose. "Sir?"

"I found that you had been employed at a cannery in Soldotna. We will hold you here at the courthouse until the authorities from Soldotna can extradite you for trial there." A couple of guards escorted him away.

The second man was another Sarah didn't know. He had been with George's party and turned out to be from the cannery in Cordova. He would be held for the authorities in Cordova for trial.

Ott pulled out the next paper. "Mrs. Leigh Annok?"

George's wife shook as she rose and faced the judge. "Here, sir."

"Your advocate tells me you were just following your husband's orders and did not partake in any of the criminal acts. Because of that and because you have three small children to take care of, I'm dismissing any charges. You are free to go home."

Leigh broke into tears on the advocate's shoulder before turning and holding out a pleading hand as she said, "George, what am I to do?" She tried to run to her husband, but the advocate escorted her out. Sarah hurt for her.

"Mr. Bobby Cusnoo and Mr. George Annok?" They stood. "We will hear the evidence gathered against you and decide if you should stand trial." He turned to the DA. "Mr. Roberts, you may present your case."

"Thank you, your honor. I wish to call Sheriff Darcy to the stand."

Amos gave Sarah's hand a squeeze and proceeded to the witness stand. He swore in and took a seat.

Roberts came up to the stand. "Sheriff Darcy, will you relate to us why you were called to the North Star Cannery on May the fourth of this year."

Amos went over the details of what he had found when the investigation started. Roberts then led him through the evidence discovered: the broken bat and the burned and bloody long coat. The subject of the jailbreak was also brought up, and the grievances against George as the perpetrator were covered. The advocates had no questions for Amos, so he stepped down.

The coroner was next, and Elmer related what he had found on the body. The splinters from the wound were also put into evidence.

Sally jerked when her name was called, and Sarah put a reassuring arm around her. Sally made her way to the stand while Sarah tried to send her some strength. Bobby glared at her, but she seemed to avoid his eyes.

Roberts went to her and said, "Tell us what happened the morning of the murder."

Sally took a shaky breath. "Bobby told me he was going into work that morning."

"Tell us what he wore."

"He put on his denims and a blue plaid shirt. He put on his mukluks, but he carried his shoes and work gloves. Over that he put on a long coat. I heard him take something out of a wardrobe."

"Could it have been a baseball bat?"

Bobby's advocate jumped up. "I object. He's leading the witness."

Roberts continued. "Did you see what it was?"

"No."

"What happened when you saw him again?"

"When I came home from work, he was burning something out back."

"Do you know what it was?"

"He said it was spring brush."

"We already know from the sheriff's testimony that the bloodied coat was burned with the brush. Do you know if Bobby acted alone?"

"I don't know, sir, but the night before, he met with another man."

"Do you know this man? And is he in court?"

"Yes. He's over there," she said, pointing at George.

"Make note that she's indicating the other defendant, George Annok. Did George plan Mr. Cusnoo's escape?"

"Yes. With the help of one of the Revenge Ravens. The other dressed like an old man walking his dog and passed messages through the bars of the cell window."

"Do you know who this man was?"

"No. I didn't see him."

"Who are the Revenge Ravens?"

"They're a group against the salmon traps the canneries have on the streams."

"Thank you, Miss Cusnoo." He glanced at the advocates. "You may cross-examine."

Bobby's advocate spoke up. "Why were you

suspicious about Bobby burning spring brush?"

"I wasn't then. Not until material from the coat was found."

"Didn't he tell you he was getting rid of it because it was old?"

"Yes, that's what he said."

"Could you be mistaken about him going to work that day? His name wasn't on the list of workers. In fact, he may not have been there at all. Do you have any proof?"

"I thought he was going to work—"

"Thank you, Miss Cusnoo."

Sally went to her seat and Sarah noticed she was pale. "Sally, you did fine," Sarah assured her.

A few other witnesses took the stand, including Mr. Perkins of the Personal ads at the newspaper, who identified George as the man who placed the ad.

Mr. Roberts stood. "Your Honor, with the evidence in front of us, I believe both of these men should be held for trial."

Ott nodded. "We will set a date for a trial to be held next month. In the meantime, both defendants shall remain here at the courthouse." He banged the gavel. "The hearing is adjourned."

Amos turned to both Sarah and Sally outside the courthouse. "It looks like we have the main group in custody, so if you want to go back home, Sally, you can."

Sarah felt a gnaw in her stomach. "I don't think you should stay there alone. Do you have anyone who could stay with you?"

"I have an aunt in Douglas who could stay for a while."

Amos nodded. "I'll help you with that. It's the least I can do. Thank you, Sally." He turned to Sarah. "I'll take her to Douglas and pick up her aunt. If you see Will, tell him I'll meet him at Millie's for dinner around five."

Sarah nodded and watched them go. A troubling weight in her gut wouldn't let go. Why was she so nervous? This case was wrapped up. Wasn't it?

She noticed Will's truck parked near the courthouse. As she moved closer, he waved her into the passenger side. "Thought you might like a ride back. Heard about the fight at the sheriff's office this morning."

Sarah gave him Amos' message. "We think we have all the troublemakers now."

He glanced at her as he pulled up in front of the office. "You don't seem sure of that."

She sighed as she got out of the truck. "No, Will, I'm not." She thanked him for the lift and watched him go before she strode through the door to her desk. She noticed Sally's suitcase next to her desk. They'd forgotten it. Well, Amos should be back around three. She'd meet him at Sally's house.

Chapter 23

Amos glanced at his watch, it was almost three o'clock. The trip to Douglas had been uneventful. Sally's Aunt Lucy was happy to stay with her for a while. Sally's home appeared over the small hill. "You two ladies stay in the auto, and I'll check the house."

Sally nodded. "Thank you, Sheriff."

He got out and looked around. Everything seemed peaceful. He took the key to the door and climbed the steps. Good so far, but the hairs on the back of his neck started to prickle. He heard an auto come from the opposite direction and stop. Amos flew down the porch stairs and saw a female form jump out of the patrol car.

Sarah's gun was drawn and she yelled toward the back of the house, "Stop! Drop that rifle!"

Amos jumped at a rifle blast and watched, horrified, as he saw Sarah crumple. Gun out, he ran around the house and fired at a figure before it could aim at him. He cautiously hurried to the injured man on the ground, rolling him over with his foot. Amos grabbed the rifle and flung it away before taking the man by his coat lapels and shaking him. "What the hell are you doing?"

Sally appeared beside them, then took a step back, astonished. "Jack? Jack Harper? Why?"

He sneered through his pain. "I was the last one who could stop you from testifying."

Amos studied his face. "You were the old man with the dog who was passing notes to Bobby." He turned to Sally. "How's Sarah?"

"Aunt Lucy is with her."

Amos took out the handcuffs and jerked Jack's arms behind him, then took out his handkerchief and tied it over the bullet wound on his shoulder. "It's a scratch, but I'd better get you to the hospital." Amos deposited Jack into the front of the patrol car and ran to where Sarah still lay on the ground. "How is she, Mrs. Cusnoo?"

Sarah's shirt was opened to her right side below her breast and an ugly hole met his eyes. Mrs. Cusnoo held a wad of material and was just placing it over the wound. "I think she needs a doctor soon."

Amos felt his face drain. "Can you stay here while Sally rides with her to the hospital?" At her nod, he gave her the keys to the house.

Sarah moaned as Amos hefted her in his arms. Sally climbed in the back with Sarah as Amos slid in and gunned the motor. The patrol car backfired and took off down the road. Within five minutes, Amos pulled into the hospital's parking lot.

Amos jumped out and bellowed at an orderly, "I've got two wounded in the auto. Get someone out here *now*!" When the man ran to get help, Amos hauled Jack out of the front seat none too gently. "If anything happens to Miss Lakat, I wouldn't want to be in your shoes, mister!"

The orderlies came out with two stretchers. Sally and Amos helped Sarah out of the back. She coughed and a pink foam appeared on her lips. With that, Amos knew immediately that the bullet had hit her lung. He had an overwhelming urge to tear Jack apart with his bare hands.

Dr. Lindsey was called, and they whisked Sarah away into surgery. Jack was treated by an emergency intern while Amos sat next to Sally in the waiting room. When the intern had done all that was necessary, Amos rose. "Sally, could you wait here for word on Sarah while I lock this trash in the hoosegow?"

Sally nodded. "I'll be here."

Amos drove Jack to the office and herded him in the door. "Sam! Lock this garbage up and put his rifle in the evidence case."

When Sam finished his task, Amos took him aside. "Why was Lakat at the Cusnoo's house?"

"Miss Cusnoo had forgotten her suitcase, so Sarah decided to take it to her. What happened?"

Amos told Sam about the afternoon's events. "I think Harper is the last of the gang to be caught. Make sure all of you watch the prisoners. Send someone to get word to Grace Lakat about her daughter. I'm going to wait at the hospital."

"Yes, sir."

Amos fought panic on the way. He sent up a prayer. *Please, God, don't let this happen again. I can't lose another woman I love right before a marriage.* Tears blurred his vision and he angrily dashed them away. He found Sally still there, wringing her hands. "Any word?"

Her lips trembled. "No. Nothing."

He put her hands on her shoulders. "Sally, take my patrol car back to the office and have two of the deputies drive you home. One of them can drive the paddy wagon back that I left there. Oh, and your suitcase is in the trunk of the patrol car."

Sally rose and Amos hugged her. When she pushed back, tears shone in her eyes. "Let me know what happens."

"I will," he said around a lump in his throat. A half hour of agony went by too slowly. He heard the door open, and Grace came in with Will.

She saw Amos and made a beeline to him. "Amos—Sarah...what happened?"

Amos put his arms around the frightened woman. "Sarah was shot protecting us from a fugitive."

Will came over. "Any word on how she is?"

Amos sighed. "Not yet. She must still be in surgery."

Another half hour went by, and finally a tired Dr. Lindsey came into the waiting room. He spotted the little group and went over. "Miss Lakat is out of surgery. She was hit in the lung, and it collapsed. We have her breathing again with both lungs, but she has to be watched for a day or so. Patients with lung injuries might develop pneumonia that could be fatal. The fact she made it through surgery is a good sign. The next few days are critical."

Amos' whole body went numb. "Can we see her?"

Lindsey nodded. "She'll be brought into Women's Ward Two in twenty minutes. Mrs. Lakat, you can stay with her, if you like."

Grace squeezed her eyes shut for a moment. "Thank you, Doctor. I will."

After Lindsey left, Grace held tightly onto Amos' hand. Will stood, then squatted in front of them. "Amos, you can have a ride with me when you're ready."

"Thank you, Will." Amos sank back into his own private hell. Scenes of the woman he loved, so vibrant and alive, played through his head.

A nurse appeared to tell them Sarah was in the ward, then led them to her bed. Amos choked back a sob. She looked so still and pale. He drew a chair next to the bed and sat to lovingly take her hand in his, gently squeezing it. He felt a light pressure back. "That's right, love, fight your way back. You can't leave me now." He noticed Grace on the other side with tears in her eyes, and his face burned.

She reached over the bed and touched his cheek with her fingers. "Don't be embarrassed. I know you really care for my daughter. She made a good choice."

After a while, Amos turned to Will. "Take me back to the office for a few minutes, and then we can have dinner at Millie's."

Will shuffled his feet. "Are you sure you want to discuss the wedding now?"

Amos moved his gaze to Sarah. "I need to think she will be here for me. I can't let myself think otherwise."

As Will drove from the hospital, he stopped the truck by the harbor and pointed across the channel to one of the islands. By an opening in the trees next to the water was a large grizzly bear. "That is a sign that Sarah will recover. That is her totem."

Amos glanced at Will. "I do hope so."

The bear seemed to gaze at them, then lumbered into the woods. Amos sank back into his own thoughts. *Right now, I'll take any glimmer of life for Sarah. If anything happens to her, I'm not going to regret what I do to Jack Harper.* An eagle soared from the cliffs.

****

Things didn't make sense to Sarah. She ceased to know what was real and what was dreamed. Sometimes one dovetailed into the other. She remembered being shot and then having a hard time breathing. Amos turned into Dr. Lindsey who, in turn, became white spirit creatures that flitted around. Amos came to her several times, then took the form of her mother. Pain in her right side came and went.

Sarah stirred in the bed, venturing to open one eye. A form sat in a chair beside her, knitting. "Mother?" she said faintly.

The form froze. "Sarah?" She dropped the knitting and stood by the bed while gently holding Sarah's hands. "You're finally awake?"

Sarah nodded. "How long?"

Her mother moved the hair from Sarah's face. "Two days. I'm going to get the doctor." She disappeared through the curtains around the bed. Dr. Lindsey came in a few minutes later.

"Well, Miss Lakat, let's see how you're doing."

A nurse came in with a tray and set it on a table. "Here are the supplies, Doctor."

The doctor loosened the hospital gown, then took the scissors and started cutting the bandages on Sarah's side. Picking up a bottle, he poured a small amount on a gauze square over the wound. "Now this may tug a bit." He carefully removed it.

Sarah could just barely see the wound. "How is it?"

"Healing nicely. Can you sit up for me?"

The nurse helped her up and slipped the gown off her right arm. Lindsey put the stethoscope on her back. "Take a deep breath with the count of three and keep doing that."

She felt sore through her right side, but she could still breathe.

Lindsey straightened up. "Fine. You can relax. You had a bullet enter below your breast and hit your lung. We removed the bullet and repaired the damage. The lungs sound clear, so I think you're out of danger for pneumonia."

"When can I go home?"

He gave her a look of concern. "Now see here. I want you to stay here a few more days and then take it easy for a month."

Sarah set her jaw. "But I'm getting married in a couple of weeks!"

Lindsey chuckled. "Let everyone else worry about the plans. I'm sure Amos wants to keep you around for a while." He turned to the nurse. "Could you replace the dressing? And give her a small amount of aspirin."

"Yes, Doctor."

He nodded toward Sarah. "I'll see you tomorrow."

Later, Amos came in. A wealth of worry, happiness, and love shone in his eyes. Wordlessly, he removed his hat and set it on the foot of the bed before he gently embraced Sarah and kissed her. When he pulled back, tears glistened in his eyes. "I love you," he said with a rasp.

Sarah felt his strength flowing through her veins. "You've helped me more than you know. It was our love that kept me going." Her fingers stroked his rough cheek.

He cradled her and rocked back and forth. "My Sarah."

Her mother appeared at the curtain. "Do you want

me to come back later?"

"No, Mother, come sit." She straightened, but Amos remained beside her.

Grace resumed her knitting. "Should we postpone the wedding a couple of weeks?"

Sarah shook her head. "The doctor said I'll be out in a few days. I'll still have time to recover enough in two weeks. We won't need to wait a month."

Amos glanced at them both. "If I may say something, I think we should wait a week and see if you're strong enough. We can make any decision then." He kissed the top of her head. "I have to get back to the office. I'll be here this evening."

She snuggled into his arms. "I'll be looking for you."

As Amos left, her mother smiled contentedly over her project. "I know now he'll do everything to protect you."

Sarah sank back on her pillow. *He never stops looking out for me.* Her happiness overcame the discomfort of the wound.

Chapter 24

Amos strode into his office feeling more relieved than he had for two days. Sam came to the door. "How's Sarah?"

Amos related what the doctor had told him. "At least she's awake. I'm sure she'll recover."

Sam nodded. "We all care for her here. I'm glad." A slow smile spread across his face. "I'm happy for you, too."

Amos cocked an eyebrow. "Uh-huh. Get back to work."

Sam had a glint in his eye as he closed the door. "Right, sir."

Amos' stack of papers rebuked him while his mind was full of Sarah. *Damn, that woman has bewitched me. I can't concentrate on anything else.* He forced himself to get to work.

About an hour later, a knock at the door caught his attention. "Who is it?"

It opened and Sam stepped in. "Sir, Assemblyman Hastings is here to see you."

"Send him in."

Hastings came in, hat in hand. "Sheriff, first I want to offer my condolences on the injury to Miss Lakat. The entire Assembly heard of her heroism."

Amos warily nodded. "I thank you on her behalf, but I don't think that's the reason for this visit."

"May I sit?" Amos waved him to a chair. "Darcy, I told you I'd tell you what the Assembly has decided as far as Miss Lakat keeping her position."

"Get on with it, man!" Amos roared.

Hastings fingered the brim of his hat, going around it full circle as he hesitantly announced, "We, the Assembly, have decided that, even though Miss Lakat has been outstanding in her duty, we can't back down on the married-woman rule. Her place would be in the home."

Amos ran his fingers through his hair, stalling for time. He didn't want to kill Hastings outright. Maybe if he started with a removal of the first organ he could get to. "Even though she is one of the best detectives I've ever worked with, you would deprive the community of her experience?"

"I'm afraid so. You see, women have to stay in their place, and their place is taking care of a home and family. Besides, she's only an Eskimo."

Amos' hands came down heavily on the desk and papers flowed to the floor like an avalanche. He practically leaped over the desk at Hastings, who fell out of the chair with a startled expression. Amos grabbed the lapels of his coat and hauled him up and shook him. "You bastard! I should string you up and let the buzzards at your carcass! That 'woman Eskimo' has saved my ass several times lately. You'd have a dead sheriff here if it weren't for her!"

Hastings turned red. "But—but—"

"If that's what the Assembly decided, you can tell the rest of the bear bait I quit! I'm not plying my trade for a bunch of jackasses!"

Amos released Hastings, who scrambled across the

floor to the door and stood. "You'll be sorry, Darcy! You won't get work in this town."

Amos threw his badge at Hastings. "Get the hell out of here while you're still in one piece." As the man hurried out, Amos swiped at the desk, and everything still there crashed to the floor. He sighed as he glanced around the shambles of the office. *Maybe I was too fast to quit my job. How's that going to look, starting out a marriage out of work? On the other hand, I couldn't work for someone who has no respect for my wife.* He shrugged on his jacket and jammed his hat on.

Amos marched out the door and swung around to Sam. "You have to take over, Sam, I just quit."

Sam gazed at his hands. "I know. We could hear." He sighed. "I'm sorry to see both you and Sarah go. I agree. The Assembly is a bunch of jackasses."

Amos half-smiled. "Take care, and I'll see you about the wedding. You're still Best Man." He started to the front door, then turned around and jerked a thumb toward the room he'd just left. "Sorry about the office." Sam grinned and nodded.

As Amos entered the ward, Sarah lay snuggled into the pillows at her back, reading the newspaper. She glanced up and smiled. "You didn't have to take the day off. I'm feeling better. Mother even went home a while to help Aunt Jane."

He took his hat off and sat on the edge of the bed. "We have a problem." He told her what had happened with Hastings. "I tell you, my love, this is a hell of a way to start a marriage."

Sarah hadn't closed her mouth as he told the story. She took a deep breath. "Can you tell Hastings it was all a mistake?"

He set his jaw. "Why? So he can insult you some more?"

"But what will we do for money?"

"Let me ruminate on this for a while. I can find a job somewhere, I'm sure."

Sarah put her hands over her face. "Maybe we should put off the wedding."

Amos grabbed her hands and pulled them down. "Listen to me. We still have money to tide us over for a while. We'll be all right."

A nurse entered the ward and looked around. She spotted Amos and hurried over. "A courier dropped this off for you." She gave him an envelope.

"Thank you." With a nod, she strode out.

Sarah watched him open it. "What is it?"

Amos quickly read the note. "It's from Sam. He wants to meet me at Millie's at five for dinner. I'm afraid I left him with a mess."

She shook her head. "I don't like this."

"Now, see here, woman. I won't put up with the blues."

"All right. I'm willing to look for a job, too. As soon as I get out of here."

Amos planted a kiss on her lips. "That's the Sarah I know."

Later, he strolled into Millie's and found Sam waiting at a table, tapping his coffee cup. Amos slid into a chair across from him. "Evening, Sam."

Sam glanced up. "How's Sarah?"

Amos noticed he didn't use his usual "sir." "Still in some pain, but she's getting better."

Sam studied his hands as Millie came over to take Amos' order. When she was on her way to the kitchen,

Sam sighed. "You know, as leader of the investigating team, you still have to testify."

"I'll be there."

"Also, you and Sarah were doing so much of the detective work, I'm standing bare naked in the middle of a field. I'm going to need help. Too bad there aren't any private detectives around here."

Somewhere in Amos' brain a light bulb lit. "You're right. There isn't an agency, is there?" He hit Sam on the shoulder. "Boy, you might have solved our problem. Sarah and I could get territorial licenses and open an agency. You could use us as consultants."

A light dawned in Sam's eyes, but then he slumped. "What can I do in the meantime?"

Amos grinned. "We can get together over dinner. You can buy."

Sam gave him a sidelong glare, but he was smiling.

After dinner, Amos made a beeline back to the hospital and told Sarah of his idea. She beamed for the first time in days. "What a wonderful idea! We can still do what we love and the Assembly can't do a thing about it." Amos gently hugged her.

"While you're in here, I'll find a storefront or office to move into. We can get our licenses fairly easily, since we were in law enforcement to begin with." He gazed into deep brown eyes that sparkled with happiness.

"I love you." She buried her face on his shoulder, and he felt the twinge of desire. To spend his life with this woman was going to suit him fine.

****

Sarah grinned at Dr. Lindsey as she placed her extra clothes in a small suitcase. "You're letting me out today?" If she weren't so weak, she'd be doing handsprings.

Lindsey's smile was bemused. "Yes, but take it easy for a while. And no wild time at your wedding."

"I hope you're able to come."

"I'll be there with bells on." He laughed.

Amos appeared through the ward door. Sarah stopped packing and went into waiting arms. "I'm discharged! I can go home now."

Amos pulled back and looked her over. "The rose is back in your cheeks. You're beautiful." He strode to the doctor and shook his hand. "You did a wonderful job on her."

Lindsey shook his head. "That was Sarah. People don't usually mend as fast with that kind of wound, but she has a strong constitution."

"Like a horse." Amos ducked as Sarah swung a fist at him. He grabbed her shoulders and turned her back to packing. "I'll take you home. Your mother will be staying at your house with you."

Lindsey turned to leave. "Let your mother do any of the work, and you can take aspirin if there's any pain."

Sarah agreed and finished putting her toiletries in. A nurse came in with a wheelchair. "Are you ready?"

Amos started out. "I'll bring the auto to the entrance."

Sarah sat with her suitcase on her lap. She gasped when the nurse opened the outside door. At the entrance was a brand new Model A Ford, with Amos exiting the driver's side. He took her case and deposited it in the back, then gallantly waved her into the passenger seat. "Well, what do you think of our new auto?"

"The bee's knees. But can we afford this?"

He slid into the other side. "Might as well get a good auto to start out. We'll probably need it quite a bit."

She looked at her shoes. "Part of me still forgets. We're out of work."

"Not for long. I've got an appointment for both of us to take the license test at the courthouse next week. That will give you time to study the rules and regulations. I left a copy at your home."

"Are you sure we can run our own business?"

"I've been studying that, too. We've got enough money to get started, and then some. Sam said he would like to use us as consultants." Amos stopped the auto in front of her porch. "I think we'd hate ourselves if we didn't at least try."

Sarah's mother came out to greet them. "Welcome home. Amos, are you staying for midday meal?"

"No, but I can accept your earlier invitation for supper. I'll be here at four-thirty." He turned a loving glance at Sarah. "Until then, woman, take care of yourself." He clasped her hand and kissed her, then tipped his hat to her mother. "Grace."

Grace put her arm around Sarah's shoulder as Amos drove off. "Come. We have much to discuss."

Later, with her feet propped up on the couch, Sarah reached for the book of territorial rules and regulations for detectives and set off on an afternoon of dry reading.

Chapter 25

Sarah turned in front of the full-length mirror and her white gown shimmered in the sunlight slanting through the window. It was sleeveless, with material draped front and back. On each side and around the squared neckline were appliqués of small brown bears.

Kata stood back with a critical eye. "What do you think?"

"I see you've brought it up to date. The sleeves were very old-fashioned."

Kata nodded. "It looks better without."

"It doesn't seem at all to be the outfit I had the first time, when I was jilted."

Kata helped Sarah remove the dress. "Since Joey is sleeping, would you like to take some tea with me? I just finished steeping a pot."

Sarah agreed while she slipped into her day clothes. Kata carefully hung and covered the wedding gown. "Since you're going to help me get ready beforehand, why don't you keep the gown with you?"

"Sure, I can." Kata slipped it into a locked wardrobe. "So Joey can't get it." She laughed. "He's such a scamp."

Sitting at the kitchen table in the Nikolaevich home, Kata poured the tea and set a plate of sugar cookies in front of Sarah, who inspected the fragrant delights. "Mmm, those smell fresh baked."

"They're Ivan's favorite. Help yourself." As Sarah bit into one of the cookies, Kata watched her thoughtfully. "Have you heard anything about the detective licenses yet?"

"We should hear soon. Amos is so confident that we passed, he's been asking around about an office or storefront."

"I'm sure you'll pass, too. The way you both brought down that murderous gang..."

Sarah shook her head. "We were fortunate Sally was willing to testify. That was hard for her, to have to face her brother in court, knowing she was surely sending him to prison—or death."

"Have you heard if the canneries have taken the salmon traps down?"

"No, they're not willing to. I think it's foolish, after all that death because of them, but I guess they think making money is more important. I hope no more of our people try to take things into their own hands."

Kata sighed. "Americans will be sorry when there's no salmon left."

Sarah gave a snort. "They'll just go after something else to make money." She took a sip of tea. "I hope you and Ivan are coming to the dinner tomorrow night at Mother's."

"Won't miss it. I'm glad Amos is becoming part of the family. This is a good way to welcome him."

Joey woke up a few minutes later, and Sarah gave Kata her thanks and goodbye. She was looking forward to the honors dinner. This would be a formal welcome into the family for Amos two days before the ceremony.

A stiff breeze from the channel ruffled her hair and threatened to lift her new cloche hat. It matched the rest of her recently purchased outfit. She had figured she should get into stylish fashion if they were to run a business. Anyway, the shorter skirts were nicer than the old heavy wool ones she'd had to wear as a uniform.

Suddenly she heard an auto horn cough that scared her to death. Amos pulled to the curb and leaned to the open window. "Hey, doll, want a ride?"

She put her hands on her hips. "Who are you? A masher or something?"

A smug expression crossed his face. "Just get your carcass in here, woman. We've got errands to run. We both passed the test."

She whooped and jumped onto the seat. "We've got our licenses already?"

Amos grinned. "Yep. We have to go to the photographer for identification pictures. Then we're going to the courthouse for a business license and our marriage license."

Sarah planted a kiss on his lips, which he didn't fight a bit. "You sure know what to say to a girl to get her worked up."

He sighed as he pulled back. "You keep that up, we'll never get anything done."

Later, on Sarah's porch, they were engaged in telling each other goodbye. She threw her arms around his neck. "The Darcy Detective Agency sounds so good. It fairly rolls off the tongue." She ran her hands over his rough face. "You know, running a business, you should keep clean-shaved."

He glanced at the toe of his boot. "If I have things on my mind, I tend to forget."

"Well, you'll have me to remind you."

"Nag like a fisher's wife," he muttered almost

under his breath.

"I haven't even begun yet." She laughed as his mouth formed a straight line.

"All right! But the mustache stays."

"Agreed. You wouldn't be my Amos without it."

His gray eyes softened. "I love you." Finding her lips with his own, he kissed her thoroughly, and they clung to each other. Sarah didn't want him to go, because he took a little piece of her every time. "I'll come for you tomorrow at four."

She sat on the porch railing as he drove out of sight. *We've been tested, but we haven't been found wanting.* She sincerely hoped the worst of their trials were over.

****

Carefully placing the honors gifts in a crate, Amos settled them in the back seat of the Ford. He knew her family well, but a certain nervousness tightened his stomach. This dinner was the first step to the wedding, and he was as jittery as a flea on a hot plate. Too much of the old life was gone. His new life was heading at him as if he were stuck on the tracks and heard the express train whistle.

He climbed into the driver's seat and felt a little better. He even hummed "Green Grow the Lilacs" because it reminded him of Sarah and their impromptu hiking song. Love for her swelled as he saw her hurry off the porch to greet him. He went around the auto to open her door and was met with a passionate kiss. "You want us to miss dinner? Grace wouldn't be happy." He blew out a breath and tried to control the intense tingling the kiss had instigated.

Sarah laughed. "I miss you when you're not

around." She gave him the once over. "I'm glad you shaved. You're so handsome that way."

He helped her into the auto and slid into the driver's seat. "I looked at several offices today and found a good one."

"Where?"

"Not far from the courthouse. It has two offices and a reception area."

Sarah bounced in her seat. "I'm getting excited about this. Our own business!"

They arrived at Grace's home with a song in their hearts. After helping Sarah out of the car, he hefted the crate. They were greeted by the family at the door and ushered in to where the table was spread with various vegetables, fruits, and breads, all surrounding a magnificent smoked salmon.

Amos rose after dinner and brought over the crate. "Will told me it was customary to offer honors gifts to the bride's family, so I brought this." He reached in and took out the first gift. "Will, you told me you wanted to carve a totem for the family, so I got some carving tools for you."

Will accepted them gratefully.

"Mary, I know you love to knit, so here's twenty skeins of the finest Merino wool from Australia."

Mary ran her hand over the yarn. "Oh, my! It's so soft."

"For the twins, the books *The Wizard of Oz* and *Winnie the Pooh*. The love of reading is the basis of a good education." He turned to Kata. "For you is a new pattern book for theater costumes."

She smiled. "I've been wanting to get that one."

"Ivan, I've got a carpenter's T-square to help with

your construction."

Ivan gave a hearty laugh. "You must have known I lost mine."

"For Joey, there's a box of building blocks, in case he takes after his old man." He handed the next item to Jane. "I know you love gardening, but you always complain about your knees. Here's a padded kneeler for working outside."

Jane stood and kissed his cheek. "Thank you."

"And for you, Grace. You told me you'd love to have the means to make sausages. I got a sausage stuffer and casings for you."

Grace rose with tears in her eyes. "You have honored this family well with your thoughtful gifts. I am happy that you are the man Sarah chose." The relations closed around Amos and, for the first time since his parents died, he felt part of a family.

****

Later, in front of her house, Sarah was ensconced in Amos' strong arms. He pulled back and cupped her cheeks. "I know there's no honors gifts for the bride, but I want you to know, all I can give you is myself. We don't have much, and we're scraping the bottom of the barrel for money, but I will always love you and care for you."

She snuggled down again and felt the warmth of his body all around her. "That's all I ask. As long as you're there, I'm at home."

The morning of the wedding, Will's truck stopped by the curb. Sarah waved out the window, then gathered her things and went out and climbed into the truck. The gloom and gray of the fog rivaled the sunshine in her soul. Amos won't run off like George did. *George never loved me. Now, he's going to be tried for murder.* Sarah felt sorry for his wife and children, but he was paying the price for his own choices. If only he would have put his family first.

Will glanced over as they navigated through the dark streets. "You seem awfully quiet this morning."

Sarah sighed. "I was thinking about George and how lucky I am to have Amos."

"I know it didn't seem so at the time, but your best day was when George left."

Sarah stretched her legs and put her head back. The shadows of the mists changed shapes and played with her mind. Phantasms lay outside, but she was safe. She didn't realize that sleep had overcome her until Will turned onto the primitive road to the meetinghouse. Bear Rock loomed ahead like a massive dark object. She breathed easier when she saw Ivan's truck. Kata was here with her gown.

In the small outbuilding opposite the meeting house, Kata and her mother helped Sarah dress. When the glistening white folds of the skirt had settled in layers, her mother opened a wooden box with a small key. "This is my headband and necklace from my wedding. I want you to wear it." She carefully lifted the items made of cobalt beads and delicate dentalium shells.

Sarah ran her fingers over the jewelry. "Oh, it's beautiful!"

Her mother tied the headband over Sarah's dark hair and clasped the ten-string necklace at her nape. "Perfect. Just perfect." She stood by Kata, and tears started to well up. "I've waited so long for this day."

Kata hurried to the door and peeked out. "Looks

like people are here now. Mary and I should get the cedar boughs." She waved Sarah over. "Amos is here."

Sarah gave a small gasp. He wore a brown-and-black tunic made of leather and cloth decorated with beads and ermine tails. A beaded leather headband was tied on his hair. The puffs of gray fog on the scene gave it a magical quality. He seemed a mythical hero.

Kata slid past with the boughs and found Mary. They proceeded into the meeting house to wave the boughs in a ceremony to cleanse the area. The guests were all in the meetinghouse and the procession was forming outside. Five of Will's friends arrived with Will, hauling the platform chair they would carry Sarah on. The chair was secured to the platform by four metal braces and screws. Three long poles extended underneath with enough coming out on either side to carry. The whole thing was on four short legs that stabilized it while on the ground.

As Amos neared the entrance to the meetinghouse, Sarah silently came out of the outbuilding to watch. At the doorway, he paused, then blew eagle feather fluff into the air to bring peace to those assembled.

By now, Sarah had moved next to Will, near the door. Amos started a respectable eagle dance, swooping and weaving to the sound of the ceremonial drum. She turned and grinned at Will. "You taught him well," she whispered close to his ear.

Will had an impish smile. "Pretty good for an American. Ready to get up in the chair?" He gave her a hand onto the platform. "Hang on. We'll be as careful as we can."

She clasped the seat and steadied herself as Will and his friends lifted the chair. An audible "Ohh" reached her ears as she sailed into the room on her flying carpet—or so it seemed. Amos looked thunderstruck, unable to take his gaze off her. Her complement of carriers set her gently down in front of the Tlingit Chief of Juneau, Ray Johns, and their pastor. She rose regally, and Will helped her down, then escorted her to Amos and joined their hands. The couple faced the pastor while Sarah's family draped her with a bear robe. Sam put an eagle robe on Amos, and Sarah knew it was reasoned that the eagle was the American totem.

The pastor proceeded with the official Christian wedding ceremony, until it was time for the vows. Everything paused as Sarah's family laid a large wool blanket over both Amos and Sarah. Then the vows and rings were exchanged.

Sarah saw great love and tenderness that she hadn't fully realized existed in Amos' soul, but it shone brightly as he repeated the vows. She choked a little on hers, because of a massive lump in her throat that threatened to give way to sobs.

After the pastor had pronounced them husband and wife, the chief stood. "I, too, give this union my blessing. This shows that our people are civilized and worthy to become citizens in their own right. May this couple be blessed with wealth and prosperity and children who will honor them."

Sarah's family then removed the wool blanket and the totem robes, and the pastor announced, "Where two came in, one in the spirit of a new family will leave. I present to you Mr. and Mrs. Amos Darcy."

Sarah gazed deep into Amos' gray eyes, finding nothing but love there. He tenderly embraced and kissed her as if for the first time. Her eyes streamed with tears at the intensity of the moment. And then the drumbeat began again, accompanied by applause from the many friends and family assembled.

Her mother stood up in the front of the meetinghouse. "You're all invited to the feast at our home to honor my daughter and son."

Everyone got into their autos and wound their way through fog to the Lakat home. Before anyone could turn around twice, there were platters of salmon and trout, surrounded with everything that was ripe in the garden. Bread and rolls of all shapes, with fresh-churned butter, added to the aroma. Summer berry pies were still warm from the oven.

Sarah laughed and hugged her mother. "Putting on an old-fashioned potlatch?"

Amos and some of the other Americans asked what a potlatch was.

Grace gave a hearty laugh. "This was done ages ago. When someone considered themselves wealthy, they would put on a feast for the neighbors. Tons of food would be eaten for the whole day. It was considered impolite if you didn't vomit."

Amos twisted his lips. "Sounds delightful."

Sarah continued, "In fact, I think the European Romans had a similar feast, if I remember my history correctly."

Amos snorted. "The Romans did everything to excess." He leaned in to her ear. "Even—I'll show you later."

Her head swirled with his words, and a tingling tightness to her chest and warm cream between her legs responded to them. She couldn't wait for the feast to be over.

Finally, they were thanking everyone and telling their family and friends goodbye. Sarah turned to her mother. "Thank you to you and Aunt Jane for such a feast."

Her mother embraced her. "I'm so happy for you, my daughter." She embraced Amos. "I'm honored to have you for a son."

He kissed her cheek. "Goodnight and thank you, Grace—Mother."

She teared up. "Go on, you two. Enjoy your life."

Amos helped Sarah into their Ford and set off for her—their—house. He had moved his things in the day before, with the help of Will and Ivan. Home had never looked so beautiful. Amos had never looked so handsome.

He helped her out of the auto and stood there holding her hand and drinking her in. "Damn, woman, you remind me of an Indian angel."

Sarah's cheeks heated. She disengaged her hand and hurried to the porch. Amos was still on the sidewalk. "Well, are you coming in, or aren't you?"

His eyes lit as he took the steps two at a time. He closed the door behind him and Sarah turned to him from the parlor. He had her in his arms in a moment. "I couldn't take my eyes off you in the meetinghouse. You were a vision being carried in."

She never had been this flattered, and she fingered the laces on the front of his tunic. "In my wildest dreams, I never pictured you like this." She worked the laces down and exposed his bare chest. Her fingers traced the taut muscles, and she noticed a twitch from his nether regions. "I remember you saying something about a Roman orgy—" As she slid the tunic over his shoulders and to the floor, he groaned and thoroughly kissed her, running his tongue to the top of her mouth.

But then he pulled back and turned her around. His fingers worked undoing the hooks and eyes on her dress. She smiled secretly. He'd soon find out that was all she was wearing. Just like the groom, the obvious wedding clothes were the only thing worn by the bride. The dress puddled to the floor and Sarah stood there in the headband and beads, her breasts jutting through the strands. He cupped them and a flaming heat hit her from head to toe. "My God, you are so wild and beautiful."

She grinned and pulled the drawstring on his pants. Amos flushed when they got caught on his male appendage. She worked them to the floor as Amos embraced her in a wonderfully erotic caress. The smoothness of his skin over the hardness of his muscles was like silk over steel.

She shed the beads and shoes, as did he, and she led him to their bedroom. As she sat on the edge of the bed, she noticed a bead of liquid had formed on the tip of his shaft. Taking her thumb, she rubbed the liquid around the head, and Amos hissed. "Keep that up, woman, and this is going to be a short session."

Lying back, she smiled. "Do what you like."

He crawled beside her and started with a passionate kiss before moving his tongue from her collarbone to her ear. Sarah's breath rasped and every nerve came alive. The place between her legs screamed for relief, but Amos was taking his time.

Her nipples hardened like rocks, and when he suckled, she arched. He moved lower and tongued her belly button. By now, she writhed with the tension. "Please, please!" she begged.

"Soon. Let me enjoy this," Amos hoarsely croaked. His fingers invaded her slit and found the sensitive nub.

Sarah moved her legs apart, and Amos dipped his tongue into her opening. Sarah exploded as he moved on top of her.

"I can't wait any longer," he choked. In the midst of the ripples, he entered her, and she continued to convulse. Moving back and forth, he seemed like a man in agony. Then he gave a cry and she felt the hot splashes inside. With a groan, he collapsed on her, and they stayed that way for countless minutes. He brushed her soaked hair from her face and kissed her. "God, you're good to come home to."

"Likewise." Sarah laughed out of pure joy.

Chapter 26

The next morning, Amos made her close her eyes as they were going downtown in the Ford. "This is silly."

"We're almost there." The auto stopped. "Now, take a look outside."

She gasped. By the courthouse was a suite of office buildings. The one they faced had a shingle with the words "The Darcy Detective Agency, Amos and Sarah Darcy, Proprietors."

Amos came around and helped her out. "Let me show you the inside." He unlocked the door. "You have to understand, it's not furnished yet, but we can do it this week."

She went into a well-lighted pleasant reception area with a low wooden gate to the back two office doors. "Two offices?"

He swept his hand. "Of course. We're equal partners. We can work on cases together or separately. We need to start with a secretary."

"I love it! Our own business! It's too bad we can't toast it with champagne."

Amos glanced around and locked the outside door. He motioned her to one of the offices. When they were inside, Sarah noticed a bucket of ice in the corner. Amos pulled a bottle out of it and took two glasses that had been set nearby. "I bought this two months before

Prohibition started." He popped the cork, and the liquid gurgled into the glasses. "Here's to us and our business."

Sarah clinked her glass to his and, when the bubbles hit, laughed with love. In the midst of the celebration, they heard a rap at the front door. Amos put everything under a towel, and they both ventured out to see who it was.

An official-looking man stood on the other side of the glass. He raised his hat as Amos opened the door. "Good morning to you both. I saw you go into this building and figured you were the Darcys. I'm Arnie Doogan." He turned to Sarah. "I assume you're Sarah."

She nodded. "Yes. What do you want?"

He thrust a folded paper into her hand. "This is a summons as a witness for the defense in the trial of George Annok on Wednesday next at eight o'clock in the morning."

Sarah's stomach knotted. "But…I—defense?"

He raised his hat again. "Good day, madam." He skittered out the door before she could finish. She gave Amos a helpless glance. "What could the defense want me for?"

Amos pursed his lips. "I have a feeling George told someone about your history together. I don't like it when they bring up personal things on a case."

A fluttering started in her chest. "Oh, no. I was so afraid people would find out why I didn't marry. The banns were posted, but when George ran off, I let things go. No one asked, and I didn't tell why there was no wedding."

He gripped her shoulders tightly. "There's nothing to be ashamed of now. You're married to me now, and this was in the past. Don't you see? George is the problem, not you."

A new Sarah was being born with this truth. She had forever railed on herself that something was wrong with her. That she wasn't worth being loved and that was the reason George didn't want her. That was driven home when she found George had married Leigh. But all this time she had been paying for his sins.

****

Sarah gazed at the courthouse looming at the top of the steps and gave a shaky cough. Amos squeezed her hand. "I'm right with you, woman. We'll get through this together."

This was not going to be like the Bobby Cusnoo trial, where Amos gave most of the informational testimony on their investigation and she gave what she had found. This one might have her airing dirty laundry.

They went through the great front door, and their footsteps echoed down the hall to the courtroom. Once inside, they slid into seats behind the prosecution. Roberts, the district attorney, came in carrying his briefcase and gave them a slight smile and nod.

On the other side of the gallery Sarah spotted Leigh Annok. She hurt for the poor girl, who looked so lost and alone. There was no hatred for George's wife. She had been used as ruthlessly as Sarah at George's hands.

The early summer mist lifted and sunlight streamed into the courtroom between the blinds that painted rayed stripes on the walls. The defense counselor came in next, with his staff and George. Sarah felt a squeeze of her hand and glanced at Amos' eyes full of love and support. She smiled and squeezed back.

The bailiff stepped to the front and called, "All rise for His Honor, Judge Henry Ott."

The judge ascended to his chair behind the dark mahogany desk and banged the gavel. "The court will come to order for the trial in the city of Juneau, Alaska Territory, versus George Annok, indigenous person, for the murder of Mr. Edward G. Thornton at the North Star Cannery. May I have the opening statements from the prosecution and defense?"

Roberts stood. "Yes, Your Honor. We are prepared to prove that the defendant did willingly plan and abet the murder of Mr. Thornton at the cannery last May tenth. He also planned and executed a jailbreak for Mr. Bobby Cusnoo, who was convicted last week of the physical murder of Mr. Thornton."

The judge nodded. "Thank you, Mr. Roberts. Mr. Connor of the defense?"

Connor rose after talking to George. "Your Honor, we will refute the evidence and prove that Mr. Annok just happened to be in Juneau when the murder and jailbreak took place."

Amos snorted and whispered to Sarah, "All Roberts has to do is put Perkins from the Personals on the stand to identify him."

Amos was called to the bench by Roberts to testify about the investigation and capture of George Annok. Back-up people like Mr. Perkins and members of the ANB who had known about George and his plan identified him. During the lunch break, Sarah gave Sally her support in the testimony that was to come.

Sally picked at her food. "I don't know how much more of this I can take."

Sarah put her hand on Sally's arm. "Just answer the

questions honestly. You'll do fine."

When they returned to the courtroom, Sally made her way to the stand when she was called. Sarah was sorry her friend had to endure all these trials, but she admired her, too. It took fortitude to face all these questions. Probably the trial of her brother had been the hardest, and that was over with.

Roberts stood in front of her. "Miss Cusnoo, who is the one that planned the escape of your brother from the jail on May twentieth?"

"George Annok."

"Do you see him in the courtroom?"

Sally pointed. "He's at that table."

"Let the record state she indicated the defendant."

"How long did you know that the defendant was involved with the plot to kill Mr. Thornton?"

Connor rose. "I object, Your Honor."

Ott agreed. "Reword your question."

"When did you first see the defendant?"

"He went with us to the social at the ANB on the Saturday after the murder."

"Why did he go to the social?"

"He said he wanted to stop the investigation."

"How was he going to do that?"

"By roughing up and threatening Deputy Sarah Lakat, who was on the case."

Sarah almost collapsed and gave an audible gasp, while Amos swore under his breath. *George was the one who tried to stop me that night!*

Roberts turned. "Thank you, Miss Cusnoo." He waved his hand at Connor. "Your witness."

Connor made notes on his legal pad. "How long did you cooperate with the then Miss Lakat on the investigation?"

Sally thought for a moment. "I guess it was until I identified Sheriff Creag as the leader of the Revenge Ravens."

Conner gave a half-smile. "Thank you, Miss Cusnoo. No more questions."

Judge Ott sounded his gavel. "It's getting to be four in the afternoon. We'll adjourn for the day and resume at eight o'clock tomorrow morning."

Sarah found Sally and gave her a hug. "You did fine, dear."

Sally nodded. "Thank you. I was wondering why the defense asked about you?"

Amos gripped Sarah's arm. "I was wondering the same thing."

Sarah gritted her teeth. "I guess we'll find out. Sally, what are you going to do after the trials are over?"

She looked at the ground. "I think I'll go back to Angoon. It's easier dealing with our own people. Thank you both for your help." They watched Sally hurry down the court steps.

Amos put his arm around Sarah's shoulders. "We can do some work on the office and then go to Millie's for dinner."

Sarah sighed. "I need something to do after sitting all day in the courtroom."

As they set out down the steps, Sarah heard a voice behind her. "Mrs. Darcy, can I say something?"

She turned to see Leigh Annok hurrying after them. "I didn't realize how terrible George treated you. I want to say I'm sorry he hurt you so badly." The poor girl was wringing her hands.

Sarah instinctively hugged the distraught woman. "Mrs. Annok—Leigh, thank you, but you don't have to apologize for him. This happened before he met you."

Leigh shook her head. "When you came to the house in Yakutat, I noticed you seemed distressed about something. I learned later what happened in Juneau, and I knew what he had done."

Sarah glanced at Amos. "As you can see, I've gone on with my life, but thank you for thinking of me. Can you manage with the children?"

Leigh sniffed and dabbed her eyes with her handkerchief. "We've moved in with my parents. We'll be all right." She stepped back. "Thank you for being so kind."

Amos tipped his hat. "If you need anything, don't hesitate to ask."

A faint trace of a smile shadowed across her face. "Good day to both of you."

As the young woman went on her way, Sarah turned to Amos. "You don't realize how much I wanted to hate her, but she was as much a victim of George's ways as I was."

Amos offered her his arm. "He sure left a trail. He thought he was just fighting the white man, but he did as much damage to his own people and his own family."

Sarah pondered this on the five-minute walk to their office. How many revolutionaries and fighters for justice destroyed their families and friends in the process? Was it worth it?

****

For some reason, Amos was worried about going to the courthouse the next morning. Why did the defense attorney subpoena Sarah? What could she possibly say in George's defense? They took seats in the gallery, and he held her hand because she kept fidgeting. Her face was pale.

The prosecution closed their case, and the defense attorney rose at the judge's bidding. "Your Honor, we call our first witness, Mrs. Sarah Darcy."

Amos squeezed her hand, and then she took the long walk to the witness stand to get sworn in. As she seated herself, Connor looked at his notes and rose.

He took his time going to the witness stand. "Now, Mrs. Darcy, when was the first time you remember encountering the defendant after the murder at the cannery?"

"He came to my house a week after."

"You didn't know it was he who attacked you at the ANB social, as Miss Cusnoo stated?"

"No, sir."

"Why did he come to your house?"

"He said he wanted another chance." Amos believed dredging this up was like digging wet muck with bare hands.

"Another chance with what?"

Roberts stood. "Really, Your Honor, what does this have to do with the case?"

Ott turned to Connor. "Does this have something to do with it?"

Connor nodded. "Yes, it does, Your Honor."

Ott waved him on. "Go ahead."

"What were you giving him another chance for?"

Sarah studied her fingers. "He wanted to start courting me again."

"Even though he was married."

Sarah smacked her fist on the railing. "He didn't tell me he was."

"When did he court you before?"

"We were engaged to be married six years ago."

"I see. When did you learn that he was a suspect in the murder case?"

"It was when Mr. Perkins of the newspaper identified him."

"But you continued on the investigation?"

Sarah took a deep breath. "Yes."

Connor slapped the note pad on his palm. "Your Honor, I declare a mistrial! She should have taken herself off the case when she found out Mr. Annok was a suspect." An audible gasp came from the courtroom. Amos almost destroyed his hat by yanking at it.

Roberts jumped up. "Your Honor, may I direct a question to the witness?"

Ott tapped his gavel for order. "Quiet in the court! Roberts, you can ask your question."

"Now, Mrs. Darcy, were you the primary investigator on the murder case?"

"No."

"In other words, you were just following the orders of the sheriff? And you were in his employ?"

"Yes, sir."

Roberts turned to Connor. "There you have it. She was following orders of her superior."

Ott stroked his chin. "Connor, I have to agree with Roberts. She was helping the sheriff in her office as deputy. This wasn't her case."

Connor muttered under his breath and threw his notes on the defense table. "No more questions."

Ott glanced at Sarah. "You may step down, Mrs.

Darcy."

Amos watched her get off the stand, and she slipped into the seat beside him. Trembling as he put his arm around her shoulders, she laid her head on his chest and silently wept. He gave her his handkerchief. *I wish it could have been me to go through that.* His throat was tight.

After the defense closed, both Connor and Roberts gave their closing arguments, and the jury retired to the jury room to decide George's fate. Amos and Sarah stepped outside for some fresh air.

Amos leaned against the stone of the building. "Are you all right?"

Sarah shook her head. "I almost lost it for us. Why didn't I pull myself off the case?" She smacked her hand against her forehead. "I should have known better than that."

Amos gently embraced her. "I would have lost my best partner if you had backed out. I didn't think of it, myself, at the time. We were so engrossed in catching the bastards, that slipped by me, too."

Sarah gazed at him with a tearful smile. "We are a hell of a team, aren't we?"

Amos kissed her. "You bet we are!" He clasped her hand. "Let's get some lunch at the cafeteria while we wait for the jury."

Time passed during lunch as they discussed their plans for the business. Amos fretted, "I'm worried about the money that's not coming in. I never started a business before, and I hope we have enough stashed away to get us through lean times."

Sarah shook her head. "We'll manage. There are enough people in this town that know us and our work."

Amos chuckled. "Thank goodness for your presence of mind to have bought a house. At least we'll have a roof over our heads."

An hour later, an announcement was made that the jury had returned in the George Annok case. They wound their way through the hallways to the courtroom and took their seats. The players in the drama returned one by one, concluding with the judge. Amos instinctively pulled Sarah close to him. *She's gone through enough.* God, he wanted to protect her from all the hurts of life, if he could.

The jury filed in from the door behind the box. Ott directed George, "Will the defendant please rise?" As the jury settled in their chairs, the judge turned to them. "Have you arrived at your decision?"

The foreman arose. "We have, Your Honor."

"What say you?"

He unfolded a piece of paper. "In the case of Juneau versus Mr. George Annok, we find the defendant guilty of plotting the murder of Mr. Edward G. Thornton."

A wail came from Leigh, who was seated behind George. Sarah slumped against Amos. A murmur went through the spectators.

The judge banged his gavel. "Order, please!" The bailiff gave Ott the paper. "Mr. George Annok, you have been found guilty of plotting the murder of Mr. Edward G. Thornton. You will be held here at the courthouse until Wednesday next, when sentence will be pronounced. Court is adjourned."

Amos watched George embrace Leigh before the guards took him away. Amos gazed at Sarah. "Let's go home."

Sitting on the porch was pleasant in the almost endless warm summer sun and the cool breezes from the sea. Amos loved the time he spent relaxing with Sarah. He could get used to this. Her summer dress fluttered as the wind played with it.

She glanced at him pensively over her cup of tea. "Would you mind if I go visit George before his sentence?"

Amos felt a pang of something. Pain? Jealousy? "Why do you want to do that?"

"Please don't be impatient. I want honesty this time. Since all the lies have been stripped away, he has no choice but to tell me the truth."

He ruminated over that. "I don't agree. You should leave him behind and not bother with him again."

She chewed her lip. "This means a lot to me."

His resolve broke down. "All right, do what you want, but I think it's a bad idea."

She sauntered over and sat on his lap, causing the wicker to protest. "I love you." Snaking her arms around him, she gave him a passionate kiss that woke up several parts of his body. "Let's go inside."

"I'm right behind you." The tea was left to cool for a while outside.

Chapter 27

Sarah sat at the table in the cell block, wondering if she was doing the right thing. *Maybe Amos was right, and I should let this whole thing go. I've got a good life without George.* The clang of the cell door brought her out of her thoughts. George entered in chains, the metal scratching across the floor. The guard took up his station by the entrance.

George sat in the chair facing her. "Well, Sarah, we meet again. Here to see the animals in the zoo? Or just the chief ape?"

She glared at him. "Don't blame me for your predicament. No, I am here to close things out, hoping to get the truth this time."

"Truth?"

"About why you walked out on me. Did you already have Leigh on a leash and you were toying with me?"

He slumped and studied her. "No. I met Leigh when I ran to Yakutat. I didn't want to marry you because you were too strong. I wanted a girl I could bend to my wishes, and I saw you were not that kind of woman."

Her hand slammed on the table. "Then why didn't you tell me? My family set up the wedding, and then you ran out. You're worse than a coward."

"You're right. I was afraid they would corner me

247

and make me marry you anyway." He stopped and looked in her eyes. "Don't stare at me that way. I didn't mean there was anything wrong with you. It was me."

"Now poor Leigh has to pay for your stupidity. Leigh and your children. You didn't put them first, did you?"

He gritted his teeth. "I was the one found guilty."

"Yes. And now she has to carry on without you. You're a jackass, and you deserve everything you've got coming." She rose. "Goodbye, George. You've got all the time in the world to feel sorry for yourself. I hope you ponder the shreds you left in your wake."

He sneered. "You seem to be doing well."

"Only because I found a good man who cares about me." She turned to the guard. "I'd like to leave now."

The guard opened the cell door and she stalked out, never once glancing behind.

****

Amos went to work on the office after he dropped Sarah at the courthouse. Hanging up his coat and hat, he rolled up his shirt sleeves. A new coat of light blue paint, modern shell light fixtures, potted ferns, and a large oriental carpet gave it a warm feeling. Amos slapped a fresh coat of varnish on the old wooden desk they would use for the receptionist behind the half wall. Before long the sharp odor on the brush was getting to be too much, so Amos opened the front door. Mr. Peter Anders, owner of North Star, was coming down the street.

Anders turned in at the entrance. "Mr. Darcy? I was sorry to hear you resigned from the sheriff's department. You're opening your own detective agency?"

Amos nodded. "Differences with the Assembly prompted it. I'll still be working as a consultant for the department, along with my wife."

"I heard you married your deputy. Congratulations. You do good work together. I wanted to thank you on the fine investigation you did, bringing those murderers to justice."

Amos shuffled his feet. "Well, I did have a lot of help from other departments around the territory, but I'll accept your thanks." They shook hands. "Anders, what are you going to do about those salmon traps?"

"We plan to leave them in place. After all, business is business."

Amos frowned. "Seems like those damn traps cause more trouble than they're worth."

Anders' mouth drew into a tight line. "Seems to me the natives upstream are too lazy to find another source of food. They rely too much on the salmon runs when there are other fish and game that are just as accessible."

Bastard. Aloud Amos said, "Tradition has a lot to do with it. I guess everything has to change with the times."

Anders tipped his hat. "Well, I wanted to express my appreciation. Remember me to your wife." He continued on his way.

Sarah came in a few minutes later, just as Amos was finishing the desk. She made a face when the smell hit her. Grabbing the electric fan, she set it on a small table near the door. "You should have done that out back."

Amos glanced at her sheepishly. "I found that out when I was halfway through." He pointed at the floor.

"I remembered to put a drop cloth underneath."

She laughed and tousled his hair. "Good for you."

"How did it go at the courthouse?"

Sarah told him about the meeting with George. "I'm glad I have that chapter closed. I feel nothing for him—except some pity. For a man who loves the outdoors so much, he won't be out for a long time, I'll bet."

"Do you still want to go to the sentencing?"

Sarah hesitated. "We've gone this far, so we might as well."

Amos gathered his love in his arms and kissed her. "I'll go with you." How George could have run out on this wonderful woman Amos would never understand.

****

Sarah was unexpectedly calm the morning of the sentencing. That George deserved whatever he got was apparently her stance. She and Amos decided to have breakfast at Millie's. The no-nonsense woman took their order. "I take it both of you are going to the court for the judgment."

Sarah nodded. "That will make our case complete."

Millie gave an aside to Amos. "When are you going to open the detective agency?"

Amos rubbed his chin. "We're shooting for next week. We've been interviewing for a receptionist who can do secretarial work. Haven't found the right person yet."

You'll find her." She slipped the pencil behind her ear. "I wish you well in your new business." Millie made her way to the kitchen with their order.

Sarah took a sip of her coffee. "Don't you have an interview scheduled for today?"

Amos slipped his black leather date book out of his coat pocket and opened it. "Yes, we do. A Miss Molly Flanagan, at one-thirty."

"We should be at the office by then."

Their order, a stack of Millie's special flapjacks, with scads of butter and warm maple syrup, fragrantly appeared in front of them, accompanied by specially smoked crisp bacon. They dug in with gusto.

An hour and a half later, they slipped into the court and took seats. Sarah noticed Leigh was there and so were many curious townspeople. This had been a banner trial. The attorneys came in and then George, flanked by two guards.

The bailiff announced the judge and all rose. After everyone sat again, Henry Ott adjusted his spectacles and opened a folder. "Will the defendant please rise." When George stood, the judge continued, "Mr. George Annok, you have been found guilty of plotting the murder of Mr. Edward Thornton." George shuffled his feet, and the shackles clanked. "Before I pronounce sentence, I have to tell you, this is one of the coldest and most calculated murders I ever had before me. I'm giving you the harshest sentence the law will allow. Mr. Annok, you will serve fifty years in the territorial penitentiary. But first you will be extradited to Cordova to stand trial there." He hit the gavel down. "It is so ordered."

George and Leigh clutched at each other until the guards pulled him away. She fell back into her chair and continued to stare at the door the guards had taken him through. Sarah and Amos made their way over to her.

Sarah sat next to her. "Is there anything we can

do?"

Leigh shook her head. "I guess I'll go back to my parents and take care of our children. I'll have to do it alone."

Amos put his hand on her shoulder. "Are you going to the trial in Cordova?"

Leigh gazed at him with a lost, empty expression. "I'm his wife. Where should I be?" She rose and gathered her things together. As she walked to the visitor door of the courtroom, she paused and turned around. "May God bless you both. Goodbye."

Sarah stood as Leigh closed the door behind her. "There's a poor soul who got stuck with the worst. Not many people like to think about that part of the marriage vows."

Amos embraced her. "I'll be stuck with poorest if we don't finish getting the office ready to open."

She patted his cheek. "Let's get going. I don't want to be married to a pauper." They laughed as they exited the courthouse. They were done with this case.

Former sheriff Creag had been given to Mahoney in Cordova because apparently Creag had masterminded all the cannery murders, with George as his operations chief. Creag would have to stand trial eventually in Juneau, because it was the territorial capitol, but unless they had to testify, Amos and Sarah wouldn't be present.

The June sun had warmed the air to seventy degrees, a very warm summer day in Juneau, until the late afternoon breezes from the channel brought in the cooler air and fog. The glaciers on the mountaintops glittered like rare diamonds set in white velvet. Sarah loved this time of year. The warmth was so fleeting, a day like this was a treat in icy Alaska.

They unlocked the front door and entered their finished reception area. The blinds in the front window had been put up the day before, and the sunlight made bright stripes in the room when Amos pulled the string.

A stack of crates stood by the entrance to the two private offices, and Sarah sighed. "Well, with our desks and furniture delivered yesterday, we can load up the drawers and shelves."

Amos dug into one of the crates of books. "This is going to take a couple of days."

She swung one labeled "office supplies" into her room. "At least." Straightening, she was aware of arms around her waist, and then Amos was kissing the back of her neck. Her body went squishy. "Longer, if we keep this up."

Amos turned her to face him. "Quit talking, woman." His lips claiming hers made her forget why she was protesting.

She pulled back. "I have to change into my work clothes. Care to help me?" Her summer dress fluttered to the floor. His hands were busy in back. She closed the office door as he shed his jacket and undid his trousers. The new oriental rug flamed under the baptism of fire that took place on it. She shattered and took him on a ride of fireworks. Then, spent, they held each other breathlessly as the office came back into view.

Amos gave her a hand up as he glanced at his watch. "Oh, damn, it's almost time—"

"Hello! Is anyone here?" came a voice from the outer room.

"Just a minute!" he answered back while adjusting his clothes. In a lowered voice, "Get your work denims on. I'll start the interview." He slid out of the office to confront a red-haired, freckled woman with her arms crossed, watching him carefully.

She gave an amused smile. "You must be Amos Darcy. I'm Mary Flanagan, here for the reception and secretary job. I hope I wasn't interruptin' anything."

"Oh—no. We were just—working on the office." *How long had she been there?* He rummaged in a drawer at the reception desk and brought out a form, as well as pen and ink. "You can sit here and fill out the application."

While Mary worked on the form, Sarah came out in her denims and plaid shirt. She looked questioningly at Amos, and he shrugged. When Mary was finished, Amos and Sarah brought two chairs to the desk and sat across from her.

Sarah held out her hand. "Mary, I'm Sarah Darcy. Pleased to meet you."

"I'm pleased to meet you, too. I kept up on what you were doin' about the murder of Mr. Thornton at the cannery. That was some fine detective work."

Sarah flushed. "Well, thank you."

Amos perused the application while the pleasantries passed between the two women. "Miss Flanagan, why did you come to Alaska?"

She sighed. "There weren't many people who would give a girl fresh from the old sod a decent job. I worked as a secretary back in Dublin, where I'm from. I'm a hard worker, Mr. and Mrs. Darcy. You'll not regret hirin' me."

Amos rubbed his chin. "Can you take dictation and type?"

Mary nodded. "Yes. I can do ledger bookkeepin',

as well."

Sarah leaned back. "How are you at handling clients?"

"Friendly, but firm, ma'am."

"How about keeping secrets?"

She grinned. "I won't tell anyone what goes on in this office."

A slight pink tinged Sarah's cheeks, but she asked, "Do you have references?"

Mary opened her pocketbook and took out some envelopes. "These are from my job back home. Most in this country didn't care. They didn't want to hire an Irish girl."

Amos took the papers and read them. "These are excellent references. The employers who wouldn't hire you were a bunch of jackasses. Would you mind if Mrs. Darcy and I confer in one of the offices?"

Mary shook her head. "No."

As Sarah closed the door behind her, she hissed under her breath. "I wonder how long she was here?"

"I was wondering the same thing." He blew out a slow breath. "Well, what do you think?"

"I like her, and she's been through enough. I know how she feels, how it was with those narrow-minded people."

Amos now knew what a bunch of idiots a lot of Americans were. "I think we can hire her. Fifty cents an hour sound all right?"

Sarah made a face. "Can we afford that?"

He paused. "We still have some reserves left. I think we can."

Sarah turned to go. "Let's tell her."

They told Mary what they'd decided, and she was

delighted with the pay. "When do I start?"

Amos shook her hand. "Next Wednesday we plan to open. Be here at seven sharp."

"And I'll be here. Thank you, Mr. Darcy, Mrs. Darcy." She gathered her things together and flashed them a grateful smile before she strode out.

Amos started back to his office, then turned to Sarah. "What do you want to do this weekend, since this is our last free one?"

Sarah sashayed to him and purred. "I'd love to go camping with you, big boy."

Her voice poured over him like warm molasses.

"Oh. Think you can handle being out in the wild?"

"I do it all the time. How about you?" Her body curled toward her office, but Amos snagged her hand.

"You keep this up, we'll never get the rooms ready." He dragged her back and kissed her thoroughly.

Chapter 28

The sun was burning off the morning fog as Sarah and Amos headed up Sixth Street with their backpacks and walking sticks on that glorious summer morning. The air was crisp and clean at five o'clock, and there weren't many people out on a Saturday yet. The aroma of bacon wafted out of several houses they passed.

Turning on Basin Road, they followed as it curved up a tree-covered knoll. In the branches, they could hear the chattering of a Steller's Jay against the *klok* of a raven that must have flown too close to the jay's nest.

A few houses and cottages dotted the road on either side, until the road ended. Sarah led the way to the wooden bridge over the tumbling waters of Gold Creek. She pointed to the opposite side. "That dark green patch is an old avalanche scar. The plants come in a brighter green than around it."

Amos chuckled. "That family of bears are enjoying it." They watched as the bears tried out some tasty summer fruits. "I've been in Juneau a number of years, but I've never come this way. I'm glad you suggested it."

Sarah started on the road that cut between Mount Juneau and Roberts Peak. Both had glistening glaciers on the top and dark green vegetation growing below. An eagle sailed off a cliff up above and glided over the creek.

About a mile or so along, they came upon the ruins of some old mine buildings. Sarah sat on a fallen log and motioned to Amos to do the same. "I thought we could take a break and I'd tell you about this area."

Amos took off his backpack and took out some biscuits and water. "This obviously was a mine at one time."

Sarah nodded. "Gold prospectors cut this road through the mountains in the winter and spring of 1881."

He shook his head. "That must have been one hell of a job."

"I'm sure. That place ahead is Snowslide Gulch. That's where Joe Juneau and Richard Harris climbed to the top and looked down into Silver Bow Basin."

"They were the founders of Juneau, weren't they?"

"Yes. They started the gold mining there."

They finished their biscuits and strapped on the backpacks once again. The trail went up hill, and in a few minutes Sarah heard the familiar roar of Ebner Falls. She grasped Amos' hand as they stood at the edge of the path and looked down on the falls, the water cascading over the rocks seeming to come from the lush tree-covered basin.

He sucked in a breath. "That's some view. Reminds me of the falls in Idaho."

Sarah indicated the path going down. "That's the way to Perseverance Basin. There are several clearings near the creek where we can set up camp. This is where my family used to come with my father and brothers to fish."

They found a clearing under some hemlock trees where a steady breeze kept the flying pests at bay, and

Sarah set up camp while Amos took his fishing gear down to the creek.

She put up the larger two-person tent and staked it. Taking the small spade, she dug out the fire pit and arranged stones around it. After gathering some fallen wood, she started a cooking fire and set the small iron grill over it. *Might as well make some coffee.* She emptied the rest of her canteen into the coffeepot and put it on a flat rock near the fire. Sitting on a nearby log, she watched the sparks flying in the air like manic fireflies when she poked at the flames.

A wistful tingle went through her as she remembered the many happy weekends she had come here with her parents and brothers, before the men in her family were taken. She and her mother would set up camp while her father and brothers provided the fish. A tear slid down her cheek. She missed them very much.

Sarah closed her eyes and let the breeze bring in the fresh smells of summer in Alaska—the green plants, new flowers, and the rich soil of the forest. Then a "halloo" broke into her reverie.

She gazed with love as her man came up the trail with two rainbow trout slung over his shoulder. She waved and then poured a cup of coffee for him, and he presented her with the fresh fish. She quickly had the fish cleaned and in the skillet over the fire. Adding herbs and salt, she poured in some rice and a can of tomatoes and sealed the pan with the lid.

Amos pulled out a bag containing several rolls Sarah had baked the day before. In a short time they had a feast fit for royalty. To top off the meal, Sarah had gathered wild berries earlier and smothered them in sugar. Crumbling some molasses cookies into a dish, she poured the berry syrup over them.

When Amos had polished them off, he sat back against a tree trunk. "I declare, woman, that's one of the best meals I've ever had."

Sarah giggled. "Thank my mother. She made this every time we went camping."

After supper, they lingered in front of the campfire until the late June sun finally slipped behind the mountains. Amos took a stick and stirred the fire. "There's something I want to know."

Sarah glanced at him, puzzled. "What is it?"

"Do you still have feelings for George?"

She paused, then poured the dregs of her coffee into the pit, causing a sizzle. "Mostly disgust and some pity. Why?"

He stared at her and in the firelight seemed almost sad. "You must have loved him before, if you were going to marry him."

Sarah looked down. "I guess I had a young woman's yearning for marriage at that time, but now I no longer feel anything for him. I matured and found a man I could trust without wavering. Amos, I can truly say I've never loved anyone like I love you."

He lifted her chin with his fingers until they were eye-locked. "That's all I wanted to hear. Dance with me, woman."

She smiled. "But there's no music."

He rose, pulling her up with him, and started singing, "Green grow the lilacs all sparkling with dew..."

They danced and sang through "Sweet Betsy from Pike" and "Clementine." Around the flickering campfire, the gruff former sheriff and the lady Tlingit did a bright two-step.

A wolf howled in the distance, and an owl hooted its intentions, but the couple danced happily in the dappled shadows of the full Alaskan moon, their laughter and song wafting through the treetops.

A word about the author...

Ilona Fridl happily resides in Wisconsin with her husband, Mark, and a well-worn computer. Due to the popularity of two minor characters in *Golden North*, she gave them their own story.

Ilona is on Facebook and Goodreads and you can visit her site on the web at:
http://www.ilonafridl.com